An Eyeful

Kirk wanted to scream, he wanted to jab hot pokers in his eyes. He didn't want to be here anymore. He wavered, staring at Sylvie as she looked around the room.

Sylvie urged, "You've got to resist him, Kirk. That's the only thing I can tell you to do. Resist! Don't let him take you. Don't!"

Kirk felt the turning, the worms eating his guts. He sank to his knees, trying desperately to turn his face away. Demon laughed, keeping his eyes open. "You want to watch, don't you, Kirkie boy? Go ahead, boy. Watch. You'll love it," Demon spat into his ear.

Kirk shuddered again. Sylvie backed away from him, afraid . . .

SINS
OF THE
FATHERS

Based on
THE OBLIVION

Sam Chupp

BOXTREE

First published in the UK in 1996 by Boxtree Limited,
Broadwall House, 21 Broadwall, London, SE1 9PL

First published in the USA in 1995 by HarperPaperbacks, a
Division of HarperCollins*Publishers*,
10 East 53rd Street, New York, N.Y. 10022

ISBN: 0 7522 0315 0

Cover illustration by Joshua Gabriel Timbrook

10 9 8 7 6 5 4 3 2 1

Published by arrangement with HarperCollins*Publishers* Inc.,
New York, New York, U.S.A.

Printed and bound in Great Britain by
Cox & Wyman Ltd., Reading, Berkshire.

A CIP catalogue entry for this book is available from the British Library

This book is dedicated to my three Fathers: may they all three be revered for all that they have given me and taught me:

My birth-Father, whose seed helped give me life, and who knows the pain of not knowing where his son is. Hi, Dad.

My life-Father, who gave me all he could afford; who gave me his cynical humor, his anger, and his sense of honor, who did the best he could with the feelings that the Marines left him with, a tough old cuss who could give the worst of Spectres a hard time.

My spirit-Father, that wild man, that Smith/Stag/Sage/Boy so long denied by us all, who has taken me in his hand and shown me what fathers used to be, and what they will be again.

I only hope to be worthy of their gifts, and to make them all proud of me.

SINS OF THE FATHERS

1

Ghost Story:
Chains Rattlin' Roof

You see, there was this guy, name of Kurt or Kirk or somesuch. He was one baaaad motha. He used to hang out at school, just hang out, rake in the dough with his beeper and his little plastic baggies. Heh. He'd stolen a key up to the roof of the school and he'd do his meetings there.

Well, one day they came for him . . . no, not the cops, but the big guys, the really big guys who didn't like him cuttin' into their business. No, they didn't. They poked a gun in his gut and finished him off up there, gore all over the place. They didn't find the body until a few days later, when blood from the corpse drained into an air duct and spilled out on Ms. Martin, the science teacher. Pretty gross, eh?

Yeah. They say that you can hear Kirk's ghost up there sometimes, cryin' for his skank girlfriend and playin' his electric guitar and, from time to time, he'll try to make you a deal. Heh. Pretty cool, eh? Wanna go up there?

Kirk hated school, hated it enough so that the fire from his hate kept him warm at night, filled his belly with a fullness that burned. Still, from his perch on top of the four-story school near Grant Park, he was able to see pretty far in the dark misty Shadowlands that he had come to call home. He was able to keep watch from any barrow-fires which might be burning through at any point—the fires of Atlanta that still burned here in this place, in his purgatory, in this hell. Kirk had spent long hours trying to figure out exactly what and where he was: as near as he could tell, he was not alive, not in any real sense. The bad dudes with the homebrewed automatic pistols had taken care of that little detail.

This demon landscape that he lived in was something like the real world he was used to, though: all the buildings were in the same place, all the places he used to hang with his buds and sell dope were still there. The world looked as if it was stuck in some kind of black-and-white movie: everything was dark, and the only color Kirk ever saw was the red fires of the barrow-flame, and he had learned long ago that the barrow-flame was a hungry fire, intelligent like a snake is intelligent, waiting to strike you, burning through you and consuming you. Kirk never wanted near the stuff again.

Kirk soon found that, although he wasn't solid to the rest of the world, the rest of the world was quite solid to him. People would walk through him if he was in their way (or sometimes walk around him mindlessly, as if they could see him but chose not to). It was disconcerting to be walked through, but not as painful as when someone slammed a door on him. When that happened, he jerked at the potential impact and felt a sharp pain all over his body. For a couple of seconds, Kirk felt lightheaded and wispy: he looked down at his hands to see them slowly fading and then, slowly reforming. The same thing happened when he tried to walk through walls. Soon, he learned how to get around without much trouble, avoiding heavy-traffic areas in the school.

Kirk had a ball, at night, walking through the corridors of his old school, walking through open doors and looking at all the crap that the kiddies left behind. He'd learned a few tricks himself, too. How to open doors. How to open lockers (which was even more fun, because it meant you could go through kids' stuff and see what kind of crap they were trying to hide: a box of condoms, dirty magazines, bootleg tapes, and unregistered pistols). How he did this, Kirk couldn't really tell: it was something having to do with moving stuff with his mind, although he couldn't do it on command. He had to think hard about it, and get a little pissed off, and then he could hit a locker and have it open in the land of the living. He could usually close the locker door enough so that the stuff wouldn't get found. To Kirk, this was one of his only entertainments. Kirk just assumed that Purgatory was supposed to be boring, and that's why he didn't make any move to do anything about his tedium.

During the day, Kirk stayed in the machine room on the roof and practiced flipping stones at the far wall, sitting on the old paint cans. He liked the darkness inside the room during the day. One day he had stuck his head out on a bright, sunny day to a terrifyingly stark world where the shadows were long but the sun burned like a great explosion in the sky and threatened to blind him permanently. It was too much to even walk around outside during a bright day. Kirk longed for the foggy, overcast days of fall, but this was spring, and it'd be a long, hot summer before Georgia's grey weather rolled in.

So, Kirk sat in his self-imposed solitary confinement, sitting with his back against the wall and watching for cracks in the ground while he kicked at rocks and trash on the floor, trying to make them move. The cracks were what really scared him. There was a crack that opened on the roof from time to time, and Kirk had fallen into it once. Holding on for dear life, he used all his strength to pull himself up. Kirk shuddered everytime he thought about what he saw in the pit that the crack revealed. Kirk wasn't sure what the cracks were, exactly, but they grew and closed up with a regularity that made them seem "natural," if anything could be natural here in Purgatory. Maybe they were doorways into Hell? They led down, and he'd heard voices and saw . . . things down there.

At night, it was okay to wander around. Kirk never felt like sleeping much anymore, although he was vaguely aware that he'd conk out every once in a while and "wake up," it didn't feel like normal sleep. Kirk was afraid to leave the school. Following his horror-movie logic, he thought that he should be confined to the place where he died. Kirk knew that there was some kind of mystic tug, a pull, something he couldn't quite pin down but kept him here. And, something that kept him from other places. He was afraid of what those places might be like.

Kirk knew that he was invisible to people: whenever he walked around the school during the day (down hall 4C, which had no windows and had a stairway leading up to the machine room), people would walk right past him and nobody could hear a word he said, no matter how loudly he yelled. At first, Kirk got a headache from hanging out with the living folks: he could hear them whispering all over the place, could hear everything with a sensitivity that he'd never experienced before. Standing at one end of the hall, he could hear the quiet whispers of passion two young lovers were exchanging on the other end of the hall, and even hear the teacher bitch one of them out when they walked into the classroom and closed the door. Kirk soon learned not to listen too hard to anything: it was difficult, especially when he began to hear whispers he couldn't shut out.

Kirk wasn't sure what it was that whispered to him. He thought maybe it was a demon assigned to torture him specifically. The demon whispered to him all the time, but Kirk couldn't see him: one time, however, he was in the boy's restroom and caught a look at himself in the mirror when the demon started talking. Something strange had happened to his face, then: a darkening, a shadowing of his face that caused his eyes to turn into hollow pits of green fire and his mouth to shape itself into a rictus of anger and hatred.

For a brief moment, Kirk looked at the demon that was constantly bothering him with whispered innuendo, accusations, and insults. Kirk thought that the demon looked much like him, only older looking and more feral. With a chill, later, Kirk realized where he had seen that face before: the pictures of his father that his mother had hidden from him since he was a baby, since Daddy had died in Vietnam. Kirk had dreamed about his father once a week for his final five years, terrible dreams. Kirk only ever forgot the black nightmares by popping a Quaalude and sleeping: those dreams dredged up the truth and made Kirk feel cold, vulnerable, and full of resentment. His father had treated him like the soldiers he had trained as a drill instructor for the Rangers. Kirk never told his gang or anyone he hung out with about the dreams. Kirk was glad to be dead, if nothing else, so that he wouldn't have those dreams anymore.

Still, his father was here in some kind of demon form, and Kirk knew that if he didn't occupy his mind with other things, the demon within him would wake up and start talking again. He'd had some luck with screaming at the demon to "shut up" before, but he got the feeling that, if it wanted to, it could ignore anything he said and just keep right on talking. It talked about things he did in life: the girls he'd had sex with; the drugs he'd sold; the things his mother had done; his sister's "job"; his little sister, who never said anything to anyone; and Jo, his parole officer, who he often wished he could hurt. And most of the things it said he didn't really want to hear anymore. After a while, he began to learn how to deal with his demon.

So he spent his time with the one thing he'd been able to find in the basement of the school: an old Fender electric guitar. He'd heard the story of the principal of the school burning the guitar in the incinerator many years ago. Well, here in Purgatory it was still there, sitting in the old incinerator, a little worse for wear (scorch marks on the finish; no structural damage) but usable. Somehow, in destroying it, the principal had sent it to Purgatory. Kirk thought that maybe those Egyptian fellas had the right idea about taking stuff with them when they died, and wished he'd had a pizza, or some weed, or a TV or something buried with him.

One night, as the heat of the summer resonated up off the street, Kirk decided to sit down and focus for a while on his new-found guitar. Kirk played with it, hearing the wires rattle without the benefit of an amp, having taught himself to play guitar a little last summer, when he had been alive and full of hope that his band would get him better drug connections and his drug connections would get his band a better place to play. So much for that.

Still, playing the music had a calming effect on him. It also helped to drive the demon inside him away. He ran through his band's play list: they'd been obsessed with heavy-metal dinosaurs and Southern rock, although Kirk liked the heavy techno and goth music himself. He played the favorite songs that every beginning guitar player learns: "Smoke on the Water," "Iron Man," "Freebird," and, in a moment of cynical humor, "Stairway to Heaven." Thoughts of playing turned him to thoughts of Cindi, his girlfriend. She was only seventeen, but she was the hottest babe he'd ever known. He wasn't sure if she was dating him because he could get her free shit, or if she really loved him. He paused and thought for a second. What was Cindi's favorite song? He began to play "Beth" by KISS, and played all the way through it before he realized that the guitar had begun to sing and 'verb as if it had an amp plugged into it.

Looking down at the guitar, he saw that it glowed with some kind of eerie light, a light that made Kirk feel a little queasy but excited at the same time. He'd been thinking of the last time he and Cindi had made love, about how they'd not had a condom, but she didn't care. About how she'd felt beneath him. That feeling, that raw emotion, was something that he couldn't deny, and it had poured out of him. Shouldering the guitar again, Kirk began to play, this time slamming into the lead part on "Through the Never" by Metallica. The sounds reverberated throughout the machine room, echoing off the walls. Although his fingers used to go numb and scream with pain while playing this song, which used lots of incredibly fast riffs in rapid succession, his fingers didn't seem to even touch the strings now. He gave himself up to the music, and somehow, the spectral guitar's music burned out of the pickups, which glowed with the energy Kirk put into the song and into the guitar. He realized that his whole body was serving as the speaker for the guitar, that he radiated the music from his skin.

Kirk turned around, still lost in the music he was playing, and nearly dropped his guitar.

Seated in a cross-legged position across from him was a young girl, nearly ten in age, Kirk guessed. She was black—Jo, Kirk's parole officer, would've said "African-American." Her hair was done neatly in cornrows, and she wore a plain white Sunday church dress. She smiled quietly at Kirk. "Don't stop on my account, mister. I just want to hear the music."

Kirk looked at her, felt the hot rage and lust that he'd been feeling drain away to nothing, and watched the guitar go from a brilliant red and white heat-lightning ax to a dull grey antique. Looking up at where she was sitting again, Kirk was surprised to see that she was gone. Where had she disappeared to?

Kirk put down his guitar and walked to the open stairwell door—he always left the door open to the roof, because he hated walking through anything if he could help it. He walked to the edge of the four-story school building and looked down to the street below, scanning in all directions for the girl.

She was nowhere to be found. Up one side of the building and down the other Kirk looked, straining his eyes to see everything. Although he was able to make out the license plate number of a car two blocks down the street, he couldn't see the girl anywhere.

"Hey, demon. This your doin'?" Kirk said, trying to sound brave.

"What do you think, Kirkie boy?" came the voice inside him.

"I think you're playin' with my head. Tryin' to get me to stop the music. You don't like my playin'," Kirk said, grinning a little despite himself.

Demon said nothing in return, and Kirk ran his hand through his matted crop of hair and shrugged his shoulders, still looking all around for the little girl.

Then, a half-second later, she was standing there, holding part of a little corn-husk doll. She smiled at Kirk, looking at him sideways. "How come you don't ever come out, like the other spooks?" she said, quietly.

Kirk looked down at her. "I ain't no spook, little girl. I'm a devil. Didn't you hear my devil music just now?"

The girl smiled. "There ain't no demons here, mister. Not 'less you bring 'em out of you. Or 'less they come up outta the ground . . . "

Kirk shivered, looking down at his feet for cracks. "Oh, yeah? What makes you so smart?" Kirk said, suddenly angry that this kid was trying to tell him what was what.

That smile again, nearly ubiquitous. "Because, mister, I've been around Marthasville for a long, long time, ever since it was Terminus. And I know a lot about it. A lot. You'd best listen to your elders, mister," she said, almost laughing.

"Shit. You ain't my elder. You're a little kid, and I ain't gonna take this crap from a little kid. See ya."

Kirk turned around and stalked back into the machine room. He turned around a few times, looking to see if the girl was following him. But she had vanished again.

Kirk felt anger welling up inside him—the girl couldn't be just a trick of the demon. She was too detailed, too real looking. So, she was someone like him. Why did she have to put on airs, callin' herself an "elder" and all? Kirk let his frustration overflow, and he turned around to kick at a paint can. With a flash of fiery-red light that burned down his leg, the can toppled over and began to roll across the room. It rolled down the stairs, stair by stair, picking up speed. Finally it slammed into the door at the bottom of the stairs, making a loud spanging noise, and Kirk watched as the beige paint began to slowly pour out of the can, glooping on the floor and flowing under the door.

"Shit," Kirk swore, looking at the mess.

Demon spoke up, "Oh that's just great Kirkie-boy. You just screwed up major big-time. Wonder what they're gonna do when they find that little puddle tomorrow morning? Huh? I'll tell you what they'll do, they'll lock this place up tighter than a drum and you're not going to like that, no boy. You're too much of a sissy boy."

Kirk ignored Demon's taunts and walked back outside, out on the roof, sitting down on the ground and watching for cracks, his favorite meditative activity. He felt Demon rattling his cage inside him— it felt like a rabid rat trying to eat its way out of his guts. He felt that peculiar feeling of fear, anger, and dread burn through him that meant that the demon was flexing his muscles. Kirk did what he could to hold on, but Demon knew when to strike, when Kirk was weakest.

He felt the slithery feeling of Demon sliding its tendrils into place all over his body, watched as the greenish grey opaque smoke billowed through his body, slowly covering it. He tried to scream as he realized what was happening, but couldn't. Demon took him. Clutching its dark tendrils around his heart, he laid siege to and broke the defenses of Kirk's mind. Demon was in control.

Demon laughed, and Kirk realized that he was going to be forced to quietly watch everything Demon did.

Demon walked over to the cans of paint and paint thinner, grinning to himself, and knocked a can of thinner over without even trying hard. The can fell over and broke open and streamed down the stairs like an acetone waterfall. Kirk could smell the bitter bite of the chemicals. Then, grinning (Kirk felt his face freeze in the rictus of a grin, against his will), Demon reached down with his hands and rubbed his fingers lightly together over the acetone. There was a curl of smoke at first as Demon rubbed, and then, suddenly, there was a spark, a tiny burst of fire. With a roar, the paint thinner caught, burning rapidly in a blue-green sheet across the floor, down the stairs, to the door, where it fanned out. The plaster began to smoke. Kirk saw licks of flame begin to dance up the wall and realized that the school, old as it was, was one huge firetrap.

The flames began to dance up the walls and spread to the rest of the paint thinner cans, which were already bulging from the heat buildup. Demon forced Kirk's body out the door, over to the edge of the roof.

Demon hissed at Kirk inside his head. "If you weren't such a friggin' freak, you'd jump, boy. That's the smart thing to do. But you're a sissy. Ain't never jumped noplace. No guts, no glory, craphead!" it yelled at him.

Kirk felt its control slipping away as he stood on the lip of the roof looking down. He saw the fire start to spread through the walls, saw smoke rising from below him. Time must have passed that he hadn't known about, or else something the demon was doing was making the building burn faster and faster.

Kirk felt a sharp pain in his middle as he realized the building's burning was hurting him—it felt like he himself was on fire. Panicking, he closed his eyes and jumped.

The fall took forever, as he knew it would, and when he hit the street he felt his vision swim as, for a second, he felt his body enter the pavement, then bounce back. He shook his head to clear it, watched as his body reformed from the impact. It was disgusting to watch: the grey plasm slowly seeping back together to form coherence under his clothes. He knew he had no bones and yet he could "feel" his skeleton inside him reknitting, could "hear" the bones cracking and popping back into place. He slowly stood on his feet, looking up as another pang of pure fire in his chest wracked him. He knew that, somehow, the pain was associated with the building, that the building itself was important to him.

Kirk wanted to scream, but didn't. He hated that school building more than anything, and now, here in death, he was cursed to protect it. What for? He wanted to grab whoever it was that was in charge of this place and shake him. Then another pang wracked him as he saw the entire fourth floor of the school in flames. Kirk put a hand over the middle of his chest, winced, and began walking down the street.

"Come on, where are you fire dudes?" he whimpered to himself as he began to run. He remembered a fire call box down the street, one his buddy Rick had pulled once as a joke. He began to run, looking for it, found it open and the handle already pulled: another joker, another false alarm.

Then, looking up, he saw an old lady sitting with her pit bull in an all-night Laundromat. Stumbling through the door, as another pang shot through him, he held himself up by grabbing the doorframe. The glass in the window was riddled with cracks but somehow stayed intact. He looked down at the old lady. She was knitting something and had a revolver on the seat next to her, probably loaded. Smart lady. As he stepped closer, the pit bull woke up from its snooze and looked in his direction. Kirk was glad for a change that he was invisible. He smiled at the dog.

"Hey, nice doggie. Nice dog," Kirk said, grinning for a second, then another pang wracked him and he knew he had to do something.

Looking at the woman, he passed his hands in front of her eyes, trying to get her attention. Why couldn't she see it? The light from the fire was clearly visible out in the street. Then Kirk realized that the school was quite a few blocks down the street, and it was only his own heightened perception that let him see from there. Still, couldn't he get this lady's attention? He tried touching her. The dog began to growl, low, looking directly at him. Could the dog see him? Kirk growled back at the dog, just to see. The dog stood up on its stubby little legs and growled louder this time, showing some of its fangs. Kirk froze in place as he realized the dog was about to pounce.

"She can't see ya. But he can," came a voice from behind him. He turned around. There was the little black girl again.

"You again? Well, you can just go ahead and do your vanishing act, cause I'm busy. . . . " Kirk felt another wave and nearly doubled over at the pain rushing through his body.

"The school's your fetter too, eh?" The girl said, wincing as well. "I didn't think anyone else cared about it."

"Fuck no, I don't care about it. But I'm stuck with it. Why does it hurt me when it's the one that's burning?" He divided his attention between her and the growling dog.

"It's your Fetter—one of them, anyway. We're tied to things, people, and places that were important to us in life. When those ties are broken, it takes away what we are, who we are. It hurts," the little girl said, wincing in pain herself.

"Damn straight it hurts! Now, if you'll just be so kind as to help me with the pooch, we'll see what we can do about getting the old bag up and callin' the fire trucks," Kirk yelled at her, feeling Demon grinning inside him. Demon wanted him to take control, tell her exactly what to do, Kirk knew that. He shook his head. "Look. I'm afraid the pooch is goin' to chew me up. I don't know how he can do it, but I just don't feel like trying him out. Capiche?"

The little girl nodded. She whistled to the dog, who looked up in her direction. "Come here, boy. Come here," she called to him. The dog began to whine, looking at Kirk and the little girl. "Come on, boy," the little girl said pleadingly, holding out her hand like she had a treat in it.

Kirk saw a flash of light inside the girl. The dog looked at Kirk one last time, scrunched his legs up and jumped to the ground, waddling over to her. Kirk took this opportunity to heave back with one hand and thrust his hand into the woman's face, hoping that it would have some effect.

The woman's glasses jumped off her nose and fell onto the floor, making her drop her knitting. She looked up, blinking, in Kirk's direction, as if she saw him for a second.

The little girl's quiet, melodious voice spoke up. "The old are closest to death and can sometimes see us if we're not careful," she whispered to Kirk.

Kirk nodded and took a step back. Getting on his hands and knees, he flicked his finger at the glasses, making them jump nearly a foot toward the door.

"Careful, don't break 'em," the little girl said. Her hand was resting comfortably on the dog's forehead now. The dog was calm, seated, resting with his head on his paws.

The lady followed the glasses, bent to try to pick them up, and Kirk flipped them again, moving them closer to the door jam. She swore once and said something about "ghosts" to herself. Kirk flicked the glasses one last time and watched them tumble out into the street. He then got up and quickly stepped outside, around the woman as she was passing through the door.

She bent to pick up the glasses, and this time Kirk put his lips to her ear and screamed at her. She looked up, shocked, looked around, and found nobody anywhere nearby. She looked at her revolver sitting on the bench inside the Laundromat and obviously wished she had it in hand. She bent down one last time to get the glasses and put them on slowly.

"Listen, *lady*!" Kirk yelled. *"Call the fire department!"* He screamed as another pang of fire shot through his heart. Kirk saw a red light go off inside him like fireworks on a summer night.

Looking down the street, she saw the orange-red glow of the fire in the school, smelled the smoke. She walked back into the Laundromat, got her dog, got her revolver (which she put in her purse), and walked out, moving across the street slowly and carefully, looking all around her. She picked up an ancient, battered public telephone and dialed 911.

Kirk relaxed, watching her talk to the fire department. He turned around and looked for the little girl: true to her style, she was gone.

Kirk shrugged, cursing to himself as the pain kept coming, but less now that he knew help was on its way. He walked back to the school, swearing under his breath. He looked up at the building and hated it, wishing somehow it would burn, if he could just get out of this curse of being tied to it.

Kirk heard Demon whisper, "Go ahead. Let it burn. Make it burn. I have the power. You do, too. I could just give you what you need, Kirkie boy. Ever see napalm go up? I love the smell. Let's make the whole thing burn, shall we, Private?"

Kirk hated when Demon called him Private, like he was some army soldier that the demon issued orders to. Kirk tried not to let the things Demon said bother him, because if he did, it always came to no good: witness the paint cans and the fire.

Kirk leaned against a light-post that had long ago been turned off to save money and now stood like a dead steel tree, never dropping its light-bearing fruit. He heard the fire trucks off in the distance, their high-pitched whine, their horns blasting as they moved through heavy after-bar traffic in the middle of the city. Kirk wished he had a watch: the one he'd had didn't come with him when he came to Purgatory. Kirk figured it was just another punishment.

Then, suddenly from the direction of downtown, Kirk heard the clippity-clop of a horse's hooves on the street. He felt a hand on his arm—the little black girl again.

"Come on," she whispered, tugging on his arm. "We gotta hide." She pulled him into an alleyway, almost against his will. But the girl seemed to know what she was doing, so Kirk let her drag him into hiding.

"He'll see us here!" Kirk whispered.

"Shush. He won't see us if you be quiet. I'm vanishin' us both. Now keep quiet," the girl whispered, almost hissing her words. Kirk was quiet, although Demon muttered something about taking orders from black kids.

A tall man on a horse, clad in black metal armor that didn't shine or even seem to clink together as he moved, was the first on the scene. He had a Confederate officer's sword on his belt. Clearly visible in a saddle-holster was a shotgun with some kind of lightbulb attached to it: Kirk saw a tiny glow coming out of the little half-sphere attached to the butt of the gun. Strung in a special harness across the rider's back was a large scythe, of the kind Kirk's country uncle had hanging up in his living room: it had two handles. The rider's face was covered with an iron mask that hid his features and made him look rather piggish: like a hungry pig looking for food. The mask was attached to an immense helm that covered the man's whole head. Kirk thought he looked like a strange Disney version of Darth Vader, and almost laughed to himself at the concept, but decided against making any noise.

Following the rider were several men in combat gear with guns that had lights on their stocks, and two men who weren't wearing shirts but were carrying several sets of heavy-looking iron chains. The rider slowed to a stop next to the burning building and directed the soldiers to split up into two patrols: they soon disappeared around the corner of the building.

It was quite clear to Kirk that these men and the horse were all like him: grey, quietly moving. They had an eerie presence. They were all dead, like him. Kirk marveled at the horse: where do you get a dead horse to ride on around here?

Kirk strained to hear their conversation. "Doubtful we'll get any souls this time out, but check around anyway. Don't want to lose a chance. Monitor! Sense the building, if you will. I have a feeling about this place."

Kirk looked over to the girl, who put a finger in front of her lips. The world flickered around them both: for a second, Kirk felt an icy cold and then everything was right again, except this time they were standing atop a warehouse across the street from the school. Kirk looked at the girl questioningly, and she just smiled and shrugged.

Kirk focused his hearing on the group of ghostly soldiers again. One of the soldiers was speaking to the rider. "Dread Knight, I report that this structure seems to be the Fetter of two wraiths. One, a newly dead wraith, and another one we know to be named Sylvie—a Renegade, master."

"Interesting. A newly dead wraith? An Enfant? Fascinating. Monitor, can you sense anything further about this Enfant?"

The little girl closed her eyes and stayed very still, while Kirk looked at her inquisitively.

"No, milord. My senses are blocked by some greater force. Perhaps the use of an Arcanos?"

The black knight laughed cruelly behind his helm. "Ah, Monitor, that is always your excuse if you cannot get your art to do what I wish. Still, the Renegades could be protecting this new wraith, having gotten to her first . . . "

"Him, sir. Very definitely a he."

"Very well, then. Him." The black knight sighed. "It's a shame that the Hierarchy cannot be everywhere at once. I would have liked to have gotten hold of an Enfant during these times. One loyal to the Hierarchy could be very useful right about now." The black knight turned his attention back to the Monitor. "Monitor! Send a message: I would like a soldier well-versed in the Arcanos of Masquers and of Harbingers to be posted to this Fetter, to await the possible return of our new wraith. It's not too late to give up on fresh blood, as it were."

A soldier approached and saluted the knight. "Perimeter secure, sir!" The other soldiers had returned from their patrol and were slowly filtering back to the street as the large red fire trucks pulled up, a flurry of firemen getting out, attaching hoses to the trucks and to fireplugs, and starting to blanket the upper floors with powerful streams of water. The grey patrol moved out of the way as more trucks screeched to a stop.

The knight nodded to the soldier, edging his horse over to the other side of the street. "Excellent. Well, too bad it's not going to burn to the ground. I wouldn't mind harming the Renegades a bit. Troops, let's move out. We've got a full third of our domain left to patrol," the knight said, and clucked to his horse, which took off at a walk, the troops and slaves following along behind.

As soon as they were out of hearing range (even for a ghost), the little girl dropped the cloak of darkness from around them both and smiled at Kirk. Kirk shook his head, running his hands over his chest, where he felt the soothing water starting to ease the pain of damage to his Fetter.

"You Sylvie?" Kirk said, grinning.

She nodded yes.

"They're lookin' for you, I'd guess, eh?"

She smiled. "They're looking for all us Renegades. But who ain't?"

Kirk shook his head again, not knowing what to think, or who to trust. Demon spoke up within him: "Oh, yeah, that's the way, Kirkie. Trust a little kid. Trust a little jungle-bunny girl. What is it? Got a little jungle fever?" the foul thing whispered in his head.

He looked up, grinning. He was starting to learn that anyone Demon didn't like must be good for him. He put his hand out to shake Sylvie's. "Nice to meetcha. I'm Kirk. I don't know where it is that I am, Miss Sylvie, but wherever it is, you've been the nicest person I've seen so far, and besides, anyone Mr. Demon doesn't like, I have to give a second chance at likin'."

"Mr. Demon?" Sylvie asked, amused.

"Yeah. Talks to me in my head. You know, used to be I'd've thought you was crazy if you'd come to me and told me that you had a man talkin' in your head—but that was last month. Now that I'm dead, I can kinda see where it might happen." Kirk grinned and scratched his chest again, still feeling the cool water's effect.

"Mr. Demon, Kirk, is what we call the Shadow," Sylvie said quietly, as if she were reciting something she herself had once been told. "He's an evil force inside you, contrary to all you are. It seeks to strip away what makes you you, and force you to become one of the mindless servants of Oblivion . . . of the nothing," Sylvie said, the words sounding strangely chilling in her mouth.

Kirk shuddered, laughing. "Damn, girl," he said, grinning. "What *is* that supposed to mean? Servants of the nothin'?"

Sylvie looked at Kirk with a deadly serious glint in her eye. "Don't laugh. It's everywhere. It's inside you. Mr. Demon— my mama . . . Inside of us all. All us Restless, anyway. Not like the lost souls or the drones."

"Oh, you mean we're a special kind of ghostie?" Kirk said.

"Very special. And very . . . caught. Other ghosts are thin and ain't worth nothin'. But a Restless like you and me, we got smarts, and powers. We got Fetters, and we got our own feelin's. Feelin's that make you strong," Sylvie said, her eyes big and round.

"Like when I get pissed off about school?" Kirk said, suddenly remembering his guitar.

"Yeah. Like when I see dollies. Like, when I can feel again. It's a pretty thing, and ya gets light for it. Light, you know—juice? Stuff. Inside you. Like this," Sylvie said, holding up her hand, which briefly glowed a cool blue-and-purple color.

Kirk nodded. "Yeah. Light. I getcha. So, all I gotta do is get pissed off. That's good."

"You can't just get pissed, Kirk. You gotta think about things and know what you're doin'. Like when you knocked that lady's glasses off. You must'a been practicin' that," Sylvie said, smiling.

"Yeah. Like when you carry us around so quick. How you do that?" Kirk said, looking at her sideways.

"Miss Cindy used to call it 'Argos'—it's the fancy word for it. I just call it travelin', cuz it can get you around places. Quick, like ya said. She's the one who kenned me out, found all the things that I could do. Taught me 'em."

"Kenned you out?" Kirk said.

"It's like, she looked at me with these pretty blue eyes and she looked through me, and then she knew all the things I could do. As a ghost. All my powers," Sylvie said, chewing on one of her braids.

"All of them, eh? Can you do kennin'?" Kirk said.

"Nope. She said it was easy for her, but it ain't easy for me. I can do a little divinin', but no kennin'."

"What other powers do you have?" Kirk asked, looking down. He wanted to know what he could do. He liked the idea of having powers, like having superpowers in a comic book.

"I can sing some, and dream some. I like to do dreamin'. It's fun. I can travel some, and give folks juice. And some divinin'. But not like Miss Cindy!" Sylvie said, grinning.

"Sing? What good is that?" Kirk said.

"You can make people feel stuff. You know, get 'em in a mood. Like that dog—I made it all happy. I like makin' things happy. I do it all the time. There's too much sadness in the world. I betcha you could do singin'. It sounded like it when you were playing your git-fiddle," Sylvie said. "And, you got the 'rage, too. That means you can hit stuff in the land of the living. Open doors, knock people's glasses off—"

"Start fires?" Kirk said.

"Yeah, if you know what ya doin'," Sylvie said. "That's a powerful power. Can you do that?"

Kirk focused on his fingers and rubbed them together like he remembered the Shadow doing. He rubbed and rubbed, but nothing happened. He looked up at Sylvie. "Ain't somethin' supposed to happen?"

Sylvie grinned. "Hey, you gotta let loose some feelin's. Some juice."

Kirk grinned. "Oh, yeah!" He got a serious look on his face and started thinking about the pain he'd felt, the school on fire, the scary man on horseback, the strange pain as the building burned. His hand began to glow red, like a heat element on a stove that just got turned on. He started rubbing his fingers together.

"You can't do that without me," Mr. Demon said, chuckling. "Of course, you've never been much without me, boy. Want some help?"

Kirk looked pained and looked up at Sylvie. "Mr. Demon says I can't do that without him. He's offerin' to help."

Sylvie shook her head. "Don't you go makin' a deal with the devil, Kirk. If he says he can help, don' believe him. He ain't never gonna help you 'less it's gonna help him. And what helps him, hurts you. Miss Cindy said that, and I believe it. I ain't never let Mama do nothin' for me, and she stays quiet about it now."

Kirk looked at his hand, glowing bright hot, and then shook his head and watched the light slowly die. "Damn," he said. "Oh, well." He looked up. "Do you think it's safe to go back over there?" He got to his feet and looked across to the school building. It was smoking, but the fires had mostly gone out.

"I guess so. What for? I don' want to see no Legionnaire over there." Sylvie stood on her tiptoes looking across at the school.

"Legionnaire?" Kirk asked.

"That guy with the horse and his soldiers," Sylvie said. She squinted. "But I don' see 'em."

"I wanna get my guitar," Kirk said. "That's all. We don't have to hang around. Say, what would they do if they caught us? They like the cops or somethin'?"

Sylvie smiled. "Somethin' like that. They're lookin' for new dead folks, just in case. They collect 'em all, and take 'em to the Citadel. From there they ride the rails to Stygia, where the Big Devil lives. Unless you Restless, like me. Like you. Then they make you swear oaths and stuff, and then you get to walk around with a Centurion and do everythin' your boss says, or you get yourself put in chains. Like those Thralls you saw—the ones in chains."

"Sounds great. Not," Kirk said. "Who died and left them in charge?" he added, grinning. "Or do they work for God?"

"Nah. They work for Charon, the Big Devil. He's dead, or gone, or somethin'. Miss Cindy used to know, but I never listened to her when she went on about them Archy folks. Scuse me, it's 'High-er-archy.' Hierarchy."

"Where's Miss Cindy now?" Kirk asked quietly.

"She's gone. Down there. Down in the nothin'," she said, looking glum.

Kirk ran his hand through his hair. "I ain't never seen this nothin' you keep talkin' about."

Sylvie climbed up on the edge of the roof. "You don't wanna. Come on, we gotta get your guitar." She held out her hand.

Taking her hand, Kirk felt a flash of total cold and pure black, and then he was through the other side, standing next to the charred remains of the machine room. Leaving Sylvie behind, he stepped inside and saw his guitar leaning up against the wall. A fireman was poking around the machine room, looking at the spilled paint cans, writing in his notepad and holding a lantern.

Mr. Demon spoke up inside his head. "See what I mean, boy? It's over for you here. Shoulda let it burn. Oh well, gimme another chance, and it will."

"Fuck you, Mr. Demon," Kirk whispered, and picked up the guitar, which seemed none the worse for the fire. Kirk inspected the strings, wondering when one of them would break—and where he'd get more when they did.

Sylvie stood at the doorway. "Want to go someplace else? I can take you."

Kirk looked back at her, then at the fire inspector looking over the burn markings. "Yeah. I do. People walkin' around make me nervous."

Sylvie nodded and extended her hand. "Okay. We'll go see some folks I know. They Renegade like us."

"I didn't know that's what I was," Kirk said, grinning.

"Renegade? Oh, everybody Renegade, unless they are with the Hierarchy. Or 'less they're with the churchy types." Sylvie grinned.

"What churchy types? Angels and stuff? I wondered what God had to do with all this," Kirk said.

"God ain't said yet. The churchy types think He has, but I ain't heard from no angel yet. I seen angels that say they're angels, but even my pitiful divinin' can tell they ain't angels. Just Restless like us, only with wings and glowin'."

"Maybe there ain't never been no angels. Maybe there ain't no God," Kirk said.

"Maybe. I dunno. Miss Cindy believed there was a God, but she didn't never say how she knew. She wasn't no churchy, though. Those churchies get strange—rantin' and ravin' and sermonin'. Lucky enough they keep to themselves," Sylvie said.

"Who we gonna go see?" Kirk asked, feeling drained, almost tired. He wanted to sleep, but the building seemed foreboding now. He couldn't sleep here.

"Duke's Circle. He's a nice man. Has a few friends. I guess we can hang with them, if it's okay with them. They have to say when they sees you. Duke has the kennin' somethin' fierce, and so he'll be able to tell ya more about your powers," Sylvie said, somehow seeming to know that would be all Kirk needed to hear for him to decide to go with her.

Kirk grinned. "Okay—can I take my guitar with me?"

"Sure. Don't weigh nothin'," Sylvie said, holding out her hand and twirling a braid in her fingers. Kirk grabbed onto her hand, holding tight this time.

With a lurch, they plummeted down—into darkness.

For a moment, all Kirk could see was blackness punctuated by skirling storms of purple—although the sense of incredible velocity wasn't lost on him. He almost trailed off behind Sylvie, but the girl's grip was firm and strong, and there was considerable power in her will.

Then, almost a second later, they were standing atop an ancient hotel, looking down. Kirk heard a gunshot go off below him.

"What was that?" Kirk asked, surprised.

"Shh." Sylvie said, bending down. "Bad news." She pointed over the lip of the building into the alley below.

Looking down, Kirk saw what had been a familiar scene while he was alive: a gang of his age faced a team of scared, but relatively well-trained, uniformed police—except that, in this case, they were

all Dead. Kirk saw that the gang's weapons were out-
lined in the darkness with light that seemed to come
from their hands, and the cops had guns mounted
with tiny starlike jewels burning furiously red.
Almost immediately, Kirk found himself appraising
the scene from a strategic point of view, muttering
under his breath, "Must be a low-ammo situation:
they're taking their shots carefully. Of course,
they're wiped if they don't watch their rear flank. If I
were the cops, I'd send two men around the building
to nab 'em from the back. Of course, the cops are
scared shitless; I'd think a little distraction would go
far in taking care of them." Kirk grinned as he felt
his anticipation of the fight. He looked up at Sylvie.
"You think they could use some help?"

She looked down. "I think so, Kirk. It'd be your
choice."

Kirk knelt down beside her. "What do you mean
by that?"

Sylvie looked up at him. "Kirk, those cops—
they're from the Hierarchy. If you throw in with
Duke's gang, you'll be marked by the Hierarchy for
imprisonment. This is where you decide whether
you're a Renegade for sure or not. There ain't no
goin' back."

Kirk shook his head, looking down at the gang,
which was losing, bit by bit. "Sooner or later, it's
gonna happen. I'm just not cut out to follow the
rules." He watched as one of the Hierarchy cops
nailed a guy in the arm: they might be dead, he
thought, but the bullets still looked painful, maybe
even fatal. Kirk wondered what would happen if he
was hit too many times.

"We're already dead, Sylvie—how are those bullets going to hurt us?" Kirk asked.

"They hurt a lot. And Kirk, there's more to worry
about than dyin', here. If'n you get hurt too bad, you

go to a very bad place. It's hard ta come back. Sometimes, people don't."

"Where do you go? The nothin'?" Kirk said, watching one of the gang members try to rush the line of cops. A bright red bolt shot into him, and he fell, clutching his shoulder. Kirk watched in horror as the kid screamed and dissolved, flowing like water down a crack that seemed to open up and consume him. A second later, there was no trace of him.

Kirk looked up at Sylvie. "You go into the Harrowin', Kirk. A place that's controlled by the Shadow. And if ya don't watch it, you're gonna go straight to Oblivion."

Kirk screwed up his face. "Oblivion? The nothin'?" Sylvie nodded. "The nothin'."

The gunshots quieted quickly. Kirk saw the gang moving down the street, backing up, taking shots as they went. He nodded to Sylvie. "Okay. Important safety tip. Don't get hurt," Kirk said, grinning to himself. He watched a few seconds more, feeling the call of battle, shaking his head as he saw the gang expertly retreat, taking shots at the cops pressing them.

He made a decision and looked Sylvie in her eyes. "Can you get me across the street into that alley, down next to that shoe store?" Kirk said as he saw the gang break up and make a defensive rear action—in other words, they ran around the corner of the building and ducked into a nearby alley.

Sylvie smiled. "Sure." She took his hand. "Beam me down, Captain!" she said, and there was a brief moment of cold discontinuity before Kirk's vision reformed.

Suddenly three gun barrels were pointing at him as he heard the word "Harbinger!" yelled. Kirk slowly raised his hands, as did Sylvie. The gang members looked at each other, then at him. Their faces were strange—it was only a second's thought before Kirk realized they all three wore masks: one a lion's head, one a wolf's head, and another looked like a monkey.

Kirk grinned. "Um, I guess you don't need no help. Ahhh, could I convince ya that I'm one of the good guys?" he said, whispering, still grinning.

The wolf-head ran to the edge of the alley and looked down the street. "We've got to go, Duke, they're coming," came a feminine voice from under the wolf mask.

The lion-head turned back to Kirk and Sylvie, shotgun still trained on them. It glowed red. "Nah, you're too stupid to be an 'arch. Anyone who'd jump down next ta some armed folks without a gun's got a screw loose, in my opinion."

The monkey-mask started giggling, crouched down as he was, but said nothing. Kirk saw that he held a grenade, the pin still in it. It glowed with a white-hot radiance.

The lion-mask turned his head back and forth between the wolf-head and Kirk, checking every few seconds. "Look, buddy, I don't know who you are, but if you'll get your Harbinger there to get us the hell out of here, I'll be glad to have a nice, long conversation with you."

Sylvie shook her head. "I can't carry you all. I don't got enough juice."

The lion-head looked down at the monkey-mask and nodded in Sylvie's direction. A spindly hand fanned open under his mask and offered a finger. Kirk thought, for a moment, that he looked like E.T. with his long, thin finger glowing red. Sylvie took his hand, and Kirk watched as fiery luminescence washed from monkey-head's fingers into her body, illuminating her from within.

Sylvie giggled. "Okay . . . I have enough now." She grabbed hold of Kirk and the man in the monkey mask.

The lion-head grabbed Kirk and stretched his arm out to grab the woman in the wolf mask, who was already leveling her pistol and starting to fire down the street. Kirk watched in amazement as the lion-head's arm snaked out, longer than it could've possibly been, to touch the wolf-mask's shoulder. As soon as Sylvie saw the contact, she raised her hands, and Kirk saw them all, one by one, fall through a hole in the ground that irised open. There was the brief sensation of falling, and then, suddenly, velocity.

Kirk opened his eyes and saw a straight, flat desert all around him, red sand, and a single black-top road. Sylvie was flying along, her braids streaming behind her; the chain of ghosts she was tugging was nothing to her. Her face was contorted in a grimace of concentration. Finally, she lifted her head up and Kirk felt the ragtag wraith-chain fly upward. There was darkness again—the nothin', Kirk guessed—and suddenly they were all standing next to a beautiful old oak tree. There were no Hierarchy agents in sight.

"Freda, can you check to see if we were followed?" the lion-head asked. He took off his mask and smiled at Sylvie. "Thanks for the save, Sylv. I didn't recognize you at first—normally you go it alone."

Sylvie nodded. "No problem, Duke. This here's Kirk. He's my friend. We share a Fetter."

Duke nodded. "Anyone who's a friend of Sylvie's can't be too bad. How are you doin', Kirk? Ain't it great to be dead?" Duke smiled, his mane of hair all white.

Kirk smiled, looking at the lion mask, and shrugged. "God, I wish I had a cigarette. Other than that, I'm okay I guess," he said, stomping his feet from the sudden cold that gripped him from his travel.

He turned away, looking out across the street. Duke was silent, but when Kirk looked up at the tall Renegade ghost, he was proffering something with his hand. "Smokes. It's not the best, but it's something," Duke said, grinning.

Kirk shook his head and put the hand-rolled cigarette in his mouth. Monkey-mask held up a finger (the same one that had glowed like E.T. earlier), and his cigarette briefly caught on fire.

"Puff on it quick, or it'll go out," Duke said. Kirk winked at Sylvie, who wrinkled her nose at him.

Kirk inhaled the sweet but bitter smoke, felt a cold chill go through him as he held it in what used to be his lungs. He realized that the smoke was moving through him, billowing out around him, illuminating him from within. Still, it gave him what cigarettes used to give him: a tinge of something crisp and something to do with his mouth while he was thinking.

Duke smiled. "So, what brings you here tonight to save our asses, Sylvie?"

Sylvie smiled. "Oh, I'm just out and about. Not doin' too much. Just givin' Kirk the tour."

"Ain't thinking he's just gonna get cut into the Circle are ya, hon? Hate to disappoint you," Duke said, grinning. He lit his own cigarette and started smoking. He pointed at Kirk. "What sort of thing are you lookin' to do for the rest of your afterlife? Hang out? Try to screw with the skinbags? Avenge your death? Find God? What?"

Kirk blew the smoke out into the dark air and spread his arms. "I dunno what to tell you. I don't want to just sit around. I want a piece of the action— I want to be out and runnin' with a gang. I'm good, but how can you know that? I'm good at the kind of stuff you guys do. I notice you're down a man. You could use me."

The wolf-masked woman turned to Kirk and picked him up by the collar of the jacket he was wearing. With one hand, she held him suspended in midair.

"Look here, smart boy. That guy was our friend. Derek was the best Breaker I've ever known, and he was ten times smarter than your pansy ass." Kirk hung there, kicking a little, looking down at Sylvie worriedly. His cigarette had bounced out of his mouth and had rolled somewhere in the grass.

"Put him down, Freda," Duke said. "He didn't mean anything by it. Did you Kirk?"

Slowly Freda, her wolf mask seemingly grinning at him, put him down.

"So . . . Kirk. Kirk who?" Duke asked. Kirk looked at Sylvie out of the corner of his eye, but she wasn't giving out any clues.

Kirk's eyes darted to Sylvie and then back to Duke. "Kirk Rourke. You wanna check my job references?"

Duke shook his mane of white hair. "Naw. This is Freda, and this guy in the monkey mask is Jojo."

"Why were those cops messin' with you?" Kirk asked.

Duke put his lion mask back on. "They caught us near one of their secret caches of equipment and stuff. We were trying to rip it off, maybe get in with the Greymaster and his gang. We ain't doin' too good by ourselves, especially now that Furman's gone. Jojo . . . can you sense him anywhere?"

Jojo shook his masked head. "No. Furman gone. Bye, Furman."

Duke slammed his hand into the oak tree so hard he went fuzzy for a moment, and then turned back to Kirk. "What can you do for us?" he said.

Kirk looked down at Sylvie, who smiled at Kirk. "I can push things around. A little singing, too."

Freda swiveled her wolf mask in Kirk's direction. "How do we know he's not an Archy plant? They've been gettin' pretty smart lately."

Sylvie shook her head. "No. I divin'ed him out. He ain't with the Hierarchy. He's a baby. I was surprised to see his Caul gone—someone musta already Reaped him. Don't know who."

Kirk turned around to Sylvie. "Hey! I ain't no baby! I'm twenty-six!"

Sylvie grinned. "You're a baby ghost, Kirk. Ain't been dead for more than nine months. Ain't even seen a Halloween yet. Heck, Miss Cindy spent four months teachin' me powers and stuff."

Freda looked up and down the street. "Um, folks, I hate to break up this party, but all we need right now is some wastrel to see us and report us, and we'll have a bunch of Legionnaires on our asses. Let's go someplace safe."

Jojo looked up suddenly. "The World is safe. Meany will let us in for free."

Sylvie clapped her hands. "Oh goodie! The World!"

Jojo danced around. "Yeah! The World. We say good-bye to Furman! We ride the Merrygo."

Duke looked at Freda, then Sylvie, and asked "Can you carry us there?" Freda shrugged her shoulders, and Duke caught her eyes rolling skyward behind her mask.

Sylvie nodded at Duke. "If you got the juice," she said.

Jojo grinned and touched Sylvie's hand again. A flash of light burned like a magnesium flare between them. Sylvie glowed all over like an industrial angel for a second, and she giggled at the power.

They stood in a circle this time, holding hands: Sylvie liked it best that way.

2

Ghost Story:
Justice Burning

And this, ladies and gentlemen, is the portrait of Magistrate O'Rourke. Jebediah O'Rourke was a prominent member of the community. Served in the Civil War as a colonel in the Georgia Volunteers and rode with Stonewall Jackson. Believe it or not, he was actually murdered here in Dekalb County Courthouse. As you see by this commemorative plaque on the wall, Jebediah was appointed magistrate of the Superior Court in 1856 and served for several years. He was supposedly killed by a group of Ku Klux Klansmen in his chambers, stabbed thirty-six times in the back and burned at the stake for refusal to cooperate with the Klan.

The really interesting part of Jebediah's story is that it's said at certain times when the light is right you can see him still sitting up on his bench, dispensing justice with a stern hand. Some claim to have seen him stalking the great hall of the courthouse, looking out the great windows and brooding over the state of the city. I wonder what he would think about Decatur now? Well, ladies and gentlemen, if you'd like to step this way, I'll show you our collection of Civil War relics. . . .

Jebediah loved his little courthouse. Loved the windows that looked out onto the street. He loved the shadows that were so cool in the day. He hated what he had to do here, hated to have to send free people into bondage, but it was the way of things. He was a judge: he was not to make laws, but to judge them fairly.

Jebediah would stalk the halls of his courthouse, climbing the spiral stair to the utmost tower room, and watch the Shadowlands of the city, watch the purplish red fires that lit the city from below and made the dark sky glow with streaks of magenta. From the top of the tower, Jebediah could almost see the nightly battles that took place in Oakland Cemetery, not too far away. He often walked down to the graveyard to see the Northern soldiers, who had been buried in Confederate graves, drag Confederates from their open crypts and do battle mindlessly. They had long since abandoned gunfire: they possessed no bullets. Still, many of them still aimed their guns and "shot," while more had come to understand that only the bayonets on the ends of their weapons mattered now. Every night there would be wholesale slaughter, and the next night the Drones would rise again to do battle once more. Jebediah watched these fights more to assuage his own Shadow, which was a bloodthirsty sort, than to satisfy his curiosity.

Still, he was always excited when the South rallied

and "won" the nightly battle. It was one such night, the same night that Kirk met Sylvie, that Jebediah used his Argos powers to travel from his beloved courthouse to the cemetery to watch the festivities.

Jebediah was troubled, because his Shadow had grown quiet in the last few days, and his dreams had turned into things of true fear: fiery maelstroms that swept the city, taking all the Restless with them in their relentless paths; a dark demon coming to him to demand payment of some kind; a familiar but strange old woman; his grandson James. Jebediah's dreams had become dire, and he felt the need to let the Shadow out for catharsis to keep it from overcoming him while he was rendering verdicts.

So he sat and watched the carnage, feeling the dark, old cloak of the Shadow mantling him, and it wasn't until the fighting was nearly over that he came back to himself to see a woman resting on one of the benches. One of the dead, Jebediah was certain—a noncombatant. Some of the women buried in Oakland were as fierce as the men, but this one was docile, quiet, her hands folded as if in prayer. She looked up at Jebediah from afar and nodded to him.

She was wearing an exquisite black mourning gown, a black neck draping and veil, elbow-length sleeves, and black lace on her kirtle. She looked ancient, one of the Travelers, obviously—one of the ghosts who had come over the sea with her family.

Jebediah was suddenly shocked as he recognized Mary Riorche, who was not only his great-granddam but also a known Heretic in the area. If he was seen with her, he would be duly censured. The Hierarchy was firmly against the Heretics, who in ancient times tricked Charon into sending them their souls only for personal gain. Although secretly Jebediah still believed in God, he would never have voiced that belief to his Hierarchy friends—then he would also be branded a Heretic and cast out.

Drawing on his Mask of Privacy (an owl's-head mask made of Stygian iron) he strode across the battlefield. Drones were known to avoid their more self-determining Restless "kin," avoiding their presence much like mortals avoided their presence. Jebediah and the lady would not be disturbed.

He bowed low to the lady in black, and she inclined her head at the same time. She wore no mask, as was customary for Heretics, but her mourning veil was firmly in place.

"What brings you to this awful place, dear Mary?" His thick Southern drawl came from behind the owl's beak.

"I come, as ye know, Jebediah, as a bearer of prophecy. From our most holy Laird. As it has ever been. I come here, knowin' as I do that you frequent this place," Mary said, crossing herself.

"I see. What prophecy do ye bring to me this time, most respected dam of my father's father?"

"Ye are to know that the Firebird has arisen. That the Curse of our line has claimed the last son of the Riorche: Kirk, his name be. That he has stepped forth from the Caul to claim his destiny, and I cannae be sure what will befall him," Mary said quietly, her melodic voice carrying to Jebediah's ears over the sounds of men fighting.

"Mary, say it cannot be! I promised I would not continue the Curse of the Dead, and yet you say it's continued without me?" Jebediah looked shocked.

"Aye, and before this it has. The Curse has been fulfilled twice since."

"Twice? Another Riorche lies now in this eternal turmoil! Give me his name!"

"James. Thy son's son."

"Then surely the Kirk-boy isn't a product of the Curse—which is said to skip a generation, from grandfather to grandchild, through the male line," Jebediah said.

"James Rourke lives on, without rest. And his pain, and his fear, and his anger live strong in him," Mary said, her head impassively turned toward the battle.

Jebediah looked up as the call for a Charge was bugled out over the gravestones. He shuddered involuntarily.

"Surely this boy Kirk has no get? Thus ends our line. Thus ends our curse." Jebediah's voice was pleading.

"Aye. And I not be the one you plead to. Plead to God, if such you must do, or to the black-hearted Celt who cursed the Riorche with Restless death so long ago. I only see God's will as described by his great Plan," Mary said, folding her hands.

Mary stood up to leave. Jebediah rose with her at once. "You must tell me more. Where is Kirk? Where is James? Sweet, young James, so strong and brave. I could not claim him as my grandfather claimed me, Mary. I do not know why he is a Restless."

"He was in a great an' terrible war, or so the angels hae told me. It claimed his very soul. Now, I must be going, Jebediah. Likewise, I think ye can set your Monitors to tracin' their places in Purgatory. For me, it is not my place. God gae with you," she said, and turned from him, her fiery red hair streaming out in the wind from under her veil. She made her way out of the graveyard and soon vanished from sight, leaving Jebediah to watch the rest of the battle alone.

Jebediah took a parcel that he always carried in his greatcoat out of the deep wool pocket and unwrapped it, checking the contents. He ran his hand across the mother-of-pearl hilt of the sword, up the blade, to the ragged tip where it had been broken. Would the Firebird come to claim it? he wondered. And what shape would its weapon take this time?

Ghost Story: The Haunted Gun

"No, man, it's not that I'm scared . . . I don't care about no stupid ghosts. I just don't want to clean the armory, that's all. So, if you do it for me . . ." Squire said.

"Me? But Sarge said for you to do it. Besides, it's a haunted gun, not a haunted armory. Just don't mess with the gun, and you'll be fine," his pal, Griff said, grinning. "Look, I'll hold your hand while we go back there . . . "

"Fuck you, man. What do you think I am, a fag?"

"Don't ask, don't tell, Squire."

"Fuck you. All right then, you . . . you stay out here, and hold the light . . . "

"Yeah, it's a good thing you don't believe in ghosts, Squire. 'Cuz the guy who used to own the haunted gun . . . Colonel Jim Rourke I believe his name was, well, damn. He was a mean bastid. I mean, just a hellacious DI and an Army Ranger and he'd as soon rip your heart out and show it to you as shake hands. And, you know about the curse, right? Anybody who goes into training with that rifle gets a medical discharge before too long: funky things happen to them. They get wonky. But you don't believe in that shit, so I'll just leave you here in the dark. . . . " Griff grinned in the doorway of the armory.

"Griff! Dammit, I'm trying to sweep here!"

His men called him the Greymaster, themselves the Grey Wolves. In the twenty or so years since his death, James Rourke had become proud of the wraiths he'd gathered from battlefields all over Southeast Asia, Korea, and even across the Persian Gulf in Desert Storm. One by one, his unit of crack troops (trained as they were in several powers of the dead each) plowed through the Shadowlands of the tropical islands, looking for the dead, the disenfranchised, the lonely soldier-wraiths who would never see their units again. He was able to give them a place, a soldier's job, which is all the Heaven a soldier needs.

His soldiers were from nearly every era. Jameson was a Confederate colonel who was killed just north of Atlanta in a skirmish, one of those that damn fool General Hood ordered. Adams was a doughboy in the Great War, who died nameless in a trench. He'd have no Fetter at all except for the memorials that dotted the French countryside. Collins was a Marine in World War II, one who fought and died on the beach at Iwo Jima. Becker was a riverine patrol officer in the 'Nam, who ran the "cruise ship Oblivion" back in the day. One or two of the men were former Legionnaires, although none of them were older than the modern age. Except maybe Dr. Teeth, but he wasn't what you'd call a soldier. He wasn't what you'd call a doctor, either.

The Grey Wolves numbered forty-three: three highly trained teams of ten, plus administrative support. What Arcanos they needed to know, they were taught. What the Greymaster asked them to do, they did, without question. That was the way of things. The Greymaster could've just as easily gone to work for the Hierarchy, except that they had pissed him off when he'd died. Some backward filing clerk in some embassy over in the 'Nam had forgotten to pick him up, so he'd had to spend two years in the Jade Empire's Hell of Burning Embers, a special Hell they reserved for the spirits of their dead enemies.

Becker and Grim (another wraith, a tall black fella who had since passed on to Oblivion) had broken him out of the Hell of Burning Embers using Becker's riverine boat (they were, as Rangers, sworn to get the last man out of there) to escape down the River. For that reason, Becker was his right-hand man and would, if anything ever happened to him, take over his position as leader.

They called James the Greymaster because he was a master of the quick fade with all his troops, leaving behind nothing but a fog. He was adept at bringing up a fog of grey smoke in the Shadowlands to cover their pursuit, and good enough at Argos, the traveling power, to move his troops through the Tempest if need be. That, and he wore an unmistakable, mirror-helm.

His troops even respected Greymaster's Shadow, which had a known Relic attached to it. When his Shadow was dominant, he would draw a black-bladed machete seemingly from thin air. None had ever been able to best Greymaster's Shadow in a fight and take the machete away from him. No one was that suicidal, not even the worst of the Martyrs, who James suspected secretly worshipped Oblivion.

They had made a headquarters for themselves in a fairly nice place. A MARTA train ran overhead, so there was instant, cheap transportation relatively available. It was an ancient warehouse, one of the many hundreds in Atlanta, a city of rails. It had been condemned several years ago, but one of Greymaster's teams had gone in, possessed the necessary clerks, and made the necessary changes. The warehouse didn't exist anywhere anymore—not even in computer records.

Greymaster had made—just for effect, mostly—a throne made out of a barrel, backed by one of Sherman's neckties. A Sherman's necktie was quite clearly a steel rail twisted into a loop, usually heated on the roadbed and beaten around a nearby tree. General Sherman left quite a few on the trees around Atlanta as he destroyed the rails, and to Greymaster, this symbolized many things at once. For one, it made clear his position on the Greyboys and their Klanriders: he'd have none of that racist crap in his organization. Becker was black, as were a few others of his men, and he couldn't afford to lose any of them. It also signified his other main goal: crippling the rails, specifically the rail line that ran from the Shadowlands to the hub of the Hierarchy, Stygia. It was a stratagem worthy of Sherman: disable the enemy's ability to make war, and he would destroy them. Without the regular supply of soulfire to Atlanta from Stygia, the Hierarchy would just be another group of trained soldiers fighting a losing battle against his better-trained troops.

Greymaster hungered for soulfire. He didn't know exactly where it came from: he was sure it wasn't an easily stomached process. Tales had been told that soulfire was the distilled essence of souls: kind of a spiritual version of Soylent Green. Soulfire was energy, passion, what the Hierarchy called "Pathos," and it was contained in special crystals mined from some hellish hole in Stygia. The crystals fed guns, cars, whatever you needed energy to run. This allowed the Hierarchy Legionnaires to use their Arcanos, their powers of hiding, moving, and magic, and their rifles at the same time.

This was an unacceptable tactical advantage to James, one he must deny the enemy. Besides, there were many other uses soulfire could be put to. It was a more ready currency than oboli. It was also needed to operate not just weapons but radios, computers, anything that once required electricity in the living world. It could also be used to drive a vehicle, sometimes a critical advantage in the lands of the dead. Attach enough soulfire to a bomb in the Shadowlands (oh, that rarest of commodities!), and you would see an explosion the likes of which the Hierarchy had never seen. Oh, how Oblivion loved a bomb, how it hungered to take the fiery power of its explosion and magnify it.

Greymaster had, understandably, become quite adroit at discovering when the Hierarchy shipment of soulfire was to arrive in town. He had operatives on the outer rings of the Hierarchy defenses in downtown Atlanta for many months, testing their response time and readiness. He had informants within the Hierarchy who themselves wanted a cut of the soulfire. He had trained his own men in several soulfire-gathering exercises. Now, all that he lacked was enough weaponry—enough guns to take the Hierarchy by storm and make off with as much soulfire as he could.

And as for that, well, Greymaster had a plan. His Wolves were incredibly efficient, but sometimes measures called for more . . . expendable instruments. James put on his Greymaster's helm, a shiny, smoked-mirror helm which reflected a distorted view of those who looked him straight in the eyes, and strode out of the tent he had erected in the main receiving area of the warehouse. Within seconds, his commands were being followed.

When the cold of the Tempest was done, Kirk and his new-found circle of the dead stood at the bottom of a huge escalator, the bottom-most part of it boarded up. The escalator reached up many stories to the World of Krafft, originally an indoor amusement park that never made it financially.

"Damn. That's what you were talkin' about. That place closed down years ago," Kirk said, shaking his head.

"Not to us," Sylvie said, smiling. "Meany runs it now. He's a clown." Sylvie looked up at the others, as if sharing a secret joke.

They climbed up onto the partition which blocked off the entrance to the escalator and started climbing the frozen metal stairs to the World. Kirk felt dizzy as he rose in height, looking down off the side. He remembered reading that this escalator was one of the largest escalators in existence, when it had been operating. It was even higher than the one in the Underground MARTA station, which took people several stories down.

A few minutes later, Kirk could make out a man standing in a blood-stained clown costume at the top of the stairs. Turning around to face his companions, he realized that this was nothing strange to them. He tried to be cool, but kept avoiding the man's gaze. It was unnerving.

The clown stood there, fingering a rusty razor blade and grinning at him as he reached the top of the stairs. Somehow his companions had maneuvered him so that he was walking in front. Just before Kirk took a step off the escalator, the clown spoke up.

"STOP! Who goes here?" he said in a high, squeaky voice.

Kirk looked back at his friends. Sylvie whispered, "Tell him your name."

"Kirk," Kirk said.

"Ah-ha! Kirk! Are you a first-time visitor to the World?"

"Yes," Kirk said.

"Ah-ha! Then your friends get in free. Come on, friends, come on," the clown said, ushering them past. Kirk started to follow them. "Now, now! Not so fast!" the clown said, interposing his rusty razor blade. "We need to have a chat. You see, everyone who comes into the World has to pay one way or another. If it's your first time, it's easy to pay. Just agree to look in Meany's Mirror in the Hall of Mirrors. Easy enough, no? Everyone here has done it. Why can't you?" the clown said, grinning at him.

Kirk shot daggers at Sylvie, but she looked very seriously at him. "If you want to be one of us, Kirk, you'll do it."

Kirk nodded. "Let me see this mirror."

The clown laughed. "All right then! Follow me, Kurt!"

"Kirk! My name's Kirk."

"Oh! Sorry!" the clown said, rushing ahead of Kirk toward the Hall of Mirrors, which was right next to the entrance. He stepped up to the door leading inside. "Do you have a green ticket?" the clown asked.

"No. I don't have any damn tickets," Kirk said, putting his hands on his hips.

"That's too bad. I always love asking that question. Nobody ever has any tickets. Okay, you can go in," the clown said, opening the door.

Kirk turned and looked at Sylvie again, who mouthed the word, "trust me" back. He turned and confronted the darkness of the Hall of Mirrors.

"Can't see anything in there," Kirk said, looking back at the clown.

"That's the idea," the clown said.

"Can't see anything. How am I supposed to find Meany's Mirror?" Kirk said.

"You'll know it when you see it. You will. I promise," the clown said, grinning wildly.

One of the mirrors in Kirk's view began to writhe.

Freda spoke up from behind the fence leading to the attraction. "Hey, Kirk—what's wrong? Afraid of a little darkness?"

Kirk ignored her. He looked at the clown, looked at his bloody costume, his knife. He wanted to kick the bastard's nuts in and run. Fear and desperation gripped him, nearly suffocating him. The darkness beckoned to him.

Closing his eyes, ignoring the taunts, the anger, the fear, Kirk took a step into the darkness. Almost immediately, the clown slammed the door to the hall. Somehow this place existed entirely in the Shadowlands, in the realm of the dead. Looking at the cracks in the mirrors and the scorch marks on the walls, Kirk guessed that, somehow, this entire place was like his guitar: part of someone else's life, so important a part that it came over with them.

Slowly his eyes adjusted to the utter absence of light, and he began to see movement on the walls around him. Fragmented mirrors, shattered long ago, danced around him, taunting him with different sizes, shapes, distorting his body as he walked by. And as he walked, he saw a dark cloud start to form around him, a dark cloud that contained within it fiery red motes of light that danced. The cloud had his father's face, a face Kirk had seen only in home movies, in pictures in photo albums, and in his dreams. The cloud was Mr. Demon, his Shadow, Kirk knew somehow. And the cloud mocked him, called to him from the other side of the mirror, beckoning him. It flitted from one shattered mirror to another, yelling at him soundlessly, as if the glass kept the voice from being heard.

Kirk walked through the maze, glad for the sturdy feeling of his guitar strapped to his back. He pulled the ax around to his front and held it by the neck, ready to bash anything that came at him.

In the center of the maze of mirrors, he came to a room with six mirrors in it, all six of them perfect except one, which had been painted black. Kirk felt strange, like he had entered someone's dream. Everything sounded hollow, and everything looked out of focus.

"Kirk. You gotta come home, Kirk. I'm really worried 'bout your momma," came a voice from behind.

He turned slowly around. Standing in the mirror behind him was Desiree, a prostitute who worked for the pimp that his mother used to date. Kirk tried to look her in the face: she was wearing nothing but a black lace bustier, and she looked real. To Kirk's eyes, however, her lungs were filled with black energy, her veins running with grey-green foulness.

"What about Momma? She smokin' again?" Kirk asked, compelled by the reality of her image.

Desiree nodded. "Smokin'. Bad. Spent all her AFDC on crack, then had to go work for J.T. for the trailer payment. Anna's sick, too."

Kirk winced. His little sister sick meant that Anna would probably linger on for months, now that Kirk was gone, before she got help. Kirk used to take her to the doctor, because ol' Mom would never do it. Even if it was free. Of course, Anna would only talk to Kirk: she'd not spoken a word to her older sister Kristy or to her mother since she was three. She was out of school most of the time because she was sick, and was constantly being held back grades because of absences.

"What about Kristy?" Kirk asked.

"Kristy's working full-time for J.T. Shootin' up, too. Only, Kirk, she can't afford a hotel room like most of us. She takes her johns home, to the trailer."

Kirk shook his head; he turned away from Desiree. "I don't want to hear this. I'm dead. Can't they take care of themselves?"

Another voice came out of another mirror. It was a strange voice, but one he'd heard over the phone and coming from his mother's bedroom many times: J.T.

"Now, Kirk, don't you worry about them girls. I take good care of them." J.T. grinned. J.T. was an immense white man with a cheap polyester shirt and black jeans bought at Wal-Mart. His rolls of fat were barely contained by the plastic buttons on his shirt.

"You fuckin' leave Mom alone, you hear me, bastard?" Kirk said, feeling his voice get hollow, feeling the black cloud start to congeal around him. He felt burning sensations inside him and saw fiery motes start to dance inside him in another mirror.

"Oh, now, come on, Kirk. Don't you know that she's my best whore? I couldn't leave her now. She'll do anythin' I ask. Anythin' for another pipeful. And you can't tell me you hadn't thought about your sister goin' into the business with me? I know for a fact you've been lookin' at her the past year or so. Just 'cause you're dead don' mean you're dead, boy. And when Anna grows up, just a little bit more, well, she can start earnin' her keep, too." J.T. grinned, showing his cracked teeth.

"You foul fuckin' bastard, I'll rip your fuckin' heart out if you so much as touch Anna, you hear me?"

J.T. laughed and shook his head. "You can't touch me, boy. You dead. Gone. I think I'll go take a piss on your grave."

Another voice: thin, quiet, hoarse, soft. "Kirk? Is that you? Kirk? Oh God, Kirk, it hurts. Can you make it stop hurting?"

The figure was lying on a bed, her arms strapped down, her tattered, straight black hair covering her shoulders. She was thin, bony, wearing a hospital gown that was soaked with blood, her knees up in stirrups.

"God, Kirk! It hurts! I can't take it," came the voice again, and Kirk realized it was Cindi. Cindi on some kind of operating table. They weren't giving her anesthetic. What were they doing?

"Cindi? I'm here. Cindi? Can you hear me?" Kirk called out.

"Oh, shit, Kirk, it hurts. It hurts. Make them stop. Make them stop it, Kirk!" Cindi called out, twisting in the straps. A nurse blew on her face.

"You're forgetting to breathe, Cindi. Breathe, dammit. Breathe through the pain."

"What the hell's going on, Cindi? What the hell?" Kirk screamed at her.

Cindi looked up at him. "Kirk—where are you? You're supposed to fuckin' be here. You did this to me. Damn you to hell, Kirk Rourke," Cindi called out, gritting her teeth as another wave of pain crashed over her. Kirk could feel the pain, stabbing deep in his bowels.

"I didn't—what the hell? I didn't do anything—that's not my baby you're carrying," Kirk said, his voice cracking. He wanted to believe it, but he couldn't.

"Just shut up. You can't help me. You can't do shit," Cindi hissed, and she bucked against the straps. "Shit, I just want one shot of Demerol. Just one. Come on, dammit," Cindi said to the nurse, pleadingly.

The nurse shook her head. "Judge's orders. No painkillers unless absolutely necessary. The doctor hasn't authorized it. Part of your probation. Besides, don't you think your baby's gotten enough drugs?" the nurse said. "Now, breathe."

Kirk put his hands over his face. He didn't want to watch the blood on the sheets. The nurse was bending over her, telling her not to push. Not to push yet.

Mr. Demon spoke up. "See, what did I tell you? No guts. No glory. Just a fuckin' sissy, that's what you are, Kirkie boy. Why don't you suck your thumb a little bit? That'll make you feel better. Come on little boy. Suck your thumb."

"Shut *up!*" Kirk screamed, throwing up his hands.

He swung his guitar around and started breaking mirrors—first Desiree, then J.T., then the mirror showing Mr. Demon clouding around him. Glass flew everywhere. He poised the guitar to smash at the mirror containing Cindi, and stopped. She was crying. She never cried before, never once.

"Oh God, Kirk. Can't you do something? Something. Make them give me something. Oh God. It hurts so much," Cindi screamed out loud, her head thrown back in pain.

Kirk put his hand on the mirror, trying to touch her. Instead of feeling her warm, soft skin, all he felt was the cold glass. Cindi screamed as another wave of pain shook her. Kirk's fingers loosened on the frets of his guitar, and he reversed it in his arms. She opened her eyes as Kirk began to play for her.

"'Beth—I hear you callin'—'" Kirk sang, playing her favorite song, and she nodded her head, listening, smiling weakly. His hands played over the strings, moving in proper time. He'd never played that way before. Grey light was dripping from his fingers, making the guitar vibrate, making the sound resonate against the mirror.

She tried to put out her hand to him, but she couldn't move. He watched her face as he played through the whole song, and when he reached the end, he started on it again, this time without the words. She hummed along, singing, thinking only of the song as she pushed, pushed, breathing like she had to, breathing with every push.

A piercing cry shattered the darkness, light surrounding Kirk's vision wherever he looked. The light was intense. It almost burned him. The light blossomed up from between Cindi's legs, burned into the room. Kirk felt the light as a tangible thing, burning him like the sun burned him. Then the light died down into a tiny, small pinkish light: faint, but steady.

Then they were releasing Cindi's arms and putting a tiny bundle into her hands. It was small, covered in blood, weak, and hungry for crack more than for his mother's milk. It was a boy.

The mirror fell silent and vanished. Only the last mirror, a single dark mirror that stood quietly there, challenging him, remained. Kirk looked down at his body, at his hands, which were still glowing from the light. He wanted to see his son—his new baby boy. He felt more attached to him than anything else, more than the school, more than Cindi. He wanted to see Anna again, see if he could protect her from that bastard J.T. He suddenly felt responsible, somehow, as if he could and should do something.

The dark mirror confronted him, and he was afraid, given what he'd seen in the others, to look into it. He felt a tap on his shoulder.

The clown stood there. Meany. He grinned. "Having fun?" He asked.

"You bastard," Kirk growled. "Did you put me in here to torture me?"

"You're doin' this to yourself, Kirkie boy," Meany said.

"Don't call me that."

"You've got one mirror to go, Kirk-me-lad, or else you'll never leave this place. And I wouldn't break that glass. Oh, no. You've already got twenty-one years bad luck with the three you've already broken," Meany said, giggling.

"What's in there?" Kirk asked.

"Your Shadow. Your darkness. Your life, your death, your regrets. All that you are on the inside, Kirkie boy."

"I said not to call me that! Fuck you. Get me out of here," Kirk demanded, grabbing at the clown.

"Tsk, tsk!" Meany said, and vanished, leaving behind a curl of smoke.

Kirk stood at the edge of the dark mirror, looking into its depths, seeing nothing. He put his hand up to its cool darkness, touching it. It was cold at first, growing warmer. His hand slowly moved into the mirror, like in *Alice Through the Looking-Glass*.

Shouldering his guitar once more, Kirk put his hand farther into the mirror and took a step through. He fell into darkness, into a nightmare, reexperiencing his death.

Rosario was mad. Well, he had a right to be. His dad owned the city's drug trade, and Kirk—well, Kirk was always the independent kind. Kirk thought he could take Rosario in a fight, but he wasn't sure. Rosario grinned at him on the roof of the school, in his nice Armani suit, his beeper attached to his pocket.

"So, Kirk. Kirkie boy. What sort of business you been doin'? I told you to stick to nickel bags and the small shit. What's this I hear about you sellin' C?" Rosario put one of his big, broad hands on Kirk's shoulder. Kirk could feel his buddy move into position behind him, and he knew that the two weren't playing this time.

"Nah, not really. Just a little bit. For a friend. Nothing big," Kirk said, trying to sound like it was true.

Rosario grinned and winked at his friend. "There, you see, Richard, he's a reasonable man. Wouldn't go back on his word to us, would he? No, no. He's a nice boy. A good man. We can count on you, can't we, Kirkie?"

Kirk grinned and nodded. "Sure, you can."

Rosario nodded again. "Count on you to fuck us over as much as you can. You see, Kirkie, I understand you've been on the phone to Miami. Trying to get a shipment in. Smart boy. Close, but no cigar. My dad's already purchased the whole load out from under you, and you ain't got nothin' comin' in on Monday."

Rosario grinned and continued. "Now, I would've gone ahead and let you get caught by the Atlanta DEA, but you know what? I'm gonna be nice to you. You see, the way I figure it, you're gonna keep gettin' out on probation and gettin' back into my supply lines, and keep showin' your grubby-ass white-boy face back in my business. And I don't like that."

"Whoa, Rosario! Let me explain. I can just tell you what's goin' on—" Kirk said, grinning, trying to move away.

Rosario shook his head. "You a fuckup, Kirk. A serious fuckup. And I ain't gonna let you keep making the same mistakes. Bye," Rosario said, turning his back on Kirk.

Kirk felt a cold muzzle pressed against his back and felt Richard pull the trigger on his bootleg automatic SMG. The bullets ate through Kirk's spinal cord, and as the gun bucked, shot through his rib cage, his skull, his heart. He fell forward onto the roof, dead.

And he fell into darkness . . .

. . . of the prison cell he'd spent a month in, the first time he was busted. He remembered the dreams he had, the dreams of his father coming to him there. . . .

The ride in the sheriff's patrol car was short. Kirk thought for a moment about kicking, about throwing his legs against the window to try to break the glass out. He seethed inside, wanting to scream out all his hatred and anger, but realized that he was bound by something stronger than the metal bands that secured him. He heard a laugh inside his head. Mr. Demon?

It was nightmarish, watching the shadows fall across his face as he rode in the back, wishing he knew where they were taking him. He caught sight of granite walls and the car slowly came to a stop. He heard the cop talking to someone else. Two deputies with truncheons opened the door and grabbed him. He blinked in the sunlight as he was dragged to the door of the prison: for some reason there were a few photographers here, catching flash pictures of him—some kind of special-interest drug story, perhaps.

Nausea gripped him as his nose breathed in the foul stench of the indoors. He was thrown into a room with a wooden bench, all of the walls covered with graffiti. He waited there for hours before someone came for him: a blue-uniformed prison guard. The guard unlocked his foot shackles and let him walk to the processing area. They asked him to remove his jeans and T-shirt and underwear: his underwear, they explained, would be returned to him after it had been washed. A trustee sprayed his crotch with some cold liquid. "What's that shit?" Kirk said.

"Crab juice," the trustee mumbled.

They gave him blue prison fatigues and fitted him with a bright red armband.

"Red for felony . . ." the trustee said, grinning. "You goin' to be with the big boys." He had a white band. "Don't take off your band, or they'll put you in solitary."

Several electronic doors opened, and they threw a bedroll at him. "Carry that thing right through there," a guard said, and Kirk walked past the main guardroom and into a long line of cold, iron bars.

Yard lights cast shafts from windows high above the floor: even those had bars on them—it had gotten dark since he last saw the sky. The stink from fifty men in close quarters assaulted him, and some of the cons began to hoot at him as he walked by. They made their way down the row until they got to a single cell, pitch-black inside. He pushed his way into the cell and tripped, slamming his roll onto a bunk.

"Y'all have a nice sleep, now, ya heah?" the guard said, smiling. The door to the cell slammed shut electronically, and the light above went off. It was dark except for the pale red light above the far door.

Kirk dreamt.

"Why did you desert your troops boy?" Captain Rourke bellowed, looking down at him, shaking his head. Kirk had run when the rest of his gang had stayed behind in the house, when the Red Dog drug cops broke down the door. "You should've stayed with them. Never desert your people. You lost them to the enemy!"

Kirk, kneeling in front of him, looked down. "I'm . . . I'm sorry, sir."

"You are sorry, son. A sorry example of a soldier. I hope no one ever finds out you're my boy. I'll have to say 'Who? Who that? Oh, no, most be someone else's fuckup of a kid.' Just you tell me how I'm supposed to stand up and be proud of a screwup like you? A wimp? A momma's boy?"

"I'm . . . no excuse, sir."

"That's right. No excuse. You no-account, no-excuse, useless piece of bird shit. Ah just a'soon get rid o' ya and start over. But I can't, now that your momma's become a worthless junkie. Of course, you had nothin' to do with that, noooo, not you. You little shit."

Kirk tried not to flinch as the captain kicked him. He felt the boot, felt the crack of bones under his nose, felt the blood running freely down his face. He looked up, his face a mess. He knew better than to wipe the blood away—that would just get him another kick. He'd grown used to these visits, in his dreams, in his sleep.

"I'll . . . do better, shur," Kirk slurred as his lips puffed up. He felt as helpless as he had when he had been paralyzed earlier in the day.

The captain lit a cigarette, grinning. "Oh, now, son, don't you take it so hard. It ain't like you're a total failure. Hell, you ran away pretty good from those ossifers. I tell ya what. Find a razor blade, somethin' nice and straight, and off yerself, okay? Save me the trouble of havin' to do it myself. That'd be real nice. Might even get ya a promotion."

The captain threw the cigarette down. "Posthumously, of course," he said, grinning even wider. He held out his hand. In it was a rusty straight razor. "Go ahead, boy."

Kirk drew cuts on his wrist with the blade, and fell back, into darkness . . .

. . . black singing darkness,
darkness that grasped,
sucked at him, darkness that wanted him . . .
he was surrounded in it,
he was being eaten by it . . .
he saw faces in the darkness,
twisted things that had no
shape or symmetry but reached
out to him.

Something stopped them, moved them aside, took his hand . . .
He heard whispers
whispers within him,
whispers echoing through him,
whispers from his past,
whispers from his future . . .
. . . and moved, as if in a nightmare,
through the tragedy of his life . . .
. . . he felt a dark hand, gloved, take his,
leading him through the darkness.

Many things moved past his eyes, not all remembered:

He saw his own grave, a space no bigger than a file drawer in a state-run crematorium. . . .

He saw his old trailer home: still business as usual with his older sister Kristy, who had found another trucker to trick with, taking his money for an hour in her bedroom. . . .

His mom spending her time planning her lottery buys for the next day and nursing a new vial of crack she'd gotten, presumably to celebrate Kirk's death. . . .

He saw his little sister Anna, who was too tired to cry, too afraid to have tears roll down her cheek, who clutched her teddy bear close, the same teddy he'd given her so many years ago. . . .

He saw his girlfriend Cindi, her face still wet with tears, slugging down hits of Jack Daniels straight and looking very long and hard at a sharp knife she had balanced on the side of the tub. . . .

He saw the roof of the old school building, where he'd spent the last months. . . .

He saw the shell of the burned-out cathedral his gang had burned to the ground when the Dragons had tried to take it over, and remembered their blind hatred of him when they'd found out he'd done it. . . .

. . . and, finally, he saw his old '67 Harley warthog motorcycle, the last remaining gift from his father, the only legacy he was ever to have. He saw it on the back of a pickup truck, burning rubber down I–20, heading toward Conyers. Out in the boondocks, where there were still trees and grass and farmland, to a place they called Competition Hills, an ancient subdivision that had failed due to the fact that the hills were too steep to build on. Now there was nothing but cracked asphalt streets and lightposts that would never see light . . . and hills. His friends drank themselves into a stupor, rigged the motorcycle to go by itself, started it rolling,

and set the thing on fire. As it burned, it fell down the ravine, trailing smoke. When it hit the bottom, it exploded, completely destroying it. . . .

The last thing Kirk remembered was a kiss, and a hand pressing something dark and hard and cold into his hand, something that slung onto his back.

Then, a hand grasped his, a small hand. Kirk stepped into the light.

Sylvie grinned at him. "Kirk! You made it through! You're one of us now! You're a Renegade!" She was hugging him. He felt somehow lighter, as if the whole experience had caused the Shadow inside of him to become weaker, drained.

"Welcome to the Circle, Kirk," Duke said, stepping forward to shake his hand. "We all said that if you came out of there, we'd let you be in the Circle. Anyone who can endure Meany's Funhouse is okay by us."

Kirk squinted in the light. "What does that mean? In the Circle?"

Sylvie smiled. "The Circle, Kirk, is what we call our family. We're all dead and, well, there's nobody to look out for us but us. You know what I mean? So we look out for each other. We're a group. Compadres."

"A posse," Jojo said, nodding, looking up from some work he was doing with his hands. Sylvie grinned at Jojo and stood in front of him as if hiding what the small monkey-masked man was doing.

Freda turned her wolf-masked head to look back at the World's entrance. Kirk now saw that other wraiths were hanging out on the old amusement rides, draped over old chairs, riding on a rickety old rollercoaster, seated on the merry-go-round.

Freda pointed at the entrance. "Looks like we got

some company." Three ghosts stood at the entrance, bargaining thick black coins with Meany for entrance. A few moments later they were admitted, Meany vanishing off to wherever he hid his wealth.

They all three dressed the same, in grey cloaks, wearing wolf masks that were quite different from the one Freda wore. She sneered behind her mask. "Grey Wolves. Greymaster's moving again. Wonder what's up."

"Play it cool, Freda. Let's let them come to us," Duke whispered.

Freda nodded, keeping her hand on her sidearm, but not lighting it with the glowing energy needed to fire it.

Kirk looked at the Grey Wolves and marveled at the effect they had on the other ghosts hanging out in the park. As they moved through the loose clumpings of wraiths, they parted the traffic like Moses parting the Red Sea. They had a presence about them that seemed to seethe with quiet power.

The three Wolves made their way slowly around, and Kirk was distracted watching them. Jojo whispered to Kirk, and Kirk bent his head down to speak with the small man. Jojo's quick hands slid a mask onto Kirk's face and he said, "Surprise. It's a present. Our Circle wears animal masks, so you get one. It's a Firebird mask. Shhh. Don't talk, here come the Wolves."

Kirk felt the mask with his fingers, but couldn't picture how it looked. There was no time: one of the Wolves strode right up to Duke and saluted smartly.

"Sergeant. It's been a long time," came a voice from behind the lead Grey Wolf's mask.

"Yeah, it has. Who are you?" Duke answered. Kirk could almost hear the cocky grin in Duke's voice.

"Inconsequential. I'm here with oboli and a job for some smart Renegades," the Grey Wolf said.

"What do I need with oboli? You think the Hierarchy's gonna let me spend them? I don't need no damn Stygian coins," Duke said.

"Then there's somethin' you do need, and we can get you that, too," the Grey Wolf said.

"What's the job?" Freda interceded.

"A simple skinriding mission. Nothing big. The way's already been primed; we've been working with these as Consorts for many months. They love to be ridden. Really get a kick out of it. And they'll do anything you want. Anything."

"So, what do you want them to do?" Duke asked, crossing his arms.

The Grey Wolf's permanent grin seemed particularly appropriate. "I want them to break into a weapons bunker. There's an old gun there, a relic, that we can't get at. Someone's warded the place."

"All of this for one gun?" Kirk spoke up. The Grey Wolf looked at him closely, silently. A moment or two passed, and Kirk wondered if he'd just blown their chance at getting the job.

"I don't believe I know you, Lemure," the Grey Wolf said. "Are you new?"

Freda took a step in front of Kirk. "He's new. Just arrived from out of town. One of our Circle, though, so you can't have him."

"My dear Freda, I would never think of stealing your Firebird friend. I was just very interested in his rather beautifully crafted mask. Where did you get that? I would like to commission the artificer myself," the Grey Wolf said, mellifluous tones in his voice.

Duke spoke up. "None of your business, Wolf. But you could do me a favor and answer his question for him."

"My, my. Touchy, touchy. All right, then. Yes, this operation is to recover a single relic pistol, very important to my master. But we need the skin-puppets to open the door for us. We've arranged to have the proper keys available. These Consorts are very easily guided—even if you've never skinridden before, you should be able to easily take control. As I said, it gives them great pleasure. They think they're some kind of superheroes or something," the Grey Wolf leader said. Then, he noticed Sylvie and bowed a little.

"Miss Sylvie. I'm sorry, I didn't see you here. I heard your schoolhouse was nearly burned. I'm dreadful sorry. You need help tracking down the arsonist?"

Sylvie shook her head. "No, thank you, Wolf. I'm perfectly able to take care of myself."

The Grey Wolf nodded. "Ah yes, but Greymaster always tells us to respect our elders, and I and my men are always willing to help out such an honored and revered Gaunt as yourself."

Sylvie smiled. "Well, thank you, sir. But I do believe I'll be just fine."

Duke spoke up. "What, exactly, are you sayin' you'll pay, Wolf? We can do this job just fine. If it's all that you say it is."

The Grey Wolf leader grinned. "Oh, it is, it is. What I'm sayin' is that the Grey Wolves will be in your debt, and we'll be perfectly willing to work out a deal for whatever you want—"

Freda spoke up. "Even souled weapons?"

Grey Wolf laughed. "If all goes according to plan, souled weapons won't be quite as rare as they are now. But if that's what you want, then that's what you'll get."

"Ooh. Ooh. Soulfire?" Jojo said, dancing a little.

Grey Wolf nodded. "Definitely soulfire. I can even provide you with some right now, if you desire a down payment."

Duke coughed. He looked at his circle, but he didn't have to. He could feel their interest and curiosity and need. His lion mask swiveled back to the Grey Wolf leader.

"Sure, we'll do it. Let's see the color of your crystal," Duke said.

Holding out his hand, Grey Wolf gestured to one of his two companions. From beneath his full, grey cloak came a small army green pouch. He placed the pouch in Freda's waiting hand. She opened it, counting to herself.

"Four shards," she reported.

Duke nodded his lion mask. "Yes, that'll do just fine. How much more can we expect once the run is done?"

"Ah, we have a prism or two for you then. Much larger. There's one stipulation, however," the Grey Wolf leader said.

"Which is?" Freda said with an "oh, boy—here it comes" tone to her voice.

"The Grey Wolves get to keep any salvage from the run. Relics, Thralls, whatever you get. Deal?" said the Wolf.

Duke glanced at Freda, who nodded almost imperceptibly.

"All right, then. It's a deal. Where are these skin-puppets?" Duke said, shaking the Grey Wolf's hand.

The Grey Wolf's directions showed them how to get to a place Kirk already knew about. Sylvie picked up the location from Kirk's head and was able to get them near it: Joe's Bar, a cheap dive just outside of Cabbagetown. Kirk was feeling woozy by the time they traveled all the way there, holding on to Sylvie through the bitter cold and dark of the Tempest. It was just one more mind-numbing feeling to add to the hundreds of emotions he'd already felt that day. Kirk was feeling empty, emotionless, despite the looks of triumph Sylvie gave him from time to time. He kept thinking about Anna and his new baby son, wanting to see them, wanting to be near them, to protect them, somehow, from the world around them. He didn't know when he'd see them again.

Behind all that feeling was the sense that the Shadow inside him, Mr. Demon, was building up energy, waiting to strike like a cobra. He felt different somehow: changed. His memory of his death was starting to come back. He found himself staring at people and places most of the time, looking through his hands at them.

"Hey, Kirk! You look a little fuzzy! Let's fix that!" Jojo said, touching him. Suddenly, like a flush of cool water all over him, he felt his vision sharpen, his wits come back to him. "You were nearly outta meat, Kirk. I'd watch that. Didn't your Reaper teach you how to heal yourself?"

Sylvie looked at Jojo sternly. "Now, Jojo, Kirk didn't have a normal Reaper like everyone else. She found him and released him. Didn't stick around to teach him nothin'. Kirk: your body, even though it's dead, is still there. It's just more solid energy now. Miss Cindy used to call our bodies 'Corpus,' but that sounds too much like 'corpse' to me, and I don't like corpses too much. Anyway, when you get tired like that, you just need to fill out yourself body-wise. It's pretty easy. Just relax and think about a full stomach, let that feeling guide you."

Kirk nodded. "Thanks, Jojo, for the jolt. I needed it. Hey! Look in there! Some of my old buds."

Freda peered inside the dusty window of the bar and nodded. "Yeah, those are our skinbags for the evening. They're wearing the Metallica jackets. You know them?"

Kirk nodded. "Yeah. I used to . . . well, I used to kind of tell them what to do."

Duke smiled behind his mask. "Well, there you go. You should take to Puppetry easy."

Sylvie put her hand on Kirk's arm. "Puppetry is the art of getting into someone's skin and makin' them do what you want them to do."

Kirk looked down at Sylvie. "You kiddin' me? Well, why didn't you tell me that? I could've puppeted that woman over to the phone to call the fire department!"

Sylvie grinned. "It's a little harder than that, Kirk. Besides, I didn't know if you had it in you or not."

Kirk said, "Huh. Just give me a chance. Tell me what to do."

Duke stepped slowly through the front door and turned around to face Kirk. The din of the bar was starting to become clearer, but he could still hear Duke easily. "Come on in, Kirk. I'll show you," Duke said.

Duke stepped into the body of the nearest boy, a guy Kirk knew as "Big John." Mimicking Big John's movements, the differences between Duke and Big John slowly disappeared, and Duke faded into Big John. Instantly, Big John began to giggle.

"Guys . . ." Big John said.

"What is it, you big ass?" Tony, a short, squat kid with an attitude asked. Tony was drinking a beer. "You drunk?"

Big John shook his head.

Kirsten, a miniature amazon in a black leather skirt, spoke up. "What is it, Biggie? You got somethin' in your head?"

Big John nodded slowly, grinning.

Monica, an even taller, darker-haired version of Kirsten, sighed. "Oh no, not more funky shit. I hate this crap. Kirk should be here—he always knew what to do."

Tony giggled. "Hey, maybe Kirk *is* here. Maybe Kirk's takin' Big John over." Tony always was a very morbid asshole—he loved to screw with other people's heads.

Then Kirk looked up and saw Rick walking to the table, his pool cue in his hand. "What's up?" He said. Rick was his old second-in-command, his best buddy.

"Big John's getting giggly. Must be something in the air," Tony said.

Rick nodded and sat down. The gang looked at each other across the table. Monica almost stood up to leave, but Kirsten shot her a look.

Sylvie stepped up to Kirk's side. "Go ahead. You take Rick. You know him, right?"

Kirk felt funny about it. Getting inside his old best friend? That wasn't something he ever wanted to do. Still, it was time, and this was the deal. Kirk slid his hand slowly inside of Rick, moving to sit down in the same chair as he was. For a second he felt like he couldn't breathe, and he almost jumped up. He felt himself sliding into place, felt his vision blur. Then, a second later, he was in Rick, using Rick's eyes, feeling Rick's body around him. Rick was smoking. It tasted so good to get real smoke in his lungs. He looked out of the corner of Rick's vision at Kirsten, who'd only sort of turned him on before, but looking at her now . . . ! So many curves! Such a hot, sexy babe! He wanted to shake his head to clear it, but found he couldn't.

Then, something clicked. His control was not total and absolute—he still felt Rick's identity just below his, watching. Still, he knew that Rick would never remember the details of the night past the moment Kirk took him—something told him that Rick would only remember this as if it were a dream.

Rick/Kirk grinned. "Yeah, I think it's going to be party time tonight, boys and girls."

Monica looked shocked. "Rick? That's not your voice. That's Kirk's voice!"

Rick/Kirk looked down at his hands. "Huh. Who woulda thunk it?" Rick/Kirk looked up at Monica. "I guess it is."

Sylvie turned to Freda. "He's got more Puppetry than I do, with no training! He's got full possession!"

Freda shrugged. "It happens sometimes. These guys are his friends. They're looking for him. Of course it's gonna be easy for him. Let's make the best of it.

Kirk/Rick smiled. "You folks miss me?"

Tony shook his head. "Rick, stop it. You're scarin' Kirsten."

Kirsten kicked Tony under the table. "I'm not scared. If that's you, Kirk, when's the first time we ever had sex?

Kirk/Rick grinned. "You know, Kirsten. Stone Mountain. Just off the walking trail. Under the stars, at night. You don't remember?"

Kirsten grinned. "Ahh, Rick, I forgot. You boys told each other everything. Probably sucked each other's cocks, too."

Rick/Kirk said, "Fuck you, Kirsten. We never did that."

Tony grinned. "Ah, there! You see, Rick! You can't keep that Kirk accent. You're fakin' it."

Rick/Kirk shrugged. "What say we go have some fun? There's supposed to be an envelope waitin' for us at the Y. Let's head over there and figure out what's goin' on. What say?"

Freda stepped into Monica, the tall one, riding along with her. Jojo leaped into Tony. Sylvie, smiling, eased herself into Kirsten. She stuck her head out of Kirsten and winked at Kirk. "Ain't never been a hot, sexy, white girl before. You think you'll take me out to Stone Mountain after this?" Sylvie said, grinning.

Kirk/Rick rolled his eyes as the rest of the group started giggling. Monica/Freda growled. "Oooh. I feel like kickin' some major butt."

Tony/Jojo shrugged. "Me, too. I guess. I feel kind of weird, actually. But okay."

Big John/Duke said, "Let's get goin'."

It was a hell of a lot of fun for Kirk, riding motorcycles again. They rode in perfect formation, his gang. He loved that. They were so cool. Kirk thought about his motorcycle . . . the one that was destroyed, wondered where it was. Unbidden, the motorcycle flashed in his mind's eye: hidden behind some trash somewhere. He wasn't sure. It was there, though. All grey, the headlight cracked, but there.

The rode across town to the Y, where Big John/Duke went in and got the envelope. Inside of the envelope was a set of keys and a map.

Tony/Jojo giggled. "Shit, man. This is Fort Gillem. That's not far from here. Shit. The big time."

Rick/Kirk grinned. "That's right. Big guns. Really cool."

Kirk couldn't help but feel that someone—something—was listening to them. He looked around, searching for the source of the feeling, but found nothing. Kirsten/Sylvie looked up.

"I don't know, Rick. I have a bad feeling about this . . . but what the hell."

Kirk/Rick laughed. "Don't worry. You guys stay here. I'm gonna go in and get somethin' out of my— I mean, Kirk's locker. It'll help." Kirk laughed to himself. Stealin' from the Army! Damn, this was going to be the biggest move since the Dragons busted into an old cop warehouse and snagged a bunch of revolvers.

A few moments later, Kirk/Rick came out of the YMCA wearing an old battered Army jacket, with the name "ROURKE" stenciled across the pocket. "Hey, what do you think? I'm Private Rourke. This is my—Kirk's dad's from boot camp."

Big John grinned and started his motorcycle. "Let's rock!" he yelled over the noise, and the gang, with their spectral puppeteers, rode off into the night.

3

Ghost Stories:
Inquest

*Q: And who, do you think, had access to the files
as to where the armament was?*

*A: Only myself, Captain Watson, and Sergeant
Bailer, sir.*

*Q: I see. And yet, you report some kind of com-
puter malfunction interrupting the system at
0413 hrs?*

*A: Yes, sir. It seems that we have some kind of
cross corruption from the /dev/null area of the
disk. "The Ghost in the Machine," sir.*

*Q: Private, what are you saying? How would
security be circumvented that way? What is
the "Ghost in the Machine"?*

*A: Sir, I don't know, sir. It's almost as if the hacker
came in from the blank parts of the disk,
trashed a few security sectors, and opened the
file from a machine-level interface. I can't see
how else it could happen. It's happened before,*

> *though. Computer jocks call it "the Ghost in the Machine."*
>
> Q: *You're saying you've had a physical security breach on a machine that's in an underground concrete bunker in Langley, VA?*
>
> A: *Sir, that's the only way I can explain it. That, or some seriously freaky kind of hardware glitch.*
>
> Q: *Thank you, Private. You're dismissed.*

Who sees a shadow? Who notices its passing? When the darkness is besieged with them, how can you tell when one breaks free and runs past? Sergeant Brian Whittaker couldn't, certainly, sitting in his post house on the grounds of Fort Gillem, an army depot in Atlanta. He smoked another cigarette and threw it out into the darkness, watching it fizz as it hit the cold, wet grass. The young shadows (with their secret skinriders) stole past the watchful eyes of the Army and off into the woods on the base, grinning to each other in the rush of danger. These young lions felt like real commandos as they made their way, in pairs, across the base, eluding the sleepy security.

Rick/Kirk led them, his left hand clutching an old Fort Gillem map that he kept tucked into a black trenchcoat of Rick's—army-issue, of course. He'd be the one to "play soldier" if they were discovered. He ran to the top of a ravine and suddenly remembered the silhouette that his gang would make when they topped it. He shot out his hand, fixing them all with a single gaze. They froze. Big John/Duke was grinning, Kirk noticed—the stupid grin that meant he was either angry or ecstatic.

"Down!" Rick/Kirk hissed.

He looked over the edge of the ravine at the

bunker—their target. It was short and squat, piled up with green grass on both sides. The gravel road around it was for patrols—Kirk/Rick knew from the instructions that the Hummer would be around shortly, in about twenty minutes, and that he had just missed the last patrol.

Rick/Kirk gave his lions the "two-by-two" symbol with his hands and rolled over the crest of the hill, getting up and dog-trotting across the intervening space. He felt the gentle weight of Rick's .38 Special riding along in the big pocket of the trenchcoat and turned to see Big John/Duke loping down the hill after him. Then Monica, Kirsten, and Tony, all very quiet. Even Big John had managed to stay quiet, although it looked like he was going to break into a giggle at any moment.

Walking up to the bunker, Rick/Kirk inspected the lock. He motioned to Tony/Jojo to hold the penlight beam on the letters stenciled just above it: A13. Without looking back, Kirk began to count out the keys on the keychain: looking for the one that was marked A13. Looking up at Tony, who had gotten his dad's shotgun and now had it hidden under his coat, Kirk thrust a key in the lock and turned it.

There was a tremendous lurching sound within the door itself, and suddenly the whole gang started as the red light on the outside of the building began to flash.

"Wait . . . that's normal. It's okay. Monnie, put that garbage bag over it," Rick/Kirk whispered.

Inside, the red glow of emergency lights beckoned the gang like the glint of gold off of a treasure. Monica wrapped the light in the bag, and soon there was nothing but a dull red dimness glowing within.

They stole quietly into the bunker. It was beautiful to them. In the living world, along one side of the wall were a row of AK-47's in excellent condition. Kirk's mind inventoried the ammunition, the grenades, even the coffin-shaped box of LAW rockets stacked to one side. Beside it was a large vehicle-mounted machine gun with its mounting assembly. On the other side were black plastic cases that he knew, somehow, had laser sights packed in them, and other high-tech toys. What really grabbed Kirk's attention and held it was the large backpack in the corner which, Kirk knew, carried enough C4 explosive to make a city block jump. Rick/Kirk looked up at his gang. They were smiling, opening up crates, examining guns, grenades, toys. They looked like a bunch of kids on Christmas morning.

Then, the strange feeling that he was being watched came again. Kirk looked up quickly, sliding Rick's head aside like one might move aside a mask—looking around desperately for the gun that was supposed to be here. This "special" gun. All he could see was an old Confederate-issue revolver hanging in the darkness, and so he tucked that inside his own ghostly pocket.

As he slid back into Rick, he suddenly became aware of the sound of a motor and tires moving across gravel outside. He ran for the open doorway and, turning around, whispered, "I'll be back. There's a car." Kirk/Rick slammed the door closed, turning the lock on it, while settling the army cap on his head and hoping that the patrol wouldn't notice it wasn't real.

A Hummer was indeed slowly making its way down the road, bouncing through the pocks in it. Suddenly its searchlight went on and shone out to hit Rick/Kirk, who saluted smartly.

"What are you doin' here, son?" the MP asked, driving the Hummer a little closer, shining a flashlight into Kirk's face, on his hat and trenchcoat. "Private . . . Rourke? I ain't never met you. What do you think you're doin'?"

Rick/Kirk looked back at the bunker, and then turned back to the MP and grinned. "Sergeant, I have no excuse, but I thought I saw some perpetrators entering the area. Civilians. I walked over to have a look, sir, but found nothing. I—"

Suddenly there was a pounding sound on the inside of the bunker, the hard sound of metal against metal, of frantic screaming muffled through the steel and earth. Kirk saw flashes of darkness rise up out of the bunker, but he knew Rick couldn't see them. Then, the entire bunker erupted in a huge gout of fire. Kirk felt himself picked up and thrown by the blast: he watched the safety glass on the Hummer shatter and the MP inside thrown back. Kirk leapt out of Rick's body as he felt the entire left side of Rick's face turn red from burns.

The fireball continued to expand up and mushroom, covering the grass around the bunker with smoking, burning debris. Kirk looked down at Rick, his body badly burned from the blast. He looked up at his Circle, who were floating just above the bunker, watching the pillar of black smoke rise up.

"What the hell happened?" Kirk yelled, stunned at the death of his friends in life.

One by one the misty shadows slowly began to materialize again. Kirk watched as the sergeant in the Hummer called the explosion in and asked for hospital assistance and the local police to come out immediately. Rick was unconscious, lying there on the ground, and nothing Kirk could do could keep him out of jail now.

Sylvie touched Kirk's arm. "Big John started playing with the grenades, Kirk. There wasn't anything we could do."

"Why did he do that? He's not that stupid. Duke?" Kirk almost yelled at Duke.

"Duke, why the fuck didn't you stop him?" he yelled.

"I tried. It was . . . it was like someone else was tugging his strings. Not me. Like he was resisting . . . but I don't know how. Like he was doing what some-one else said. I'm sorry, Kirk." Even Duke's lion mask looked a little sad.

Jojo became solid and spoke up, "Eh. I've got a feelin'. Grey Wolves on the way."

Suddenly, out of the Tempest, six grey-cloaked figures emerged and materialized. They were carry-ing their weapons "lit," that is, charged with the energy needed to shoot. They obviously expected trouble.

Duke turned to the leader. "Are you the same Grey Wolf we spoke to earlier?"

He bowed. "I am. You folks have done a wonder-ful job. Thank you very, very much. Here is your payment in full." The Wolf threw down a black plas-tic vinyl bag with a zipper. "Soulfire for everyone," he said.

Jojo scrabbled down and grabbed the bag, grinning.

Kirk watched as, one by one, the Wolves shim-mered with their own energy. Their cloaks became mirror-bright, almost reflective, and they walked slowly into the flames, searching for debris.

Kirk bent down to Sylvie, who was also watching them. He asked, "What are they doin'?"

"Looking for Relics. Stuff brought over by the dead. And for souls," Sylvie whispered back in the ultra-quiet voice that only another wraith could hope to hear.

Kirk, beside himself with anger, strode into the fire, feeling a tingle and a shock, watching as his body discorporated. He was screaming at the Grey Wolves, but his voice was as insubstantial as his body. One of the Grey Wolves gestured at him to leave. As he grew solid again, Sylvie grabbed him and pulled him out of the fire.

"Smooth move," Duke said. "That's not going to get you anywhere. Kirk . . . your friends are dead. There's nothing you can do for them now."

Kirk felt the bottom drop out of his soul, felt darkness overtake him. His eyes burned like cinders. His hand clutched around the Confederate revolver in his pocket, and he took it out and aimed it at Duke's mask. But it wasn't his voice that spoke. It was Demon's. "I want to get them, you see? Never leave your team behind, Private. Never desert your people. Understand?"

Duke shook his head. Looking down at his own hand, he watched as it began to glow with a fiery-red energy. Duke slapped Kirk across the face.

"Snap out of it, cheesehead!" Duke yelled. He slapped Kirk again.

Kirk shook his head, the blackness dropping away instantly, Demon's control broken.

"What did you do?" Kirk asked, incredulous.

Sylvie grinned and took Kirk's hand. "Duke's a Pardoner among other things. He slapped th' Shadow outta ya."

Kirk looked back at the Grey Wolves in their mirror-bright cloaks and watched them emerge from the fires carrying several boxes of equipment from within the bunker. He turned around and saw Rick being loaded into an army ambulance, the MP's having arrived. He watched as the door to the ambulance slammed closed and it slowly drove away.

The leader strode up to the Circle. "You folks still here? We had a nice haul from that little venture. Too bad about the skinpuppets, but then again, these days they're a dime a dozen. Say, Firebird! I see you found the revolver. Very good. I'll just be taking that," he said, holding his hand out.

Kirk grudgingly turned the revolver around and gave it to the Wolf. He knew it was the object they'd been sent to find, at least ostensibly, but he felt that, somehow, the revolver was his. That, at the very least, he'd earned it through the blood sacrifice of his friends.

"Now, we were about to go have a victory celebration at the Den. Would you like to come along?"

Freda coughed. "No, we'll just be going, actually."

Kirk turned to Sylvie. "I want to go with the Wolves."

Sylvie looked up at him. A smile creased her features. "I thought you'd say that."

Freda shot daggers at Kirk with her eyes. Duke, ever the peacemaker, spoke up. "Ah, Sylvie, why don't you go along with Kirk? We'll head on back to the hole and rest up. We can even ride the bus. That'll be a decent change from swimmin' through the Tempest."

Sylvie nodded. "Okay, Duke. We'll meet up with you tomorrow night?"

Duke nodded. "Come on folks," he said, and began walking toward the gates of the base.

When they had vanished over the hilltop, the leader looked down at them. "My Harbinger or yours?" he said, his voice silky.

"Yours," Sylvie said, smiling.

The Thompson Railroad Warehouse was built in the early 1920s. Then it was a sturdy brick-and-steel structure, built to last. Now, however, the warehouse had gradually eroded over the years, and several load-bearing girders had begun to buckle and bend from the weight. Still, it was a highly defensible structure with many windows, and the Grey Wolves had made it their headquarters, training grounds, and communal Haunt.

In July 1977, Thomas Heck had killed three teenagers, the Stanford brothers, in a rather brutal and perverse way (the investigator found genital body tissue stuffed into every available orifice), and ever since that brutal act of mindless violence the warehouse had gained the reputation of being "haunted."

The other strange thing about the place was that a fog would invariably rise up around it at sundown and wouldn't go away until the sun rose again, every night, even on the hottest, clearest nights of the year. Folks in the area stayed away from the Thompson Warehouse, which was just the way the ghosts who lived there wanted it.

Jameson's Wolf patrol, back from the raid at Fort Gillem, materialized out of the Tempest, the dark holes temporarily created by their travel closing as they appeared. Six Wolves, plus two "passengers."

Instantly the Wolves' security routine went into action. Three Wolves strode out of positions around the arrival zone to examine the passenger-wraiths and get a report from the leader. Jameson smiled to the boys on guard duty. They examined Kirk and Sylvie, took a small black knife from Sylvie and the guitar from Kirk, and the officer of the watch nodded Jameson onward as the other Wolves in the team began to carry the armament they'd gleaned from the explosion into the warehouse by a different route.

They walked across the remainder of the field toward the warehouse. Kirk couldn't help but notice the layers of defense the Wolves had set up: what looked like old, discarded cars and railroad ties stacked haphazardly became a maze which any ghosts attacking the warehouse would have to negotiate.

Several times Kirk got the sense that they were being watched, examined by hidden eyes, but no one challenged their progress toward the building, walking as they were in front of the Wolves. Kirk felt like he was entering a military installation, not a

haunted house. Still, the overall effect of the place—
a rotting warehouse with the stench of bad chemical
spills and death running through it, the slight fog that
wreathed the building, the thousands of watching
eyes—had their effect on Kirk, who had not yet gotten used to any of it. Kirk couldn't help but continue
to think of his dead friends, of Rick (was he still
alive?), of Cindi and his new son. He couldn't help
but wish he was anywhere else. But something compelled him to continue moving forward, something
told him that it was important for him to go through
the giant warehouse doors and confront whatever
was inside.

Sylvie helped: she was always by his side, quietly
walking. The other ghosts seemed to defer to her quietly. They didn't like to have to show such courtesy
to what appeared to be a child, but every single ghost
they walked past on their way to the entrance turned
his head in deference to her. Kirk wondered if there
was something beyond her apparent age that caused
her to have such respect among these wraiths.

They stopped in front of two huge double doors,
and when a word was given from within the building, the doors slowly slid open, somehow operated
in the living world by an unseen operator. Perhaps it
was something as simple as a ghost punching an
"open" button like Kirk used to knock people's
glasses off. Or perhaps it was some magical power
these ghosts had that Kirk had never seen.

The doors opened slowly, but Kirk began walking
as soon as there was a large enough opening to do
so. He was impatient. Something inside him was
ticking off the seconds, watching, waiting. He knew
Mr. Demon had a hand in this, but didn't know
exactly what.

The light inside the warehouse was minimal,
although Kirk could see several small lights placed in

various parts of the room. At the far end was a strange-looking chair, a throne almost, with a large rail of steel twisted into a loop behind it.

Kirk looked at Sylvie several times in the intervening space, walking the length of the large warehouse, to see if she would give him a sign as to how to act. Kirk refused to look at the throne, knowing that the one who sat there was the reason he was here. He looked at Sylvie, who smiled at him: quite a child's smile, a smile which didn't acknowledge the fear boiling up inside of Kirk's gut. The fear which threatened to consume him. Kirk felt icy cold shiver through him as he looked at the throne, finally seeing the man sitting there.

He was a tall, immense man, with a well-defined but not overly developed musculature. On his head was a helmet that was also a mask: a grey-steel thing that was shined to a mirror polish, reflecting Kirk's image back at himself. The two wolf masks standing next to him were also fully articulated heads, with mouths that moved as they talked and ears that twitched like a wolf's does, ruby eyes, and a foggy breath which issued from their mouths whenever they spoke. One of the wolf masks bowed to Jameson, who bowed back, saluting the man. "I've brought someone for an audience with the Greymaster. Is that possible?" Jameson asked.

"I believe it is, Jameson. You're dismissed," came a chillingly cold voice from within the mirrored mask. Kirk felt Demon inside him start to rattle its chains, laughing to itself.

Jameson stepped forward and offered the Confederate pistol to one of the wolf masks, who inspected it and handed it to the man in the grey mask.

The Greymaster turned to look at Kirk. "I understand that you played a part in our raid tonight. Very well done."

Kirk shook his mask. "I . . . wouldn't describe it that way, sir."

"What do you mean? The team recovered my pistol, and managed to pick up a few guns and ammunition. I would term that a success."

"Sir, I lost several friends in that explosion. I would like to know who was responsible," Kirk said, his voice rising as he spoke.

"Now, boy, don't go usin' that tone with me. You'll keep your respect or leave here without your tongue," the Greymaster hissed.

Kirk shook his head, looking down at Sylvie, who looked back at him in alarm. He turned back to the Greymaster.

"Sir, I just want to know why they had to die, and who killed them," Kirk said quietly.

"They died because they were stupid, boy. They died because they liked to play with guns where they shouldn't be played with. They died because kids like them don't have enough sense to pour piss out of a boot before putting it on. That's why they died, and if you don't like it, boy, then well, I guess you can join your pals in Oblivion, because that's where they've gone," Greymaster whispered, his voice full of cynicism and hatred.

Kirk nodded. "Well, sir, that's what I wanted to know. Thank you for your time."

Kirk turned around and began to walk out.

"Wait." He heard.

Turning slowly, he said. "Sir?"

"I didn't dismiss you, son," Greymaster said, unmoving.

Kirk turned around. "All right." He bit down on the anger that flared up inside of him.

"Who are you, boy?" Greymaster asked, standing up and stepping down from his throne. "When did you die?"

"I died . . . I don't know, sir. About nine or ten months ago, I guess. But I don't believe I should tell you who I am, since I don't know who you are, sir," Kirk said quietly.

The Greymaster swiveled to peer, faceless, at Sylvie. "You've trained him well, Miss Sylvie. I wondered when you would repay the debt you owe Miss Cynthia by takin' a Lemure under your wing. Now I see you're coddlin' street thugs. Not the kind of people a nice girl like you should be hangin' out with, don't you think?"

Sylvie smiled. "He's a nice boy, sir. I enjoy teachin' him."

The Greymaster put a finger under Sylvie's chin. "You always was the cutest little thing. Anytime you want a place in my organization, you've got it, ya heah?"

Sylvie smiled, but it was the fake smile that children wear for their aunts and uncles at Christmas.

Greymaster turned back to Kirk. "Where'd you get that mask, boy? It's awful pretty."

"A friend of mine made it, sir," Kirk said.

"Boy, do you know what the Firebird means to us Wolves?" Greymaster whispered quietly to Kirk.

"No, sir, I don't," Kirk said. He tried not to shake as he felt the man's presence move closer.

"There's a prophecy that the Firebird will return to this place, and cause the whole city to burn. Last time the Firebird was here, the native ghosts were driven out by the Hierarchy. The Firebird is a harbinger of change, boy. Great change. Now why do you reckon your friend gave you that mask?"

Suddenly, out of nowhere, Mr. Demon spoke up. "Because, boy, you is gonna bring destruction and Oblivion to everyone. Ain't ya?"

Kirk jumped, as if someone had shocked him with a bolt of electricity. He looked around, looked straight at the man in the grey mask.

The voice within his own head, his own Shadow-voice, was that of the wraith in the grey mask. Without question, Kirk knew it to be true.

"I–I don't know, sir," Kirk said.

He could almost feel the smile coming from behind the grey mask. What did it mean? Mr. Demon sounding like Greymaster, Greymaster sounding like Mr. Demon. Kirk was afraid and intrigued at the same time. Did he know Greymaster from another life? Did Greymaster know things about him that he didn't?

Greymaster said, "Well, maybe one day you'll find out, boy. Thank you again for gettin' my gun. This gun was my father's gun, given to him by his grandfather Jebediah. Pretty ain't it?"

Kirk nodded, looking down at Sylvie who, despite her normal maturity, had begun to fidget.

The Greymaster paused for a moment, and no one filled the space with words. Looking at them both, Greymaster shrugged his shoulders. "Well, I guess that's it. You've been paid, haven't you?"

Kirk nodded.

The Greymaster whispered something to one of his guards, then turned back to Kirk. "I would like to offer you a place among us, Firebird. As a good luck token if nothin' else. You see, we're about to make a major raid. I'd like for you to be in on it. Lots of loot, lots of fun. Could be that our troops would like to see the Firebird out there with us, fighting alongside us. Just might shake the Hierarchy up a little bit." Greymaster paused for a second, obviously waiting for Kirk to accept.

Kirk spoke up slowly, carefully. "I-I'm sorry sir. I'll need a little time to think about it, if that's okay."

Greymaster ground his fist into his palm. "What's to think about?"

Sylvie looked up at him. "Now, sir . . . that was a legitimate answer don't you think? Firebird's still young. Let's let him make up his mind on his own time."

Greymaster nearly growled. His aura changed to a cool, dark blue. He smiled slowly behind the mask and nodded. "Well, Miss Sylvie, if you think so, then I don't see what the harm is in lettin' him have a few days to think about it. Son, the raid has to be fully planned out and practiced by the next new moon. Keep a watch for the dark of the moon, and when it happens, come back here and tell me your answer."

Kirk nodded. "Yes, Captain," he said without thinking.

Greymaster paused for a moment. "How did you know I was a captain, boy?"

Sylvie smiled and spoke up. "The boy's got a bit of kennin' to him, sir. Doesn't know how to use it yet, 'sall."

Greymaster nodded slowly. "I see."

Sylvie curtseyed to Greymaster. "Can we go now, sir?"

Greymaster nodded. "Remember, Firebird . . . the dark of the moon!"

Kirk nodded, then turned with Sylvie to walk out. As they walked, her hand in his, they slowly slid into the Tempest and were gone.

The Wolfguard to Greymaster's left spoke up. "You want me to find out who he is?"

Greymaster shook his mask slowly. "No. No, no need to waste time and effort on an unknown Lemure. Turn your attentions to finding the site and drilling the patrols!"

As the Wolfguards left, Greymaster reclined on his throne, his hand on his chin. He thought for but a moment longer, shrugged, then turned to address other, more pressing problems.

Kirk and Sylvie jumped to a building across the railroad tracks, far away from the Wolves' warehouse. Sylvie smiled at Kirk as he sat down on the roof, looking out across the city. "What's wrong, Kirk?" Sylvie asked.

Kirk looked up at Sylvie. "Sylvie, things have been happenin' left and right. I don't know what to do." Looking up, he saw the sun peeking over the edge of the horizon. *What a night,* he thought to himself.

Sylvie blinked, dazzled at the sunlight. "That's the way things happen sometimes, Kirk. You just have to accept them. What do you want to do now? We don't have to sleep if you don't want to."

Kirk looked at her. "There is one thing I really want to do."

"What's that?" Sylvie said, smiling, as if she already knew what it was.

Kirk smiled. "What?"

Sylvie shook her head. "Go ahead."

Kirk grinned. "Ah, I was hopin' to go visit my little boy in the hospital."

Sylvie grinned back, nodding her head.

Kirk looked puzzled. "How did you know about my son?"

Sylvie put her hand over her mouth. "I . . . I don't know, Kirk. Ahh. Oh, heck. I can't lie to you. I was with you, the entire time, when you were there in the mirror room. I had to see what happened to you. Are you mad?"

"No. I ain't mad. That's okay, Sylvie. I like you a lot. You've helped me out a lot. What do you get out of it?"

Sylvie grinned, looked down. "Nothin'. I just . . . Kirk, like the man said, I got a debt to pay. I don't mind doin' this for ya. If it weren't for Miss Cindy, I would still be a clueless spook."

Kirk nodded. "You must be pretty damn old. Most spooks like you a lot."

Sylvie put her legs together and smiled, looking down. "Yeah. Well, I am a lil' old. But the old folks, they think if you've stuck around, you is wise and powerful. I ain't powerful. I'm just Sylvie."

Kirk shook out his hair and looked hard at Sylvie. "Don't you be lyin'. I know you're powerful. You do all this travelin' stuff, and kennin'. Stuff I ain't never heard about. Say, why did you lie to that Greymaster guy for me? About the captain part?"

"Because, Kirk, you don't know who Greymaster is. And you don't want him to find out who you are, yet," Sylvie said, her voice sounding hollow and resonant.

"What the hell was that?" Kirk said, stepping back.

Sylvie grinned. "That? Oh, that was my voice-o'-reason, I call it. It's my kennin' voice. You see, Kirk, when you gots kennin', you just lissen to your heart. That's all, that's it."

Kirk grinned. "Oh. Do I have any kennin'?"

Sylvie peered at him. "Not a lick."

Kirk nodded. "So no fortune-tellin'?"

Sylvie grinned. "Maybe I'll teach you. One day. Not today. Oh, Kirk, ain't the sunrise pretty? Makes you feel good."

"Makes me feel good to be dead," Kirk said wryly.

Sylvie looked sharply at him. "You can't be talkin' like that. Just because you dead doesn't mean that you gotta be a sourpuss." She punched Kirk on the arm.

"Ow," Kirk said, rubbing his arm.

"You want to go see your baby now?" Sylvie said, her braids flipping around as she tossed her head.

Kirk nodded and yawned sleepily.

Sylvie grinned. "Oh, boy. Baby ghost all sleepy?"

Kirk shook his head, yawning again.

Sylvie touched Kirk and a flash of light shot into him. He jumped.

"How's that?" she asked, grinning.

"What did you do?" Kirk said, now wide awake.

Sylvie smiled, slipping into her old-life dialect. "I calls it 'ghost coffee.' It's just a little wakeup call. Nothin' big. Part of the dreamin' powers," Sylvie said, shifting her weight from foot to foot. "Let's be goin' on," she said, looking expectantly at him. "I love babies," she admitted as Kirk extended his hand to her outstretched fingers.

Then they vanished.

The morning sun was painting golden colors on the red brick of the hospital and shining in through the high skylights, making shafts that pierced the inner gloom and somehow made the antiseptic interior welcoming. Out of the shadows stepped Sylvie and Kirk, Kirk still shivering from the cold of the Tempest.

He looked down the hall one way and then the other. "Where is he?" Kirk asked.

Sylvie smiled. "Just listen to your heart, Kirk, like I was sayin'. Follow your nose. Just walk, you'll find him."

Kirk began to walk down the hallway, out of the bright sunlight, which dazzled him. He walked past rows and rows of doors with charts tucked next to them. The floor smelled of antiseptic wash and the air stank of hospital smell, which almost made Kirk gag. He looked down one corridor, then back down another.

Then he heard a tiny, shrill cry. The sound made his whole body quake. He looked down at his hands, not realizing to what depth his feelings reached. For a second he felt filled with energy, as if the sound alone filled him with light.

Kirk turned and entered a room with its door open, followed closely by Sylvie. There was Cindi with a tiny, utterly tiny, baby in her arms. She looked so frail, so thin. Sitting there in the darkness of the room with its drawn curtains, Kirk thought for a moment that Cindi had already died and that she was a wraith like him. Her hollow eyes looked as though she had just about given up.

She held the tiny baby woodenly, although Kirk could instantly see that her touch was helping the baby. He was calming down, moving his tiny fists against her cheek, her swollen breasts.

Kirk moved aside as a nurse stepped into the room. "It's time for a check. And medication for you," the nurse said.

Cindi nodded like a robot, letting the nurse take the child from her arms. The nurse weighed him, checked his blood pressure and heartbeat, looked in his eyes.

"He's doing fine. Has he slept much?" the nurse asked.

Cindi shook her head "no," looking down at the floor. The nurse nodded. "Well, you're going to have to take your pills. This is an iron pill: you're very anemic right now. And this is a pill which will help dry your milk up."

Cindi looked up at the nurse, moving a strand of her hair out of her eyes. "I can't breastfeed him?"

The nurse shook her head, giving the boy back to her. "Normally we'd let you have a choice. But the doctor wants to be sure that the baby's not getting any more contaminants. I'm sorry."

Cindi nodded woodenly and took the pills. Satisfied, the nurse turned and moved to leave. "You want the door closed?" she asked.

"No. I don't care. Whatever," Cindi said, still holding the tiny baby.

The nurse stopped for a moment. "Have you named him yet?"

Cindi shook her head. "The doctor says he might not make it past a week. I don't see that there's much of a point giving him a name just yet."

The nurse turned wordlessly, shocked, and left the room. Cindi held on to the little boy, who began shivering in her arms despite how warm it was in the room. Cindi closed her eyes and held on, waiting for the baby's wail. He cried out, as much as his little lungs could scream, throwing back his head in need, wanting something that he couldn't have, something he'd never tasted.

Cindi sobbed as she held on to him, but she didn't have any tears left. She tried to offer a tiny bottle of sugar-water to the boy, but he wouldn't take the nipple.

Kirk sat down next to the caterwauling child and his mother, on the chair opposite them. Her eyes went dull, glassy, looking out to the middle distance as the baby screamed, weakly trying to reach out and grasp what it needed.

Sylvie shook her head. Kirk saw a little drop of light at the corner of Sylvie's eye, and watched as she wiped the tear away. "What do you think, Kirk? Do you think he'll live?" Sylvie whispered.

Kirk looked at the boy. His boy. He could almost feel every heartbeat of the boy—a rapid thrumming which seemed to echo through his tiny rib cage. Kirk looked closely at him, touched him on the back. The boy instantly stopped crying, tossing his head around a little, lolling over to the side.

The boy hungrily sought the nipple of the glass jar with the sugar-water in it, and began to drink the glucose solution thirstily.

Kirk drew back his hand from the soft, exquisitely delicate skin and saw a strand of light drip from his fingertip. Sylvie looked up, eyebrows raised, eyes large. "Kirk! Kirk! Look! Your lifeweb! Look at it!"

Kirk looked down and took the strand of light in his fingers. "What is this?"

"That's your lifeweb. It's so close to your boy that you can see it. You can see the energy streaming down it to you. Look at it. That's your connection to him," Sylvie said, smiling.

"You mean . . . I'm connected to him like I'm connected to the school?" Kirk said, his voice belying the confusion he felt.

"Yes. Yes. Exactly," Sylvie said. "You have to protect him now, Kirk. Your Fetter's moved from mother to son."

Kirk looked up at Cindi. "You better treat him right," he said to her.

Cindi blinked. "Fuck you," she hissed.

Kirk looked surprised. "You can hear me?"

"Where the fuck are you? Not here. Had to be some goddamn cowboy, movin' in on Rosario's turf. What the fuck did you think he was gonna do? Send you a fuckin' engraved invitation?"

Kirk swallowed and looked at Sylvie. "Can she see me?"

Sylvie shrugged her shoulders. "Mothers are funny folks. 'specially new ones. It could happen."

Kirk turned back to Cindi. "I—I don't know what to say, Cindi. What do you want me to say?" Kirk said.

Cindi shrugged her shoulders. "It don't matter. Maybe I should smother him and jump out the fuckin' window."

"You better not!" Kirk yelled.

"Who's gonna stop me?" Cindi said, her eyes bloodred and starting to tear up in.

"I will, Kirk said, his voice turning hard. "You don't want to be here. This place sucks."

Cindi laughed. "Anyplace has to be better than this place."

As if on cue, the boy stopped drinking his water and started to scream again, screaming like someone was pushing a needle through his tiny foot.

Kirk shook his head. "He screams a lot, don't he?"

"It's the crack. He wants some. Wants more. Fuck, I know how he feels, Cindi said, laughing humorlessly. "Maybe I should get him a little baby-pipe, she said, continuing to laugh.

Kirk shook his head again, looking down. "Just . . . hold him."

Cindi held the baby close. "It doesn't help."

The boy screamed again, and again, each breath expended completely before he screamed again. Cindi heard his voice start to go harsh on the end of the scream.

Kirk reached out with his hand, humming as he did. There was no song, nothing he could think of, it was just him, his hand shaking, wanting to do anything to calm the little boy down.

"Ain't that sweet, Kirkie boy? Why don't you breastfeed him?" Mr. Demon said, his voice dripping with hate.

Kirk growled. "Shut up, Demon. Shut. Up." Kirk's fists clenched as he shoved the demon back deep into himself.

The demon was silent. Kirk relaxed, humming, humming a tuneless melody, reaching over and touching his son, feeling his tiny hummingbird heart through his skin.

The boy instantly quieted. Kirk hummed a song, which was not so much a lullaby as a gentle song of hope, born out of the driving need to see him calm, alive, happy. Kirk could feel his insides churning. As he touched the boy, he saw light streaming down his arm. He looked at him, watched his reaction to the tune.

The boy yawned a large yawn, squeezing his eyes closed a few times. His head lolled over to the side and his mouth groped on Cindi's collarbone, looking for a nipple. Cindi put the plastic bottle nipple in his mouth and watched as he sucked. She held him, rocking him slowly back and forth, cooing to him now that he was quiet. She was shaking, but at least the baby was quiet now.

She put the baby down in his crib and tucked a blanket around him. She lay back on the bed, looking nearly dead herself. "Kirk. I want to die. Please," she said, looking up at him.

"No, Cindi. No. You have to stay alive. Not for me. For the baby. For the boy." He looked down at the child, who had already snuggled down under the blanket, quiet, asleep.

Cindi looked up at him. "I love you, you know, Kirk. I really love you."

Kirk nodded. "I—I love you, too, Cindi."

Cindi laughed. "Don't lie to me."

Kirk shook his head. "No. I'm not. I—"

"I know you were fuckin' Kirsten. That's okay. You're dead now, not much I can do, is there?" Cindi laughed bitterly.

Kirk shook his head. "Not much." He felt a wave of guilt wash over him, felt cold, icy despair building inside of him. Cindi laughed again.

Kirk turned to Sylvie. "I think I want to leave now."

Cindi sat up slowly. "No, Kirk. Don't leave me. Don't leave me again, dammit."

Kirk looked at Cindi wordlessly.

"Kirk, you have to promise you will come back," Cindi said quietly. She looked like she was about to cry again. There was a manic edge to her voice.

Kirk looked at Sylvie. Sylvie whispered, "Watch what promises you make to the living, Kirk. They have a way of binding you. It's bad luck to break your promise to a mortal."

Kirk looked down at his baby son. He saw lines of

grey streaming through the boy's skin, grey that threatened his life, grey that wanted to grow and consume him, snuffing out his tiny light forever. He looked up at Cindi, saw perhaps for the first time that same light echoed in her: the light of life, the light of love that she must feel for him, despite her bitterness and pain. He looked through to her heart and saw her lonely and alone, terrified.

Kirk looked back at Sylvie for a second, searching his young-looking mentor's face for some hint of what to do.

Then, something within Kirk shifted. He didn't care anymore, didn't care whether or not it was wrong. It felt right.

"I promise. I'll be back," Kirk said quietly.

Cindi nodded and began to cry again, dry sobs wracking her. "Oh God, Kirk. I'm dying here. God, I want a smoke so bad," Cindi said, shivering.

Kirk put his hand on her shoulder and she shivered at his touch.

"Kirk . . . could you . . . could you do what you did to Jeb to me?" Cindi said, looking up at him.

"Jeb? You've named him? I thought—" Kirk started to say.

"An old lady came in this morning, wearing black. Said he was a beautiful child. Gave me a flower. She asked me what his name was, and I—I didn't know what to say. She told me to name him Jebediah. Jeb. That was a good name for him, she said. Since then, that's what I want to call him," Cindi said, sniffing, blowing her nose on a tissue.

Kirk nodded. "Jeb. Sounds good to me."

Cindi shivered again. "Please?"

Kirk nodded again. He began to hum, putting his hand over Cindi's forehead. Sylvie smiled, climbing up on the bed, and put her hand on top of Kirk's, smiling at Kirk.

Cindi gently let out a deep, deep sigh as Kirk fed her the same quiet, gentle, nervous hope that he had given little Jeb. Sylvie seemed to be growing less distinct as she touched Cindi, but Cindi's aura began to lose the blackest of the dark streaks. Soon she fell into a deep sleep. Kirk stood up to go quietly, but Sylvie stayed seated.

Running her fingers over Cindi's eyes, she blew a soft breath onto her face. Kirk watched, wild-eyed, as Sylvie gently pulled a dim image of Cindi up out of her body. Sylvie hugged the filmy spirit-version of Cindi, and whispered something into Cindi's spirit-ear.

Cindi's spirit nodded, then slowly sank back into her body.

Sylvie got up off the bed and looked seriously at Kirk. "Now, don't we have some other places to go?"

"What did you do?" Kirk asked.

"I told her soul to have peaceful dreams only. It's part of the dreamin' power. Don't pay it no mind. She's going to be just fine," Sylvie said, smiling, another tear forming in her eye. "That's a pretty little baby. Looks like his daddy," Sylvie said.

Kirk looked down at the sleeping Jeb. "Yeah. He's a cute thing. Tiny, though."

Sylvie shook her head. "Babies are strong, Kirk. Very strong. He'll live. I know he will. Now I know he will."

Kirk nodded. "Where else do we have to go? I'm bushed."

Sylvie smiled. "Oh, that's right. Little baby ghosts have to sleep a lot, too. I tell you what, why don't you sleep here? I'll pick you up tonight."

"I—I want to go see Anna. As soon as possible," Kirk said, starting to leave.

"No, Kirk. No. Anna's in school now, anyway. Let her have a full school day. She's just as likely to see you as Cindi is: kids are like that. You have to watch it around them."

Kirk nodded, yawning again. "Okay. Okay. I'll sleep here. On the floor or something."

Sylvie smiled and hugged Kirk around his waist.

"Hey! What was that for?" Kirk said.

"For doing the right thing. For once," Sylvie said, grinning.

Kirk looked down at Jeb again, nodding. "Geez. I guess I'm a daddy now."

Sylvie smiled. "Yeah. I guess you are," she said.

Kirk turned back to thank Sylvie for helping him, but she was already gone, vanished into the Tempest.

Kirk dreamt.

Warmth. Lights. Cookies. Tinsel. Candles. A fire in the hearth. Mistletoe. Holly. Ivy. The pungent scent of a young Georgia pine. Softness. Music, drifting through the house. The cinder block family housing on the base was tiny, but better than anything else they'd had.

Outside, it was raining a bitter cold rain, one that could turn to ice at any moment, but inside the smell of nutmeg and cinnamon permeated the house. Kirk lay awake on his bed, listening to the rain, listening to someone sing a song about a White Christmas he'd never known. He tried to sleep, knowing that the next day he'd wake to a floor piled high with presents but, most importantly, he would see his father the captain. He had been due to come home, away from the jungle and the fighting, and be with his family for the whole Christmas season. Although the date had been put off, time and time again, and it had begun to look like he'd not be there at all, the Marines had called that morning to say that Captain Rourke would be there as scheduled, on Christmas morning.

Kirk snuck out of his bed, quietly creeping into the living room, hoping to get a look at the presents that were laid there for him. Looking up at the fireplace, he saw his favorite teddy bear resting in the stocking there—Bearegard—only looking new, with a bright red ribbon under his stocking with the glitter-cursive "Kirk" written on the white band of fake fur.

Kirk hid behind the tree, pretending he was his daddy, who he knew was famous for hiding behind trees and sneaking out and killing everyone. He was good at that. One day, Kirk would be good at it, too.

The doorbell rang, and his mom came out of the kitchen like a rocket, trying to not look excited, trying not to anticipate anything. She threw the door open.

Out of the rain, the blackness, two men stepped. They were dressed in their shining dress blues underneath their rain gear, the blues that always excited Kirk because of the beautiful Marine sword that went with them. He stood up.

"Daddy!" he yelled, and ran for the door.

His mother's shaking hand pushed him back. "No Kirk, no, no . . . just go . . . just sit down . . . just . . . no, no honey, no."

They were speaking words he could not understand, words that were black and heavy with iron and the tang of gunpowder, the stench of the jungle and the sickly-sweet smell of orchids on the altar. They were words that carried daggers that thrust into his heart and made his mother cry. He wanted to make his mother stop crying somehow, but even trying to hug her wouldn't help.

The door closed, and Kirk watched his mother fall to the floor, crying, beating her fists against the floor until her nails cracked and her hands turned black.

Kirk woke with a shock. Looking at the window drapes in the room, he saw daylight still illuminating the edges of the curtains. He shook himself further awake and felt another shiver go through him. In his sleep, he had floated down through the floor. He remembered Sylvie telling him to follow his heart to find his son before, so he decided to walk aimlessly for a little while.

Turning the corner, he found himself in a red-walled area that was clearly the Intensive Care Unit, and looking up, saw a name that instantly captured his attention: Rick Lehrer, his buddy. The federal marshal posted outside his door confirmed it.

Kirk walked into Rick's room quietly. Rick wasn't in good shape: much of his body was burned. He had apparently inhaled some flame: he was on a breathing machine. Kirk looked closely at him and saw the black streaks of death all over him. His lifelight was slowly dying out.

. Kirk took off his mask, holding on to it. "Hey, Rick . . ." Kirk whispered in Rick's ear, trying to get Rick to wake up.

Rick's eyes fluttered open, although his mouth was stuffed with apparatus. Kirk felt Rick's pain as his drugged brain swam into consciousness. Much of Rick's face had been badly burned: he couldn't move his jaw or talk. Kirk looked down at him, seeing the death in him and wondering if he would survive this. Reminding himself that he was the cause of Rick's burns—that if he hadn't have been so willing to use his friend's body, this would never have happened.

Rick slowly smiled at Kirk, his facial bandages moving a little. Kirk tried humming his little ditty, trying to calm Rick down. But Rick wasn't having any of it: he knew he was dead already. Knew that nothing would prevent him from being a vegetable. Rick had already given up and was just waiting to die.

"Do you have the guts?" Mr. Demon asked. "Do you have what it takes to put him out of his misery, Kirk?" Demon taunted.

"I thought I told you to shut up," Kirk said quietly.

"You did. I'm back. Did you miss me?" Mr. Demon said.

"Miss you? Fuck no. I want you to go away forever," Kirk muttered under his breath. Kirk put his Firebird mask back on and turned to the heart-lung machine.

Kirk put his hand on the heart-lung machine, looking at it, watching the dials move. One flick of a switch, and it would flip off.

"Not good enough," Mr. Demon said. "Heroic measures. They'll take heroic measures to restore him. No, you have to hurt the machine that's keeping him goin'. Reach in and shock the heck out of it. That should do it."

Kirk's skin crawled with the thought of how he was listening to Demon, but this time what Demon said seemed to make sense. He wished Sylvie was there: she would know what to do.

Rick moved a little and moaned as the pain from moving wracked his body.

Kirk moved his hand slowly inside the heart-lung machine. He could feel the moving parts, the electronics zapping their tiny currents through the silicon chips. He clenched his fist and pulled, giving as much energy to his hand as he could muster. He watched as the indicators suddenly froze, looked up at the heart monitor and saw that Rick's heart was already beating slower. But no telltales went off: those, too, had been short-circuited.

Kirk watched as Rick's lungs began to fill with liquid, his breathing became ragged and shallow, burbling as the lung machine stopped making him breathe correctly. Rick began to shake in his restraints. For a second his eyes flew open again, and Kirk thought Rick recognized him standing there.

Suddenly, a doctor with a white lab coat and a clipboard strode into the room. Instead of rushing to his side and attempting to revive Rick, however, he simply watched as Rick died, as the black veins in his aura covered him, finally reaching his brain.

As Rick closed his eyes, the doctor bent over and grabbed up his soul from his body, like Sylvie had done earlier with Cindi. Rick's soul was covered in a kind of body bag of blackish, greenish slime, but it was definitely Rick. This doctor was dead—a wraith—like Kirk!

Then, a group of nurses, orderlies, and the marshal charged into the room, trying to save him, to no avail.

"What the hell are you?" Kirk said, looked at the "doctor" incredulously.

The doctor turned around, surprised that Kirk had spoken, and nearly dropped Rick as he did. "Oh, no! I thought you were just a relative. I didn't realize you were dead. Are you his Reaper?"

Kirk looked at Rick, whose eyes were still closed inside of the slimy body bag. He looked down at Rick's dead body. He looked up at the doctor, considering what the word "Reaper" meant. Had he Reaped Rick? He wondered for a moment, and then made up his mind.

"Yeah. I'm his Reaper," Kirk said, quietly.

"Good! Good! I was just about to call up the Hierarchy Reapers, but since you're here, I guess you get claim to him, eh? Where's your chains?"

"Chains?" Kirk said.

"We want to keep him from slipping into Oblivion—these Cauls sure are slippery," the doctor said.

"Oh. Yeah! Well, mine are currently tied up. Could you lend me a set?"

The doctor nodded, smiling. "Okay, but you'll have to bring me a cut of the oboli when you get paid for him. I don't mind lending out chains as long as I get them back. You stay here, and hold on to him real tight. I'll be right back."

Kirk grabbed ahold of the very slippery, slimy shell of Rick's soul. Looking through the greenish transparent slime, he saw Rick's face, still asleep, but healed of its burn damage. Kirk wondered what he was getting himself into, but he wasn't about to turn his friend over to those Hierarchy bastards.

The doctor came back with a set of black chains and linked them around Rick, locking them with padlocks of strange manufacture. Then, smiling, he looked up at Kirk. "So, are you a Harbinger?" the doctor asked.

"Harbinger? Oh, you mean, those guys that travel around? Nah," Kirk said.

"Oh, well, okay. I'll take you to the Citadel. But you'll have to cut me in for a little more, eh? This is gonna be great. Maybe they won't turn down my application to become a Reaper when they see me help bring in a soul like this. This is great. Let's go!" the youngish doctor said, smiling at Kirk, and reached out to grab Kirk's arm where he was holding onto Rick.

Before Kirk could speak a word, he, Rick, and the doctor were already in the Tempest on their way to the Hierarchy Citadel.

Jebediah stirred in his attic room, where he stayed in the courthouse during the day. His Legionnaire sentry coughed and waited to be recognized. "A Centurion to see you, sir," the sentry said. "Are you awake enough to receive him?"

"Certainly, Legionnaire. Thank you," Jebediah said, pulling on his stern Mask of Justice, the badge of his office.

The Centurion was a man who had fought with Jebediah at Leggett's Hill against the Yankees—the bonds of esprit d'corps made the man something of an informant to Jebediah about goings-on around the city of the dead—the Necropolis of Atlanta.

The Centurion saluted smartly. "Sir. An entire weapons bunker was destroyed last night, presumably many of the weapons will be gatherable. We have reason to believe that the perpetrators used skinpuppets to move past our Monitors there."

Jebediah nodded slowly. "Yes, well. I do believe we're seeing more Renegade activity these days: we shall have to take steps against them. Is there anything else, Centurion?" Jebediah asked.

"No, sir. No souls were gathered as far as we know. We have reason to believe that the Grey Wolves perpetrated this crime, although there have been some confidential reports by snitches that an unknown Renegade Circle was involved."

"This is very interesting, Centurion. " Jebediah shook his head slowly.

"You know I wouldn't have come to you, Jebediah, if it hadn't been important," the Centurion said quietly.

"I thank you kindly, brother Centurion." Jebediah bowed to the grey flannel-clad warrior as he spun on his heel and left.

So James, did you finally make your move? Jebediah thought, his brow creased. Opening up a pouch at his side, he removed a pack of cards wrapped in a white cloth. Closing his eyes, he opened himself to the lines of Fate, the possibilities of the web of life and death and all that lies in between.

He had learned this particular art from a visiting vagabond in exchange for her continued freedom: he knew that it would only be a matter of time before she was brought before him again on similar charges against the Code. Justice would eventually be served. He normally hid the talent from his Hierarchy friends, as he was certain that it was against some obscure portion of Charon's Code to know and use it. The cards had been a gift from Mary, of all people, who had given them to him without word or comment.

Jebediah laid out the cards in silence, looking at them for a moment to confirm his suspicions. The Monument was reversed in the Future position. The Charon card, reversed, was in the Final Outcome position. Jebediah's art read not just the cards, but the pattern of Fate that ran behind them.

Mary had been right. The Curse was not over. Jebediah sensed a great change coming. He knew that nothing would be the same as it was before.

He had wanted to wait before looking for James and his son Kirk, but now he realized that they had something to do with this great change. He knew that he would have to act quickly, or all that he had ever worked for, fought for, believed in, would be lost to the nothingness that hungered for it.

Jebediah put aside his Mask of Office and picked up his Mask of Honor, the one he had earned in the Fifth Maelstrom when he and many other Hierarchy wraiths fought for days against the Spectres that the storm had brought. The mask was deep black Stygian iron, marked with symbols of his prowess and honor.

As always, whenever he put it on, his Shadow laughed and attempted to frighten him with scenes of the Maelstrom, which had been caused when the atomic weapons were detonated at Hiroshima and Nagasaki. Suddenly, for the first time, people began to believe that everyone in the world could die at once, and Oblivion loved that.

Jebediah stood still for a moment as he watched the scene of the great purplish black wave of

Oblivion-energy crashing across the Necropolis of Atlanta, watched as it saturated the streets and made even the Shadowlands friendly to the Spectres who swept toward the Citadel like a cavalry charge. The Shadow within him was using its power to show him these scenes, and they affected him as if they were real. He shuddered as he remembered the utter chaos of the Maelstrom. If he could have broken a sweat, he would have. Then he felt a little sad as he remembered the brave members of his own Circle who had been swept out with the Maelstrom, or who had died later in the hellish barrow-fires that had raped the land after the Maelstrom had left. Then, slowly, the vision faded, and Jebediah settled the mask comfortably on his face.

Stepping outside, he spoke to his sentry.

"Take me to the Citadel, Legionnaire," Jebediah said." There is much to be done before the sun goes down."

TRAVELS AND
TRIBULATIONS

Sometimes God just doesn't come through . . .
                                    —Anonymous

Ghost Stories:
Hewitt's Folly

*"You ever been over on track number six?" Beau
asked as they were walking to their trains, their
MARTA train operator caps tucked under their arms.*

*"Track number six? What the hell? There ain't
no track number six. Track number five. Track
number five-A, yeah. There ain't no track number
six," Simone said.*

*"Oh yes, there is. Track number six is where
Mr. Hewitt got himself killed," Beau said, grinning.*

*"What you talkin' about, fool?" Simone said,
making sure his hair was perfect in the mirror as
they descended onto the platform in the elevator.*

*"They was building the Five Points Station,
see, and they ran into some trouble gettin' some*

103

*bedrock outta the way. Well, Mr. Hewitt, he was
a determined ol' cuss. He got himself some plastic
explosives, even killt himself a lamb and smeared
blood all over the place. He was gonna break that
rock, by God,"* Beau said as they stood on the
platform waiting for the subway trains to pull up.

"What happened?" Simone said, standing
there with his hands on his hips.

*"What happened? Crazy white man killt him-
self, he did. Blew the charges the wrong way. The
whole tunnel collapsed on him. That's why they
have track five and track five-A. And I wouldn't
do my inspection over near track six. They say
you can sometimes see ol' Hewitt, still stuck in
the rock. Those deep parts where the old maintenance area was—those parts are downright
scary. You ain't gonna see me goin' over there,"*
Beau said. He was grinning, but he was serious.

Simone shook his head. *"Beau, you is crazy,
man. Believe all that shit. Damn."*

Kirk and the doctor materialized on the bottom-most
train platform of the central MARTA subway station
in Atlanta: Five Points Station. Trains have always
been important to Atlanta: Five Points Station used
to be the roundhouse where trains would come in
and get placed on different tracks, the commercial
center of the city, if not the geographic one.

Kirk held on to Rick as he waited for the doctor to
show him where to go. The doctor turned to him.
"Oh! My name's Shaw. What do you call yourself?"

Kirk thought for a second. "Firebird," he said.

Shaw nodded. "All you freelance Reapers have
cool names. I wish I could carry that off, but I'm just
a doctor. Always have been. Well, so, ah, let's go on
down, shall we?"

Kirk nodded, waiting for the doctor to move. Shaw moved past Kirk and starting walking across the platform, toward a door marked MAINTENANCE PERSONNEL ONLY.

Shaw stopped as a MARTA train pulled into the station and a wash of people streamed out of its doors. He turned back to Kirk. "You've never done this before, have you?" Shaw said, smiling.

Kirk nodded. "Yeah, well, I'm new in town."

"Oh, so you've Reaped other places?" Shaw said, watching the people move back and forth, standing as still as possible so that someone wouldn't walk through him. Several people walked up to him and, mysteriously enough, moved aside and went on their way.

Kirk nodded. He was glad for the mask: it protected his face and kept people from knowing when he was lying. He liked that. Kirk wasn't sure what the doctor could see in his eyes, which were visible through the mask, but he was willing to take the chance. All he could think about was being there for Rick, making sure that no one treated him badly.

Shaw nodded. "Well, for a better cut, I'll make sure you don't get taken advantage of in there."

Kirk grinned behind his mask. "Is there a reward for finding a dead person?"

Shaw looked puzzled. "No, there's a reward for turning him over to the Hierarchy for processing."

Kirk cursed under his breath. Sylvie had told him about this, the other night, and he had forgotten. He remembered now and felt a cold chill run through him as he realized what the doctor thought they were there to do.

"He . . . he was my friend. Can't I keep him with me?" Kirk asked.

Shaw shook his head slowly. "No. You can't. You wouldn't be able to keep him from going to Oblivion. He's not a wraith like you or me. He's just a soul. No Fetters. Nothing. He would fall into Oblivion right this minute if you let him out of those chains," Shaw said.

Kirk nodded. He looked over at Rick. Kirk knew that the doctor was one of these Hierarchy guys, and that if he refused to let the doctor take Rick to the Hierarchy, it might just cause a problem. A stink. A fight. Kirk didn't want to get into a fight here, where, supposedly, there were a bunch of Hierarchy types, maybe even the soldiers or the cops that he saw earlier. Kirk suddenly realized that he was in a lot of trouble. What was worse, he realized, he had brought Rick into death just to have him potentially end up in chains for the rest of his existence. What was he thinking?

Kirk turned back to Shaw, who was obviously beginning to suspect his identity. "Yeah, well, okay. I tell you what. You help me out and you can have all the money I get. Okay?"

Shaw nodded. "Great! Sounds great. Let's go. This way."

They walked up to the door and through it, Kirk shivering as he passed through. Walking down the stairs, they stepped into a series of maintenance corridors, catwalks, crawlways, and rail access doors. It was a maze of accessways, and Kirk immediately knew he'd get lost without help. Kirk followed the doctor into the darkness. He turned down a corridor and there, in the corridor, was a man in full army fatigues carrying a rifle with a bright white crystal attached to the butt.

"Hold," the soldier said.

"Hello, Legionnaire. It's okay. I'm a citizen—a Monitor, actually. This is a Reaper. We've got a Thrall for—" Shaw began.

"I can see that, sir. But Acquisitions is down the hall that way. This area's restricted." The soldier pointed back down the hall the other direction.

"Oh! Oh! Well, that's fine. Thank you, Officer!" Shaw said, turning around and walking back down the corridor. "Must've moved things around since I was last here," Shaw muttered to Kirk.

They turned and walked down a set of stairs into a large open room. Inside were many ghosts like Rick: people encased in slimy-looking body bags, standing or lying on the floor listlessly, enchained.

The smell was almost worse than the sight: there was the chemical smell of some foul waste here. Men dressed much like the soldier in the hallway moved among those who stood next to their enchained charges, men and women who carried their own weapons, wore armor, and acted like loners. An officer approached Shaw and Kirk with a clipboard of his own.

"Who's the Reaper?" the officer asked.

"He is." Shaw pointed at Kirk. The officer nodded. He indicated Rick. "He have any Fetters?"

Shaw shook his head. "Nope. I'm his Monitor, actually."

The officer looked tired. "Why did you come with the Reaper? We don't need that many personnel hanging out down here." Rick and Shaw stood quietly by, not answering the officer, who didn't seem to really want an answer.

"Okay, I'll give you two oboli for him. He looks like he's got a bit of Pathos to him. Let me get him linked to a line," the officer said, gesturing to some chainmongers who carried large reels of dark chains over to where they were.

"Wait a second—what if I don't want him to be taken?" Kirk said.

The officer waved off the chain men. "You gonna sell him to someone else? Look, Reaper, this is the only game in town. Unless you're with the Renegades?"

Kirk shook his head. "No."

The officer sighed. "Then, are you gonna give him up?"

Kirk looked down at Rick, who still slept inside his body bag. He hugged him, standing up. "Yeah. I guess so," Kirk said, looking out at the entire room. Everywhere he looked he saw people in chains. He saw a line of chained ghosts resting against one of the walls. Kirk felt only disgust, at himself and at the Hierarchy and their practices.

The officer pulled two large black coins out of a pouch and gave them to Kirk. "All right. Thanks. See ya later," the officer said, moving on to the next Reaper.

Kirk looked down at Rick in his bag, whispering, "Stay cool, dude."

Turning, Kirk then strode out of the room, Shaw following rapidly behind him. "Hey! Hey! What the hell? You gonna give me my coins?"

Kirk turned around in a rage. He punched Shaw in the face, kneed him in the gut, and threw him against the wall. He discorporated, looking at Kirk, shocked.

"You fuckin' bastard. That was my best friend back there. Fuck you." He threw the two coins down on the ground. "There you go. There's your god-damn money."

Shaw looked confused as he slowly reformed. He crawled across the floor to pick up the coins, his body turning black. Shaw cringed, his hands becoming claws. "S-s-s-sorry . . ." he hissed. "I'm so s-s-s-sorry," Shaw said, now a twisted, foul-looking creature.

Kirk took a step back. "Look, I'm just going to leave. You stay here, and I won't hit you again."

He turned around and ran down the corridor, following the path he remembered—the path back to the surface, leaving Shaw far behind him. Shaw didn't seem to follow him, but Kirk was sure that he'd go to the guards to report the incident.

Turning the corner, he found a stairwell and began climbing stairs. Stepping through another door, Kirk stood stock-still as he heard a voice. He was in some kind of maintenance corridor, just off a storage room that apparently was being used as an office by the wraiths there.

Standing quietly in the hallway, he listened to the wraith's conversation.

"So, you want me to search for someone, Jebediah?" a female voice asked.

"Yes. His name be Kirk. Kirk Rourke. He is supposed to be one of the Restless. I'd ask that you keep this quiet, Sophia. I would like this to be conducted with great subtlety. I would like it to be conducted before the next shipment of soulfire arrives," a male voice, soft and very Southern, replied.

Kirk peered around the corner and into the room, where he saw a man with a full white beard, long white hair and a black mask of some kind.

"Certainly, sir. I'll get right to work on it. Although, I must warn you, a search of this kind—might take a while. It depends on how close he is, and how stationary . . ." came the female voice.

Kirk didn't wait to hear any more. He ran down the hall, and, closing his eyes, dived into the wall. He flew through it, sliding through walls of cinder blocks, electrical wires, and brick, until he finally broke free in darkness, landing on his feet and slowly becoming substantial again. His guitar had fallen free from where he'd tied it to his back; he resecured the bonds quickly. Then, looking up, he saw the train tracks with the third rail humming nearby. He climbed a set of access stairs to the bottom floor platform, just as the southbound train pulled into the station. Kirk had learned from years of life on the street to not look back, to move nonchalantly. He quietly moved onto the train, standing in one corner, trying not to be squashed by the people there.

As the train pulled out of the station, Kirk thought he saw Shaw flicker into existence on the train platform, looking around for him. He stood stock-still, sure that Shaw couldn't see him. Shaw was still turned in the other direction when the train moved into the darkness of the tunnel. But he did see, out of the corner of his eye, a flash of light illuminating a sign which said TRACK 6, CLOSED. Then there was nothing but darkness, and more train stops.

As the passenger load thinned out on the train, Kirk began to notice an old lady sitting with a lot of bags on one of the seats. She was obviously a bag lady, a homeless person. For a long time, Kirk thought she was just like the other homeless people who hung out on the train—then he realized (looking through her at the afternoon sun) she was one of the dead. He switched seats to sit with her, and she grudgingly made room for him.

"How is you, young man?" she asked him.

"Just fine, ma'am. Just fine. For bein' dead," Kirk said, smiling.

"Bein' dead ain't so bad. Not so bad as Jessie thought it would be," the woman said, smiling.

"Who's Jessie?" Kirk asked.

"Jessie? She's me," Jessie said, smiling a graveyard smile.

Kirk nodded. "Ma'am, can I ask you somethin'?"

"You can ask me somethin' and somethin' else again. Cause you already asked me somethin' when you asked if you could ask somethin'. If ya follow me," Jessie said, grinning again.

"Ma'am, do you know a Jebediah, an old-lookin' ghost with white hair?" Kirk said.

The woman thought for a moment, nodding to herself. "Yes, I do believe. I do believe that sound like Magistrate Jebediah. He runs a court over in Decatur. Why do you want to know, son? You ain't in trouble are ya?"

"No, ma'am. Not that I know of. Thank you, ma'am," Kirk said, moving away from her.

"Now, shug, don't you go on and run off. Jessie wants a friend. You come on back over here and let's us talk together for awhile. Where you from, boy?" Jessie asked.

"Atlanta, ma'am. Lived here all my life," Kirk said.

"You sound like a South Georgia boy to me," Jessie said.

"My momma's parents are from South Georgia. St. Mary's," Kirk said.

Jessie nodded. "I rode the rails down there once. Very nice place. Pretty beaches. Do you like pretty beaches, son?" Jessie asked.

Kirk shrugged. "I guess. I didn't visit too many beaches when I was alive. Now that I'm dead, I figure I won't have to learn to swim."

Jessie shook her head, grinning her ragged-teeth smile again. "No, now, son, learnin' to swim is a good idea even when you're dead. That's what movin' through the Tempest is, anyway—swimmin'. Or like enough to it. You look real young. You ain't a baby-ghost are ya?" she said quietly.

Kirk considered what to tell Jessie. He hadn't wanted to blow his cover, but if he ignored her, she'd clearly get annoyed with him, and that would be just as bad.

"Yes, I am," Kirk said.

She laughed. "You seem to want to think about that a bit. Like you weren't sure what you should say. Well, you can just not worry about ol' Jessie. She's a good lady."

Jessie bent down to Kirk's ear. "Good Christian lady, Jessie is. That's right. I don't think God's gone and turned His back on me, no suh. If'n His eye's on the sparrow, you can be sure His eye's on me," Jessie whispered to Kirk.

Kirk had heard of the so-called "churchy" types from Sylvie. He remembered what she had said earlier, about how they believed in God and that angels talked to them.

Kirk looked at Jessie, sizing her up. He wondered if she believed in angels, too, but she didn't look like someone who was bad, or harmful.

Jessie looked at him and smiled, putting something in his hand as she did. Kirk looked down at what she had placed in his palm and saw a tiny, rusty steel cross—real enough.

"God wants you to know he cares, my boy. God cares about you, even if you are dead and lost to him right now."

Kirk nodded, looking at the cross.

"You got any kin among the dead here in town?" Jessie said.

Kirk shook his head absently, then thought about Greymaster for a minute and wondered if he counted.

Kirk began to think, not answering Jessie. Was Greymaster his father? It sure seemed like it. Somehow it had to be true. It was so strange, Kirk thought, about how it seemed that Greymaster knew him so well, about how his dreams were so realistic and how his father was so true to what he was now. His mother had always described his father as being a very gentle, sweet man: who was this monster who wore the grey mask?

Jessie smiled. "I'm prayin' for you, son. You got a lot on your mind, don't you?"

Kirk nodded. His mind jumped around: his new

friends, his old friend Rick, his new son, Sylvie. Greymaster. Jebediah. Jeb . . .

"How is it that they got the same name?" Kirk asked himself, aloud.

"What's that, sugar?" Jessie said as the train car pulled into the next stop.

"Oh, nothin'. Just thinkin', like you said, Jessie," Kirk said.

Jessie stood up with all her packages. "Well, now, boy, Jessie gonna have to take off now."

"Where are you goin', if I can ask?" Kirk said.

"Susie's Bar. It's a Haunting place. You're welcome to come along, although you gonna have to listen to more of Jessie's talkin' about God and all."

Kirk smiled. "Sounds okay by me, Jessie. I was raised Southern Baptist, but I ain't been to church in forever, not since my grandma and grandpa died."

Jessie nodded. "That's all right. God looks out for ya, even if you don't come to church."

At that, the train pulled into the station, and Jessie and Kirk got off the train. Kirk watched as she waddled up the stairs, and then followed the rather large ghost up to the street level. She smiled at Kirk as they walked down the afternoon street, keeping to the shadows of the buildings, until she turned down an alleyway and led him into near total darkness. She sighed as she did, saying, "Ah, that sun's just too bright for the likes o' me, Lord," to herself.

Susie's Bar was an old, boarded-up pool room and bar that had been shut down years ago. In the perpetual darkness of the alleyway, off the beaten track of the street, it was apparently one of the most favorite "public Hauntings" of the ghosts of Atlanta who didn't congregate around the Necropolis or with the Hierarchy. Kirk wondered if the Hierarchy even knew about it.

He heard music inside: Dixieland jazz playing sweet and clear. He followed Jessie through the door, stood behind her as the rest of the wraiths in the bar greeted her. These were the ghosts who lived in the shadows of the city: Kirk saw they weren't as polished or solid-looking as the Grey Wolves or the Hierarchy wraiths he had seen. Most of them were dim, transparent. Hungry-looking, they scrabbled back and forth in the room whispering to each other, trading slivers of coins and tiny Relics with one another. Jessie led Kirk over to the corner table, where she sat him down.

"This ain't a drinking bar anymore. It's just a cool place on a hot day," Jessie said, sitting down with all her packages.

Kirk looked at the band, who were playing old, battered instruments. They ended their song and started playing the blues, deep and throaty, and some of the other wraiths in the bar looked up and nodded their heads in time with the music.

Kirk looked all around him. "Why do these people look so bad? Missing fingers, hands, parts of their faces?"

Jessie shook her head. "When the Maelstrom came, Kirk, these people were shut out. Unwanted. The Hierarchy wouldn't let them into the Citadel 'cause they won't sign up with them, and the Renegades had their own requirements. There weren't no place for them to go. So they got caught by it, out in it. Many of 'em got gone, right quick. Most of 'em didn't, though. Hung on, in pain, in need, floatin' listlessly. Until Susie found this place, an' she told 'em to come on here. That's why she run this place. To protect those who ain't gettin protected by nobody," Jessie said.

"Which one is Susie?" Kirk asked, looking around the bar.

Jessie pointed to a massive woman, a huge, naked woman with immense breasts, seated on a low cushion and holding a "court" of sorts: wraiths approached her now and then, spoke with her, and then departed back into the shadows of the bar.

Susie turned her gaze to Jessie's corner of the bar and nodded at her. "Best go and say hello, boy. It's good manners. Don't worry, she won't ask you your name. She don't bite."

Kirk nodded. Shakily, he got up and crossed the room, brushing past the tattered wraiths who scrabbled around at his feet.

Susie looked up at him, grinning. "Well, hello there, handsome. What can I do for a cutie like yourself?" she said, looking him up and down. "And I hope it's somethin' dirty."

Kirk would have blushed if he could have. He looked down at Susie, not able to keep his gaze from wandering to her breasts and back up to her face. Even though she was physically repulsive to him—her body immense and bulbous with welts and strange creases and tattoos—there was something going on in her voice, in the way she spoke, that made him vaguely (and even more disgustingly, to him) attracted to her.

"Just sayin' hello. My friend Jessie asked me to come over here and say hello," Kirk said quietly.

Susie nodded. "I'll have to thank her sometime. She's a dear. But we've met before, I think. Haven't we?" Susie said, smiling.

Kirk shook his head. "Nah. I ain't never seen you before, ma'am. No disrespect intended . . . "

Susie grinned. "None taken, certainly. But I do think that you have been here before, son, you just don' remember it. Cause you were under a Caul then, and didn't remember much a' anythin'. Good thing your Reaper took care of ya."

"Reaper? I don't remember any Reaper, ma'am. I just died and woke up one day on a roof someplace," Kirk said, puzzled.

Susie grinned. "That's okay, boy. It ain't always easy to remember time under the Caul. You can wander around for awhile, have dreams and enter them, and never know what's goin' on for real around you. But I want to tell you that you did come through here. And I do know who you are, so there." Susie grinned again, shaking out her long, stringy hair. "What's the matter, boy? Don't like naked ladies?"

Kirk shrugged. "Whatever floats your boat, ma'am. I guess you don't have to wear anythin'— you are dead and all. I guess things just aren't like they were."

"Ain't that the truth," Susie said.

Kirk looked in her eyes. "Is what you said the truth? I was here before? You weren't shittin' me?"

"No shit. Just truth. You were here, boy—oh, about six months ago."

"Six months, eh? And who was I with?" Kirk said.

"Yo' Reaper. You don't remember any of this, boy?" Susie said, shaking her head slowly, starting to look concerned.

"No, ma'am. I don't remember nothin'. Honestly," Kirk said.

Susie nodded. "Hum. Well, then, boy, I gots information for you, but I don't give info away for free."

"Well, what do you want me to do?" Kirk said, sighing. "I don't got any coins."

Susie shook her head. "Nah, I don't need no Charon-head coins. What I want is a song, boy. You a musician, or do you just carry a guitar around for pretty looks?"

Kirk grinned. "I know a few songs, ma'am."

"Well, why don't you go on over there to the band and see if they know any of the songs you do?" Susie said, and waved him on. "Then, I'll tell you all about your Reaper and everythin'. Deal?"

Kirk smiled. "Deal."

Kirk walked over to the band and said hello. The three ghosts, whose names were Blind Louie, Willie Whistle, and Bangup Benjamin grinned and welcomed Kirk. They whispered among themselves, and finally Kirk admitted that he knew the riff from "Mannish Boy."

He turned toward the dark bar, smiling to himself, and began to play the bluesy riff, backed up by Bangup's drums and Willie's horn. Kirk's guitar glowed bright blue-green with the light that was shining inside of it, and as he played, he felt the sound envelop him, shoot out in all directions, filling the patrons of the bar with passion—energy of a palpable kind. The wraiths nodded their heads as he played, a few of them changed shape in their seats, moving like flowers that stretch to catch the sun: they bent to catch his music. He felt the energy of his comrades, felt the blossoming of energy within him as he played for the sheer love of playing. Blind Louis sang, "Ain't that a man? Way past twenty-one . . . "

The entire crowd moved with them as they played. The gloom of the bar became lit with blossomings here and there of energy within: people remembering their past lives, experiencing the light of life, the fire of emotion deep in the bar.

Kirk played past the point where his fingers were cut and abraded by his guitar strings. He moved his fingers in an easy manner, one that he realized Blind Louis was matching as he played. Was Louis somehow orchestrating it all? Kirk didn't care. It felt right, and for that moment, there in the darkness of the bar, every wraith within earshot could hear the sound of hope in the darkness.

Willie hugged Kirk when the song was over, and there was a smattering of wraithly applause and a tinkling of metal in the bucket that hung on the wall for the purpose of collecting tips for the band.

"You gots to stay, boy, stay and play. Don' worry 'bout all that other crap. You ain't needin' to go off fightin', are you?" Blind Louis said, his sightless eyes seeing more than Kirk could know.

Kirk shook his head. He wished he could stay here all the time, just playing music, learning from these three incredibly talented musicians, learning about the roots of the music he loved. But he couldn't make himself forget all the things that had already happened to him: his death, the death of his friends, the birth of his son, the treatment his friend Rick got, his sister Anna. He couldn't leave them all behind, although he seriously considered it. He just smiled and shook Blind Willie's hand.

Kirk strode back across the bar to Susie as if he owned the place, many wraiths reaching up to touch him in appreciation.

"Havin' that git-fiddle helped wake those boys up, Kirk. You should stay and play with us," Susie said, grinning with her tombstone teeth.

" 'M sorry, Susie, but there ain't no way—hey how'd you know my name?" he asked, grinning.

From around Susie's other side came Sylvie, grinning and looking cute. "Hi, Kirk! Nice playin'," Sylvie said.

Kirk hugged Sylvie when he saw her. "Damn, girl, I missed you. I've been out and about. Gettin' into trouble."

Sylvie nodded. "I figured as much, Kirk. You ain't ever not gettin' into trouble."

Kirk turned to Susie. "Hey. What's the story? You were gonna tell me about my Reaper . . . "

Susie nodded and looked at Sylvie. "She don't think it's a good idea. Afraid you'll get the big head."

Sylvie looked down at the floor, then looked up coyly at Kirk. "Well, I was just worried that . . . well, I guess you need to know. I just don't want it to change nothin'."

"Why the hell would it change anythin'?" Kirk demanded.

"Well, boy, come on into Susie's office and we'll talk about it. I owe you that after that song. Geez, you made half the bar light up," Susie said, ambling through a door that had half-fallen off its hinges, on into the backroom where, away from the prying ears of those who would normally listen in on such things, they could talk in private.

Kirk sat cross-legged on the floor, idling toying with his guitar (which seemed to lose its tune faster now than ever before) and listening to Susie.

"Well, you see now, boy, I was just sittin' here in my bar, mindin' my own business, when a Ferryman showed up. Now, I don't know if you know what a Ferryman is . . ." Susie said.

"Nope. What is a Ferryman? Besides a fairy-man, which I know about already, and don't need to know anythin' more about," Kirk said, grinning.

"You hush and listen to Susie, Kirk," Sylvie chided.

"Well, you see, Charon was the first Ferryman, many, many years ago. The Lady of Fate—" at this, Susie paused, smiling at Sylvie "—came out of darkness and decreed that Charon was the man who'd be put in charge of helpin' souls get wherever they's supposed to go. He came upon a few more like himself and asked them to help out. Each one of these wraiths, back then, was given a reed boat and a pole and a scythe, and took to wearing hoods over their faces so that no one could tell who they really were. They served humanity by getting them down the river to where the Sunless Sea was and telling them how to build their own boats to get across the sea. Later on, on that same spot where the river meets the sea, that's where Charon built his city, Stygia.

"Now these Ferrymen, you see, they were impor-tant in that they helped people get right in their heads where it was they wanted to be goin' and helped 'em get that way. And after Stygia was founded and all this other stuff started happenin', well you know what? The original Ferrymen, they didn't even know what it was, but they didn't want to hang around Stygia when Charon was takin' over and makin' demands outta everyone. They weren't gonna be a party to the mass gatherin' of souls. Instead, they used their power, wisdom, and lore, and were able to continue to help individuals here and there that could use their help.

"But legends, they run deep, Kirk. And even though the Ferrymen aren't a part of the Hierarchy anymore, they are respected by all the wraiths—respected, feared, and revered. Ferrymen can do just about anythin' they want, really. And this one, her name was Sharon, I think, took you under her wing and Reaped you. She showed you a lot about the world, that I know, because she was carrying you along with her. Taught you how to use puppetry pretty well, showed you some Outrage, a little Keening such as you used here. That's how I knew you could Keen. She said you had the mark of the Firebird on you, and there ain't nobody here that ain't heard the prophecy about the 'son of the Firebird' bringing great change to Atlanta. Atlanta's the city of the Firebird, dontcha know. We've been burnin', rebuildin', and burnin' again for the longest time. And we'll keep on, keepin' on. I've seen it once, twice, three times, and it'll keep goin' on."

Kirk just sat there. "So this woman Sharon—she was a Ferryman? She's been alive that long?"

Sylvie shook her head. "She was probably one of the younger ones, actually, Kirk. What they do is train up those they think can do what it is a ferryman does, and lead them into an initiation at the secret Ferryman places all throughout the

Underworld. Secret places where no one else can go, secret waystations that let them vanish into nothingness if people chase after them."

Susie nodded. "That's right. Them Ferrymen are powerful folks. They gots Arcanos that nobody else got: things that let them know the rightness of things, that let them keep track of people no matter where they are in the Death-lands."

Kirk sighed, holding his head. "This is too much, Sylvie. What does it all mean?"

Sylvie smiled and pinched Kirk on the arm. "Stupid. Haven't you been listenin'? What it means, Kirk, is that you're special, dammit. Not just any Ferryman chooses someone to be Reaped. There's somethin' special about you, Kirk. And I see it even if you don't."

"Special? Heh. What's special 'bout a fuckup who got himself killed just because he couldn't keep his nose out of other people's drug business? Who left behind a baby sister who's gonna get turned into a prostitute and a baby son who's gonna grow up without a father. Pretty darn special, yeah," Kirk said, anger tingeing his voice. He was feeling sorry for himself.

"That's up to you, Kirk. You can forget him and never see him, and not ever be a father. Or you can do like you been doin' and watch over him. That's the key. Watchin', protectin'. But you're right: you're gonna have to face up to what you did. You're gonna have to understand what it is to be a dad, gonna have to know that demon inside you before you can do anyone else any good," Susie said harshly, but then she smiled again.

Kirk smiled, too, shaking his head. "You mean I gotta bring Demon out and talk to him or somethin'?"

Susie put a soft, gentle hand on his shoulder. "You gotta know him. You gotta talk back at him. If he tries to make you do somethin', you turn it right back on him. Know him. Know what makes your

Shadow tick, what it is he wants. Kirk, that's the only way you can get anyplace," Susie said quietly.

Kirk nodded, listening to it all, feeling a growing fear inside of him. Could he take that? Could he see all the anger, and hatred, and what-have-you that was inside of him? Could he deal with it? Wouldn't it be easier just to keep quiet, to fight him off when he got out of hand? Still, there was tremendous truth to Susie's words.

Sylvie hugged Kirk from behind. "Kirk, you're very special, very special to this city. And you can either help destroy it, or help change it for the better. Now, I heard tell you went on over to the Hierarchy this mornin'. It's gotten out. The Circle—Freda, Duke, and Jojo—ain't happy with you, Kirk. They think you've sold out. I told them you didn't, that you just had to get somethin' done, but I need to know what it is you did."

Kirk looked shocked. "Sold out? Fuck no. Rick died. My friend, you know, the one who was burned in the raid?"

Sylvie nodded. "Yes. Where did you find him?"

"He was in his hospital room. He was in a lot of pain and, well, it seemed like the right idea at the time, so, well . . . I turned off the machine that was keepin' him alive."

Susie chuckled, shaking her head. "Oh my, my."

Sylvie looked very concerned. "You killed him, Kirk? Why?"

Kirk shrugged. "It . . . seemed like . . . well, he was in a lot of pain. I just wanted to give him peace."

Sylvie shook her head. "Kirk, did Mr. Demon put you up to this?"

Kirk thought back. He remembered Mr. Demon asking him to do it, taunting him. "I reckon you're right, Sylvie. He did. Does that mean it was bad?" Kirk felt a pall of guilt fall around his shoulders.

Susie spoke softly. "It's always best to leave the living to living, as long as they can, Kirk. If his soul was still in his body, then there was a chance for him. You never know what a person's Fate is until you actually see it happen. You joggled Fate's arm, Kirk. Made him die early, maybe."

Kirk looked down. "Yeah, well, the Hierarchy has him. I wish it had never happened, but there's nothing I can do about it now."

"There's a few things you can do about it. But Kirk, you shouldn't have done that. Specially since Mr. Demon was suggestin' it—that shoulda tipped you off right there."

Kirk heard Demon chuckling to himself and shook his head, hanging it in shame.

"Don't give me that puppy-dog look, lookin' like you're all sorry you did what you did. I know you're sorry. It doesn't change what you did. Still, I might have done it myself if I were in your shoes, Kirk. I understand what you did, I just don't agree with it," Sylvie said.

Kirk nodded slowly. He looked up at Sylvie. "I hate the Hierarchy. They suck. Do you see how they treat people? Puttin' them in chains, shippin' them around like cattle. I can't believe that shit."

Sylvie nodded, looking around nervously despite the fact that no one but she, Susie, and Kirk were present. "Yeah, I know, Kirk. I ain't too happy with them myself. But it seems to me that some of the Renegades are just as bad. I can't trust any of them."

Kirk nodded. "I know what you mean. I don't think I'm with any of them. I'll stand next to my friends—you, Sylvie, and maybe the rest of the Circle if they'll get their panties unwadded, but dammit, I'm just not a big joiner. Still, if I have to, to find out what I am, and to rescue Rick, I'll join the Wolves."

Sylvie smiled. "I can understand that, Kirk. I wouldn't ask you to turn down a chance to learn about what you are. You need to. It's important."

Kirk nodded. He stared off into the darkness of the back room, his eyes glazing over as he thought. He turned back to Sylvie. "Is Greymaster my father?" he asked, quietly.

Sylvie didn't answer. She looked at Susie quietly, smiling.

Susie smiled, waving her hands, getting up slowly. "That's my cue. I'm outta here. Y'all have a good talk," she said, trundling into the front of the bar.

Sylvie waited until Susie was gone, then whispered so that she couldn't be heard from the other room, "Kirk, that's for you to find out. I can't help you with everything. I will tell you that I think if you want to join the Wolves to find out about your life, and your destiny, then I say go for it. You have to understand, though, that it's getting close to the end of the time that I can be with you and tell you what all to do. You've come very far, very far in the past day or so, ever since you went from bein' a layabout on that roof of yours to bein' a free spirit. Now you know a lot more than you did. You gotta do somethin' with that knowledge, Kirk. You can't just stay the way you are. You have to go on. I'll help you whatever way I can, but I can't do it for you," Sylvie said, smiling.

Kirk nodded, thinking. Questions were boiling up inside him, and he asked them whenever he could get ahold of one long enough to understand it. "Am I gonna hurt that little baby if I keep hanging around it? Is it a good idea for a ghost like me to hang around a baby?"

Sylvie shook her head. "Not unless you decide not to work on knowing your Shadow, knowing what it'll do, and knowing what it won't do. You won't help that boy if you're not able to protect him from your demon. But Kirk, you were right about one thing: that boy needs a father. Needs a real father, not the kind of father that abuses or ignores his kid. A father that loves him, really loves him. Can you do that, do you think?" Sylvie said, looking into Kirk's eyes.

Kirk nodded. "I . . . it's scary, Sylvie. But I can do it. I . . . feel something about him. It's very strange. It's not like anything I've ever felt before. I guess I feel . . . responsible for him. Like I need to protect him."

Sylvie nodded. "Those are good feelings. They do you credit. Now, you wanted to go and see Anna, make sure she was okay? I can take you there if you want, but I have a feelin' that you're not gonna like what you see."

Kirk nodded. "I want to go. I have to go. I want to see my sister."

Sylvie nodded. "All right, then. Let's go." She offered her hand to Kirk.

"Sylvie? I just wanted to say thanks. I realize that you do a lot for me. A lot of work. I've seen what the Hierarchy is like: everything is all cut and dried, pay for this and pay for that. You ain't never asked to be paid. I want you to know I appreciate all that you've done for me, and for my—for my family."

Sylvie smiled. "Kirk, would it hurt your feelin's if I told you it was my job?"

Kirk shook his head. "Nah, but isn't it a shitty job? Helpin' out dopeheads who fuck up things?"

Sylvie smiled again. "Nope. I wouldn't trade this job for anythin'."

Kirk shook his head again, looking down. "Thanks again, Sylvie."

"You're welcome," Sylvie whispered. "Now, can we get goin'?"

Kirk nodded, and they vanished.

———

There were always two or three cars in the Rourke's driveway inside Royal Pines Trailer Park, next to the double-wide that Mama Rourke had bought on the money from her widow's military benefit. The cars were of various different makes and manufactures, some luxury cars in good condition next to trashed-out Toyotas and Buicks. The neighbors had gotten used to the comings and goings that always seemed to be going on around that trailer: people arriving and leaving in cars all night long on the weekend. And one of the windows on the trailer always had light coming from it and the music of some blues CD of one kind or another. The smell of incense wafted out into the night— that and heavier smokes. The Rourke family didn't own a drier: their clothesline on Monday afternoons looked like a what's what of trashy lingerie: tiger-print teddies, black leather bras, nylon panties from Wal-Mart with holes cut out of the crotch. Red candles burned in the window, and everyone knew what went on there. As long as they didn't do what they did out in the open, people in Royal Pines were willing to let them keep doing it. It was their way of makin' a living, and who wanted to be responsible for ruinin' someone else's livelihood? Most of the men who drove up to the trailer on the weekends were nice enough, quietly entering the trailer and just as quietly leaving.

J.T., the landlord of Royal Pines and biggest cheese around there, took a cut of the business that Kirk's sister generated and fielded any complaints the neighbors had. Usually all it took was offering the complaining woman's husband an hour with Kristy and the problem was solved—after all, they were proper ladies who always "obeyed" their husbands, weren't they?

Kristy was sixteen going on thirty. She'd gone to work part-time for J.T. last year, making money on the side while still going to high school. But this year things were so tight for their family, with Momma being on AFDC and smokin' crack, that she dropped out of school when she turned sixteen and went to work full-time. She would sleep until noon or one o'clock, wake up, eat a double Whopper with cheese for breakfast (which J.T. brought every afternoon) and service J.T. (he always demanded one free fuck a day as part of his fee—luckily he was pretty easy to please). Then she'd take a scalding-hot bath, shave her legs, and get ready for her first customer. She'd sit and watch MTV and read trashy novels that J.T. brought her until her first john showed up. When Anna came home from school, she'd stick Anna in the back room (it did have a bathroom, after all) and tell her to watch TV. Anna had learned a long time ago to take the frozen dinners out of the freezer and nuke them in the microwave, so she only had to worry about some strange man lookin' at her funny when she did it. Anna had gotten good at being really hard to see and really hard to hear. She knew somehow that the way J.T. looked at her was unhealthy. Luckily, she never had to speak to anyone, never wanted to speak to anyone, didn't think she could remember how to talk, not since Kirk had left.

Anna would nuke her dinner, then walk to the back room, lock herself in, and watch the same videotape over and over on the VCR: a collection of *Barney and Friends* videos turned up loud enough so that she didn't hear the sounds from her sister's business. She loved Barney, a purple dinosaur who loved everyone. She couldn't wait for the song that told her she was loved everyday. She wanted to believe Barney, but when her mother would come home from work (either at the paper factory or at the "lingerie model studio" that J.T. ran over on Cheshire Bridge Road), she'd usually come home in a bad mood. That meant a beating for Anna if she interrupted Mommy's smoking, or her shootin' up, which she usually did in the kitchen.

When Kirk and Sylvie materialized outside the trailer, Kirk shook his head at the three cars that were in the small driveway. He looked over at Sylvie, who looked concerned.

"Kirk. There's something you gotta know. I know you know how to do stuff—powers and all. I want you to know that everytime you mess with mortals with your powers, where you touch them, you give your Shadow a chance to screw with them. You need to watch how you use your powers around the living. Especially out here where people believe in ghosts and they're lookin' for any reason to get into the *Weekly World News* or something. Do you understand?"

Kirk nodded. "No fancy stuff. No showy stuff."

Sylvie nodded. "That, and no skinridin'. What you see, you have to accept, Kirk. You can't change it quickly, and you can't change it using your power. You have to fix things a different way."

Kirk nodded. "All right, then. Let's go see what's what. Looks like Mom's not home yet."

Kirk stepped through the closed door of the trailer, feeling a pang of familiarity at the place. He saw his Elvis collector's plate on the wall, saw his Atlanta Falcons pennant that he had gotten the first time he saw them play at the stadium. But his attention was distracted as he heard the door to his sister's room open up and she came walkin' out, a cigarette tucked daintily between two fingers. She was wearing a purple nylon teddy with a black garter belt, and stockings that had runs in them. Her face looked like an Avon lady's nightmare, although Kirk could see where her customers might see it as being "exotic." Two guys were flanking her, wearing nothing but their white T-shirts, boxer shorts, and boots.

Kirk shook his head, not wanting to see what she was going to do with them. She unfolded a futon in the living room, grinning wickedly as she said, "Now, y'all know there's an extra charge for two guys at once. I don't do anythin' kinky without chargin' for it. Why don't y'all just put your money down first, before we get started? That way, we don't have to worry about it later."

The two big country-lookin' guys went for their wallets (they kept them tucked in their boots) and counted out a hundred dollars each. "Is this enough?" one of them asked, grinning.

Kristy nodded, brushing one of her peroxide-blond strands out of her face. She walked back down the hallway and threw the bills into her money jar. Kirk turned his face from what happened next, walking down the hallway. He peered into his sister's bedroom and saw that she had taken his TV and had bought a brand-new VCR (the box was still next to it) that she was using to show porn videos. Kirk walked past his door, which was padlocked like he had left it. He remembered the drugs he had stored in there, wondered for a second if he could somehow get in there and get those drugs. He realized Mr. Demon was chuckling to himself.

"I'll help you get that door open," Mr. Demon said, laughing.

Kirk shook his head. That time was past: how was he gonna be able to deal dope from beyond the grave, anyway? What was he thinking? He did worry in the back of his mind about someone finding the drugs and busting his family, but then realized that it was probably only a matter of time before they were busted; either that, or J.T. was also payin' off the cops to keep them out of trouble. That would be his style.

Kirk walked to the rear of the trailer. He saw Anna, her knees tucked up underneath her, clutching her Barney doll and singing quietly along with the video. The TV screen was the only source of light in the room, and Kirk felt a pang of fear for his little sister. She was so small, so delicate. He smiled as he saw the teddy bear he'd given her so many years ago (now old and battered, with an eye missing) enjoying a place of honor next to her pillow.

Sylvie whispered to Kirk, "The innocent can see us sometimes, Kirk. Be careful."

Kirk took off his mask, and looked at Anna closely. He didn't want to scare her, but he desperately wanted to talk to her.

Anna looked up from her video and glanced around the room as if to see where the sound had come from. She looked right at Kirk.

"K-Kirk?" Anna said, looking at him wide-eyed.

Kirk nodded. "You can see me?"

Anna nodded quietly.

Kirk smiled. "How are ya, pooh?" He sat down on the bed next to her.

"Not so good, I ah, I've been sick. Had the flu or somethin'. J.T. won't take me to the doctor, keeps makin' me drink Nyquil until I go to sleep. I hate him. I thought you were dead. That's what Mama said," Anna said in a nearly monotone voice, one that belied the intensity of the emotions underneath.

"I am dead, Anna. I'm just here for you to see me," Kirk said. "I'm wantin' to help you get out of here. Do you want to go?"

Anna nodded slowly. "Yeah. I don't like Kristy's job. J.T. looks at me funny. And Mama been takin' too much medicine lately. Kirk, are you gonna take me away?"

Kirk shook his head. "No, sugar. I'm not. But . . . but I'm going to get you out of here somehow. You might have to be here a little longer."

"What are you gonna do, Kirk?" Anna asked, her brown eyes wide with wonder.

"Somethin'. I don't know what, not yet. I'm gonna find someone who'll take you out of this place," Kirk said.

"Oh, I don' wanna go to no foster home where they make you go to bed early and don't let you watch Barney! I heard about that from a kid at school," Anna said.

Kirk grinned. "Well, we'll see what I can do, Anna. I just want you to hang tight here, okay?"

Anna nodded. "Have you seen Daddy?"

Kirk looked over at Sylvie, then back at Anna. "Why do you ask, Anna?" Kirk said, trying to hide concern from his voice.

"Oh. Because I figured you'd see him, since he's dead, too. Is he helpin' you?" Anna asked.

Kirk shook his head. "Nope. I . . . I don't know if Daddy is here or not, Anna. Not for sure."

Anna nodded. "You remember when you used to tell me stories about him being brave and strong and good? I used to believe that he watched over me, even though he was dead. Like you. Now that I see you, I guess I was right. He did watch over me. Right?" Anna asked.

A cold shot of fear ran though Kirk. "I—I guess so, Anna. Have you ever seen Daddy, like you've seen me?"

"Daddy? Oh, no. I've only seen the Wolfman, like you. He comes and watches Kristy work sometimes. He likes to watch her. Then he watches Mommy take her medicine and sometimes yells at her. But Daddy's never been here," Anna said.

Kirk nodded, a dark chill rushing through him. "Does this Wolfman sometimes wear a mirror-mask?" Kirk asked.

"He has a mirror-mask that he puts on when he leaves. I saw him leave one night when I was outside playing," Anna said quietly.

Kirk felt the cold of Oblivion stealing through his entire body. He clenched his teeth, trying to force it out of him. He turned around to Sylvie. "Does Greymaster have a Fetter here?" Kirk asked.

Sylvie wasn't surprised at the question, but it was clear that she wanted Kirk to come by the information he was seeking through his own efforts. Sylvie nodded slowly, in the direction of the hallway.

Kirk turned back to Anna. "I have to take a walk now, Anna. I'll be back in a little bit."

Anna nodded and went back to watching her video.

Kirk walked back into the hall, followed by Sylvie. He could hear the grunts and cries coming from the living room and shuddered. He felt Demon inside him waking up at that sound: heard him whispering something foul about going and watching it, but he wouldn't do that. He stood at the door of his room, looking at the LEGALIZE POT NOW! sticker on the door, and looked at Sylvie, who nodded. "It's in there," she said.

Kirk stepped through his door and suddenly was in his old room. Looking around the room, he realized that nothing in it was really that important to him. His bed was still unmade, his clothes were lying around. No one had come in to clean the place up, or clear out his stuff. It was as if he had just left it and was going to be right back.

Sylvie held her hand out, slowly moving around the room. "I'm looking for the Fetter. It's around here someplace."

Kirk nodded. He felt the demon churning in his stomach, whispering to him, "Listen, listen." Kirk could barely stand, feeling the feelings he felt. His eyes blinked; he cleared his vision. What was that? What was it that memory denied him?

A hand, holding his. He looked down, down at the bed, sitting there quietly, his sixteen-year-old blood pumping, roaring through his veins. Kristy was there, she was moaning, she was moving hard against the man in her bed, her body covered in sweat.

A hand, holding his—a gloved hand. "How long would he watch?" his demon asked. He shuddered. He felt Demon making him watch, chittering as he watched, laughing at Kirk's reaction, watching his sister.

Kirk wanted to scream, he wanted to jab hot pokers in his eyes. He didn't want to be here anymore. He wavered, staring at Sylvie as she looked around the room. "Are you okay?" Sylvie said. "Oh damn, Kirk. You're not okay."

Now Kirk wasn't even seeing Sylvie. Kirk was looking down at his bed, watching as his sister changed positions and started moving again. His aura was dark, fiery motes dancing within him.

Sylvie sighed. "You've got to resist him, Kirk. That's the only thing I can tell you to do. Resist! Don't let him take you. Don't!"

Kirk felt the turning, the worms eating his guts. He sank to his knees, trying desperately to turn his face away. Demon laughed, keeping his eyes open. "You want to watch, don't you, Kirkie boy? Go ahead, boy. Watch. You'll love it," Demon spat into his ear.

Kirk shuddered again. Sylvie stood back away from him, afraid of what his Shadow might do to her if she got in its way. Kirk stood up and walked to the closet. His hand glowed with fire, and Sylvie saw it open. From out of the closet a sword floated—a military sword: a Marine sword. Even though it was tarnished and old, it was still clean. The sword floated to Kirk's hand. He stood there, fire in his eyes, holding the sword, watching as fire danced down the blade.

Sylvie realized that the sword was a physical object, something in the living world. Looking at it with her lifesight, she suddenly realized that the sword was the Fetter that Kirk was looking for. Greymaster's Fetter.

As Kirk made contact with the sword, flames danced down the blade. Suddenly, in the darkness of the room, he erupted into fire, burning bright. Wings spread from his back, and Sylvie's eyes got bright and large as she looked on the power of the Firebird.

Then, suddenly, the sword fell to the bed below it, and the fire burned off like fog on a summer morning.

Kirk looked hard at Sylvie, having shaken off Mr. Demon once again. "That's the Fetter, isn't it?" Kirk asked.

Sylvie nodded.

"My father's sword. I got that sword from the guys at his funeral. He had said he wanted me to have it. Hmm. Wonder why," Kirk said cynically.

Sylvie nodded. "Let's go, Kirk. It's not good to talk around someone's Fetter. They can sense it. I'm not sure if he can sense what just happened, but I think you shouldn't touch it again."

Kirk nodded. "I'm done here. I want to go to the Grey Wolves' place. I know what I have to do."

Sylvie nodded, unwilling and unable to change Kirk's mind.

"So, Firebird, you decided to return to us, did you?" came his father's voice from behind the grey mask.

"Yes, sir. I've seen enough of the Hierarchy to know that it's full of shit. I'd like to join contingent on guaranteeing some aid from you," Kirk said, Sylvie standing beside him. They had traveled through the Tempest easily and had been admitted to the Greymaster's presence almost immediately.

"What aid would that be?" Greymaster asked.

Kirk pushed a hank of his hair out of his face. "I

want to go in and rescue Rick, my buddy. He was taken by them."

Greymaster nodded his agreement. "Sounds fair enough. Gentlemen, if you will, get this soldier a kit and a gun. Will you be staying with your charge, Miss Sylvie, or do you trust my tender mercies?"

Sylvie looked at Kirk, who nodded at Sylvie. "I think he'll be all right on his own, Captain. I don't expect he'll be needin' my help no more."

Greymaster nodded. "We'll whip him into shape. Give him basic training in five days. That should teach him all he needs to know."

Sylvie nodded quietly, trying not to get emotional in front of the Greymaster. She looked worriedly at Kirk, but realized that this was the path of his destiny. He must walk his own road. Sylvie stood on her tiptoes and hugged Kirk, holding him briefly before releasing him.

"You know what to do," Kirk whispered in Sylvie's ear. They had discussed a few things during their travel, and Sylvie had agreed to every one of them.

Kirk stood staring at the Greymaster, wondering how much the man knew about him. Wondering if he knew that Kirk was fully aware of who he was. Whatever the case, Greymaster was playing his game very well, treating Kirk as any other Lemure he might take under his wing. But Kirk could feel Greymaster's eyes on him wherever he was in the room, and knew that something must be apparent to the wraith who was his father.

He could only wait for him to reveal his hand. Until then, Kirk would be the best damn little soldier that his father could ever want. Kirk was sure that he could do anything the man asked of him, and desperately wanted more training in the secrets of the magical arts that allowed wraiths to do special things.

Kirk was given a bedroll, a rifle, and a pale white cloak. He waved good-bye to Sylvie as they marched him off to his barracks. He couldn't help but wonder if this was, in some strange way, helping the demon inside him.

In the darkness of his barracks, he thought he could hear his sister, Anna, crying. He also wondered when he'd see his son again.

5

FATE AND
THE FATEFUL

One two three four
Every night we pray for war
Five six seven eight
Rape. Kill. Mutilate.
　　　—U.S. Marine Corps training chant,
　　　　　　Camp Pendelton, quoted in
　　　　　　the *San Francisco Chronicle*,
　　　　　　　　　　　January 6, 1989

Ghost Story:
The Swamps of Parris Island

You there, recruit. Do you want me to tell you that
your mother loves you? That you are her bestest
boy? Well, I won't. I won't, and you can hate me
for that. I give you permission to hate me, recruit.
In fact, if you can stop whimpering and sucking
wind long enough to find the energy to hate me, I
will be duly impressed with you for the first time
in your miserable life. But you should take heart,

*recruit. Do you know why? Because I am not the
DI in the swamp. I am not that man out there who
rides boys like you until they are nothing but
bloody flesh hanging off bones. I am not that man,
because if I were, they'd lock me in the brig. But,
son, let me tell you, if you ever decide that this is
too much, that my tender mercies are too harsh,
just tell me. I'll be glad to let that DI in the swamp
take a crack at your hide.*

*Now why don't you get down there in that mud
and give me fifty just for puttin' your filthy eye-
balls on me. Let's go!*

Kirk had become the subject of one man's torment.
Something that was supposedly called "training."
During the day, Kirk was forced to run the interior of
the warehouse repeatedly, until he nearly discorporated from fatigue. At night, Kirk was given over to
the tender mercies of Dr. Teeth and his unique
teaching techniques.

Somehow, Dr. Teeth had managed to capture the
bare essence of every power known to ghosts in the
Shadowlands and store the essentials of them in his
skulls: head bones he found floating in the Tempest,
and some others that he collected himself. The
skulls' eyes were the portal through which the unini-
tiated learned the secrets of power. But each time
Kirk looked into the eyes of the skulls, Mr. Demon
would come out of the black pit in the center of his
skull and begin screaming in Kirk's ear. He would
pass out, unconscious, and awaken the next morning with a severe headache. At first he didn't think it
was having an effect. Then, one morning, Kirk was
late for muster. He missed the morning call because
he had to polish his boots and his mask. He was terrified to be late, not knowing what the DI (a terrible

man from the swamps of Paris Island named "Gunter") would do to him if he was late for muster, but knowing that it was something he'd rather not do. However, being late entailed more than just not being there. AWOL was not being at the right place, at the right time, in the right uniform. So even if he skipped shining his mask, he would be AWOL.

Still, as he finished the last buffs of the mask, he put it on carefully and then began to run toward the parade ground out in front of the warehouse, in the old parking lot. Instead of running, however, Kirk suddenly found himself flickering through the Tempest and materialized just as the call to muster ended.

Gunter didn't let him off easily for that almost failure, however: sensing Kirk's lateness and his tension, Gunter rode the recruit the rest of the morning. He forced Kirk to stare at the bright sun until he was blind, then made him find a way through a rope maze. He hobbled Kirk's legs together by thrusting a Relic iron pin through them and then forced him to fight off two other armed soldiers. They beat him to a pulp, although Kirk learned that Gunter was even more sadistic than he thought: Gunter had Usury, the power to give back Corpus when it had been taken away. Gunter was able to essentially "heal" Kirk's wounds, thus enabling him to further torture the boy.

Several times Kirk felt like just giving up. But a feeling deep within him wanted to get through this, knew that his father would, somehow, respect him more if he did. And there were other things: his promise to Cindi, the hope that his son would still live. He knew he couldn't let them down.

Greymaster remained aloof, watching Kirk from afar, speaking with his instructors privately, treating him like every other new recruit. Kirk watched him out of the corner of his mask every time he was nearby, simultaneously attracted to and repelled by the man's presence. He knew that everything he was, and everything he could be, counted on him surviving this training.

Gunter gave him hell for his Firebird mask. He called him "birdie-birdie" most of the time, making him tweet and "flap his wings." Once, he threw Kirk from the roof of the warehouse to see if he could really fly. Gunter told him that he wasn't worthy to wear the wolf mask, that he would never be a Grey Wolf. Kirk took the curses in stride: inwardly he knew that the Firebird was his symbol, that he was the Firebird no matter what anyone else thought. It was not Mr. Demon's symbol: it represented something greater and more powerful than him.

The demon within him loved Gunter. Loved the torture that Kirk was going through. It grew strong; Kirk could feel it like a lead weight inside of him, a burning weight that curled up in his bowels like a fiery enema. Demon began to whisper taunts, curses, taking its cue from Gunter. They worked together: one hammered him from without, the other from within.

Still, Kirk never lost the feeling that something else was at stake here. He dreamed about his baby boy, dreamed about a new life for little Jeb and for Cindi and for Anna. The short minutes of slumber he got every day were filled with moments of pure peace, as if something was reaching out from Heaven to touch him. He wasn't sure what to think about that, but he did come to associate sleep with an almost reverential sense of worship. Sleep and dreams became the food and drink of his soul as his ghostly body was pounded, worked, tortured, trained, thrown, and burnt.

But, he learned much. He learned how to charge a gun with Pathos, the energy within him, "juice" his DI called it. He learned how to use a gun with soulfire attached. He learned about darksteel, what it was, how it felt (he carried around a wound made by a darksteel dagger for three of the five days). He learned the proper names for all the powers of the dead, called Arcanos by the Domem (the older wraiths). He was told the complete history of Stygia, the Hierarchy, the Heretics (those churchy types that Sylvie had told him about), and the Renegades— from the first Renegades who escaped the tyranny of Stygia after the fall of Rome to the brave hordes that attacked the Onyx Tower just before the Third Great Maelstrom. He learned about Maelstroms, about the Nihils, which were gateways to the Tempest. He learned what the Tempest was: a place of chaos bordering on the "nothing," the Oblivion deep at the pit of everything. He was told that no matter what or in whom he believed, he'd better keep his beliefs to himself—the Grey Wolves weren't interested in any Heretic warriors among them. They were a mercenary company, pure and simple, working for themselves for the greatest part, except when Greymaster dictated otherwise. Greymaster had no serious political agenda—he simply wished to overthrow the local Hierarchy and take all the souls gathered there for himself, letting the bureaucracy of the soul trade handle the system just as it did now.

Kirk was forced to listen to long indoctrinations that several Wolfguards (the wraiths closest to Greymaster) gave to him and some of the other, lesser-ranked Grey Wolves. He became convinced that, even if they were not the Hierarchy, they would be just as bad or worse. He became hardened within himself as he entered the fifth day of training, realizing that, in order to continue, he would have to bury his true feelings deeply. The Ceremony of Initiation was nigh, something that the DI and Dr. Teeth had mentioned in passing several times: it was the ceremony which would make or break him as a Grey

Wolf. He would either be accepted into the group, the Cohort (which was what they called themselves) or he would be denied and destroyed. Kirk quaked with fear when he thought about the latter prospect.

Kirk had been assigned cleaning duty in the weapons locker, and he was cleaning the weapons with a dirty rag to keep the Oblivion crud off of them so that they didn't jam when they were fired. There was a large steamer trunk there, one that Kirk had never looked in, because it was always locked. On the fifth day, however, it was not locked like it usually was; he opened it up with a gasp. There in the steamer trunk was the backpack of plastic explosives that had been in the bunker: enough to make the entire warehouse jump in the living world. No telling what would happen if it was detonated in the Shadowlands: Kirk had learned that Maelstroms often resulted from terrible explosions in the Shadowlands. He had also learned that Pathos would be required to fuel the chemical reaction for the explosives. Kirk wondered what use Greymaster had for the bomb backpack, but didn't linger long looking at it, as his DI was soon back on his case, demanding that Kirk clean all the guns again.

As night fell on the fifth day, the call went out to summon all the Grey Wolves for a meeting. The moon was new: no light shone in the sky. One by one, the Grey Wolves flickered into being around the warehouse, adjourning within. The Greymaster sat resplendent on his throne, looking out at his crack assortment of troops, relishing the moment of them all being gathered together. Their grey cloaks, each of them a special artifact made by Dr. Teeth, shone mirror-bright in salute as Greymaster stood and called the meeting of the Cohort to order.

"Tonight we invite one of the Restless to enter our number, as once we all were invited. This is a special privilege at this time, just before our greatest triumph. Tonight, the operation we have been conducting for the past six months will come to fruition. Thanks to the diligence of our intelligence corps, we stand ready to proceed. We have but to initiate our own, and then send our teams out into the night, to secure the most precious objective we have ever sought—the power we will need to dominate this city and deny the Hierarchy their advantage. So, now, without further words, I give you Dr. Teeth for the initiation ceremony."

A low howling noise issued forth from the Wolves' masks, an eerie sound that made Kirk tremble within. Dr. Teeth emerged from behind a curtain, carrying a cup of strange liquid. The liquid burned from within: a kind of plasm mixed with "juice," was what Kirk made it out to be.

The cup was brought to the Greymaster's hand. "Thus we seal the training of this Wolf with the drink of fire. Let his true nature be revealed."

Greymaster handed Kirk the cup, which felt warm in his hand and steamed. Kirk looked at the drink and smelled the noxious fumes, and he tried in vain to hide the disgust he had for it. Then he realized what the cup meant: he would have to unmask for everyone to see while he drank.

Kirk slowly, carefully slid his Firebird mask up on his forehead. Looking warily at the rest of the Grey Wolves, but turning away from the face of the Greymaster, he tilted the cup and downed the whole drink.

Fire burned through him. He wanted to scream in pain, but he held it in. He felt the fire inside of him, burning, eating, desperately wanting to break free. He put his hands down by his sides, but the pain wracked through him and he went to his knees. The fire inside of him was vicious, angry, almost like drinking barrow-fire: a sentient kind of flame, it ate at him.

The scream that was building in him became too

much to contain, and he screamed aloud, an ejaculation of raw pain. As he screamed, he realized that fire was shooting up and out of his mouth. That he was spreading his arms, which were becoming fiery wings. The rest of the Grey Wolves stood back, moving away with great respect as his scream went off the high end of the human scale and became a screech. Fire boiled through the room.

Then, as quickly as it happened, it was over.

Kirk stood in the center of a ring of wraiths, who, swords drawn, had already committed to destroying him should he attack Greymaster. And in the silence that followed the great fire, there came a low chuckling sound. For a second, Kirk couldn't tell whether it was Greymaster or Mr. Demon chuckling. But soon Greymaster began to laugh even louder, and he stepped forward, through the ring of warriors, striding into the center of the circle and grasping Kirk by the arms.

"Kirk! Kirk! My son! You!" the Greymaster said. "Look at them! You scared the fuck out of every single one of them. They'd have shit their pants if they still did that sort of thing. Look at them. Well, my great Grey brothers, this here is my son—my son! Come to join our grand and glorious organization! Well, boy, I had no fuckin' idea. I had no idea who you were. You've changed quite a bit, you have. Where's that half-assed drug addict I used to know, eh? Eh? I know where he went. He got ate up, chewed up and spit out, didn't he? Didn't he? Gunter took right care of you, didn't he?"

Kirk was grinning, but it was a false grin, one that he sincerely hoped his father couldn't read. As his father unmasked himself, Kirk suddenly felt a wave of hatred and fear boil up from within him. "Hello, Father," he said quietly.

"My Wolves! Welcome my son into our ranks! He's survived the initiation, and it's time to link his lifeweb to the Wolf," James Rourke said, his grey mask now cast aside.

A curtain was pulled in the living world, and a terrible sculpture was revealed above the Greymaster's throne. It was a large, ravening, slavering, enraged wolf's head, a mask made of pure iron and steel that had been forged in the living world and hung there.

Kirk looked at the monstrous thing and thought, *Geez. How stupid . . .* for a moment. Then the thing looked at him. Looked into him. It seemed to move in the shadowy light, beckoning him forward.

Kirk walked toward the great wolf-head. Dr. Teeth motioned to two Wolfguards, who came to stand between him and it. They touched Kirk, pulling as they did a single strand of light from him, a strand which stretched thinner as they pulled. They placed the two strands in the wolf's mouth, and it closed shut.

Suddenly, Kirk felt drawn toward the wolf, as if it were pulling him closer and closer. The rest of the wolves howled as he was pulled up and into the wolf, vanishing from sight.

Kirk felt, for a moment, completely subsumed by the intensity of the energy flowing through him. He looked down at his body, at the center of forty separate strands of light, all of them radiating out from the center of the wolf mask. Kirk felt himself being connected to the mask in some tangible way, felt his consciousness extend to it and its vicinity just as the forging was complete.

Kirk knew, without a doubt, that the wolf mask was now a Fetter for him; a weak one, true, but one nonetheless.

So, Kirk thought to himself, *this is how they achieve such complete unity and operate so closely together.* A central Fetter would allow them to do many things, including defend their headquarters even when they were away. Kirk had learned much from Dr. Teeth's teaching skulls: much information that came unbidden to him when he chose to concentrate.

Feeling the connection complete, Kirk emerged from the mouth of the mask and stepped down to the floor below. "You are now one of us, a Grey Wolf," Greymaster called out. "We salute you!"

The Wolves howled, their voices carrying out into the night. Kirk howled back at them in response and was admitted into their midst, one of them, belonging but not belonging. Kirk donned his mask again, shaking hands and being welcomed by all those around him.

He couldn't help but think of the day, soon, when he would get to the truth of it all.

The Midnight Express is one of the mysteries that the dead live with on a nightly basis. When one is dead, the strange and bizarre seem commonplace: it's not hard to accept that a ghost train boils up out of darkness each night at midnight, as it occurs all over the world. The train follows midnight as it strikes on clocks all over the planet.

The express has cars from virtually every decade since the locomotive engine revolutionized travel in the early 1800s: boxcars from the infamous Holocaust trains to Auschwitz, cars from the Simplon-Orient Express, Pullman cars, cars from the Old West, cars from circus trains. No one in Atlanta knew how Engine #13 was assembled, only that a Ferryman ran it, and it was always, *always* on time.

Because it was run by one of the Ferrymen, Kirk knew that very few wraiths were willing to risk the power of a Ferryman and attack the train. It was something usually reserved for fools and crazy wraiths to try. And yet, tonight, because of the shipment of soulfire that the Grey Wolves had discovered would be on the train, they were willing to take the risk.

Greymaster briefed his troops in the shadow of the great wolf mask. One of his Wolfguards wove his own energy into the essence of dreams to show a diagram of the attack site, painstakingly memorized and carefully recreated. The diagram was three-dimensional: it was of the Avondale MARTA station—several stops before the Five Points Station on the east line.

"At twenty-three-thirty hours this evening, we will ride the MARTA to the attack site, all cloaked. Utter silence should be in effect. The train will appear here—" Greymaster indicated the spot with his finger on the three-dimensional image, which flickered and grew in size as he spoke. "It will slow to a stop inside the Avondale Station, at which time Team Alpha will cause a diversion for the skinlanders on the bridge, here." Greymaster pointed to the bridge which spanned a highway, connecting the station with the parking area.

"Then, Maslow, your team will be responsible for skinriding any cops in the zone and clearing the platform. This is important, as we don't want any Hierarchy types who might show up interfering with the activity. It is imperative that the platform get clear, and get clear quickly, before the train arrives. The train will pull into the station at roughly twenty-three-fifty hours, as it will still be scheduled to make its stop at twenty-four hundred hours in the Five Points Station. I know J.W., the conductor, and he's a stickler for the train being on time. And, of course, unless he and his Ferryman put up a fight, we shouldn't be a factor in delaying the train. Let me make this absolutely and positively clear: in anyone's dealing with the train, you're going to have to keep in mind two things. First, do not under any circumstances threaten or attack the train itself unless you get word from me. Now you know why some of you who've got particularly gung-ho Shadows have been assigned to Team Alpha: we can't have you Shadowing out and attacking the train. I have heard tales of the power of the Ferryman who runs the express: he's got Arcanos that we've never seen, and his scythe has been known to shatter wraiths into a thousand shards, making ghost hamburger before reforming. This guy's a major player, and I don't want to tick him off in the least. Well, not any more than we're already going to just by doing this. Second of all, and this is important, too: don't delay the train. Don't get in its way, don't stop it. Don't try to get someone else to stop it. This will also piss the Ferryman off. In my experience, he doesn't mind fighting going on inside the train and on the platform: he takes offense when someone attacks the train or makes it late. So let's not offend him, gentlemen. Now. We have reason to believe that a special Hierarchy freight car will be attached to the express this time. The freight car will hold not only the soulfire but roughly ten to thirteen Hierarchy Legionnaires guarding it. It's important that Team Beta be on deck and ready to move against this car as soon as possible. If all goes well, our operative aboard the express will have secured final plans and all will run well.

"Beta: you folks are in charge of engaging the Hierarchy people inside the freight car and keeping them busy for the two minutes that the train will be paused at the station. That is all. There's nothing else for you to do. We'll take care of the rest. Now, who's not taken care of by this?"

Kirk raised his hand. "What team am I in, sir?" Kirk asked quietly.

"Kirk, you're with me. Command and control. We'll be monitoring things from the other side of the tracks, encloaked."

Kirk nodded. He couldn't help but feel the sudden wave of jealousy that swept through some of the Wolves.

"Anyone have a problem with that?" Greymaster asked, looking around. "Truth be told, I can't trust a green recruit to anything complicated. This mission is too important. So, if you folks think I'm playing favorites, you've got another thing comin'," Greymaster said sternly.

The Wolves stood quietly. Greymaster nodded. "Good. Good. I'm glad we're all in agreement. It's important for this job. Now, Team Delta, you folks are the rear guard, support, and in charge of moving HQ. I imagine the Hierarchy already knows about this place, and besides, we've been here too long anyway. You folks have been assigned some skinpuppets to drive the mask and the rest of the Relics to the new HQ. I want you to be in touch by Harbinger as soon as you're in position, and I want it to be by twenty-two hundred hours, at the very latest. Make sure you're not followed. Folks, I believe we all know our jobs here, so let's get cracking, and we'll close the operation down by oh-two hundred hours. Vanish well, my Grey Wolves. Don't disappoint me," Greymaster said, and there was a roar of men running to various positions, forgetting for a moment that they were soldiers who had died once already—like all good commanders, Greymaster had convinced them that they would not die this time.

A light rain was falling. Inside her hospital room, Cindi held on to her baby, rocking him quietly. She pulled the covers up around him. He was sleeping, a blessed event. He had screamed all day long. She thought back to the night she'd given birth, the vision of Kirk she'd seen and the promise he'd given, to always be there.

"Well, Kirk," Cindi said quietly. "Well. If you are keeping your promises, which I doubt, you're around here someplace. Someplace. You better be, damn it. Can't you do something to help keep Jeb alive? They tell me he has an even chance to live, but Kirk, that's not good enough. An even chance to live is an even chance to die, Kirk. You have to know, you have to know how to help him," Cindi said, looking out the window, tears mirroring the raindrops on the glass.

Then, somehow, Cindi knew he was there. Somehow, he was there, listening to her. She felt something—a presence—in the room.

"Kirk?" She spoke quietly.

Kirk had felt the pull all the way from the warehouse, and knowing what he knew about Argos, he didn't need Sylvie this time to visit Cindi. He simply wished himself there, and he was flying through the cold of the Tempest. Standing in the hospital room, looking at his little boy, at his girlfriend, he took a step toward the tiny light with the dark streaks running through it. He looked at Jeb, lying there, asleep on his mother's tummy, and felt a pure twinge of love as he looked at his gentle, delicate face and little hands. He wanted to hold the boy, to caress him, but couldn't. Somehow, he knew that's what the boy needed the most.

Cindi relaxed as she felt his presence, although Kirk felt her will flagging and realized she could not hold the child in her arms forever.

Stepping out of the room, Kirk walked down to the nurse's station. The only person there was a hospital volunteer, a woman dressed in a peach blouse and slacks, her grey hair up in a bun—someone's grandmother.

Kirk sat down next to the woman, who was knitting something. He could feel the loneliness dripping off her like rain off of an old tenement building.

Looking at her, he could tell that she had raised many children, loved them all, and watched them leave the house, one by one, forgetting about her.

How many times had she sat, lonely, like this? Kirk didn't know. But he knew that she needed something Kirk could offer her.

Kirk took off his Firebird mask and set it on the file cabinet. He clasped his hands together and quietly began to talk to her, humming phrases of music as he did, whispering in her ear. He felt the fullness of his idea, of his need, begin to cause his own energy to be released: he saw it as streaming blue and green light out of his hands and his throat as he hummed. As he spoke, his words became her ideas.

"You need a new person to look after, ma'am. You were always looking after children, and now your children are all gone. They're too busy to have children of their own. You need to hold a baby, listen to its heartbeat, listen to him breathing. Now, ma'am, there's a baby just down the way, just down the way. Do you remember the new baby just down the way? The baby which was born hurt. He needs so much attention. Do you remember?" Kirk whispered into her ear, hoping that at least her heart would hear. For a moment, she did nothing.

Then she looked up, put down her knitting needles, and walked over to the floor registry. Looking at the list, her finger slid down it until she reached Cindi's room. Kirk nodded, walked up behind her. "Yes. That's it. Go for it," he whispered into her ear.

Whether or not she heard him, she glanced at her watch. Shaking her head, she started to walk back toward her seat. Just at that moment, Jeb woke up and down the hall came the sound of an infant screaming. Kirk could feel the anguish and the need in that cry. The woman shook her head again and started to pack up her knitting for the night.

"No! You can't! You can't just turn your back on him. He needs you," Kirk yelled at the woman.

She looked up, as if she had heard, but then turned back to her bag again.

Kirk cursed under his breath. Jeb let out another long wail. "Please. I need you," Kirk said quietly.

"You can't force her to love someone, Kirk," came a voice behind him. He whirled, his grey cloak flowing behind him. "Who said that?" Kirk said.

"It's me, Kirk. Doncha remember Sylvie?" she said, stepping out of the shadows. "My, my. Don't you look nice? All dressed up," Sylvie said. Her voice and manner did not match her congratulatory words.

Kirk turned around. "Something has to be done. I can't keep leaving you as a baby-sitter for them both."

Sylvie shook her head. "That Cindi girl's on her last legs, Kirk. I don't know if she's gonna make it. She's been playin' with fire in her head, thinking death thoughts. The power to change is still hers, but . . . Fate doesn't smile on that child. Not unless somethin' changes soon, Kirk."

Kirk nodded at the woman, now waiting for the elevator. "That's what I'm trying to do."

Sylvie shook her head. "It has to be her choice to get involved, Kirk. You can't make her. You can't force people to do what you want. Do you want your son to start down the path you're on?"

Kirk turned to look at the woman, then whirled on Sylvie. "What do you mean? What path?"

Sylvie shook her head slowly. "I—I—can't say, Kirk. I've made a promise. You have to understand that."

Kirk nodded slowly. "All right. So you know I'm doing something wrong, but you can't tell me what?"

Sylvie gritted her teeth. "No! I can tell you. I told you. Don't force it. The living must go their own way. You can suggest. You can ask. You can plead.

But you can't force them to do what they should. That is the way of things."

"Who says?" Kirk spat.

"I say," Sylvie said quietly.

"That ain't good enough," Kirk growled.

"It has to be. It used to be." Sylvie stood quietly in front of Kirk, watching as the storms of his Shadow started to move, like an advancing front, across his countenance.

Sylvie held up her hand, watching as the elevator door opened and the woman stepped inside. Kirk was almost growling as he watched the elevator door close. He turned on Sylvie, who stood with her arms folded.

"Look how you've changed, Kirk. How much have you been changed in the past five days? What about the plans you and I made? Have you forgotten?" Sylvie said accusingly. The door to the elevator bank next to them opened, and the night nurse came on duty, cursing quietly that the volunteer had left her post early.

Kirk watched her and turned back to Sylvie, standing well out of the way of the mortal. "No, I haven't forgotten. I—I just want to know how he's going to stay alive. I don't want him to die." They continued standing in the hall, looking down it and listening to the cries of the baby in the background.

"Jeb? Kirk, Jeb's got a fightin' spirit, somethin' fierce. He's got a fire in him. Just like his pa. He's gonna do fine, if we can find him some help. If we can get someone to watch over him. And I want you to do that. But you got things to do right now. Things you know you should do. Things you can't turn away from. It's your Fate," Sylvie said again, this time more firmly.

Kirk's eyes squinted. "I don't believe in Fate. Ain't no such thing."

Sylvie nodded. "Perhaps you're right Kirk. Fate's not a strong argument anymore. But look inside yourself. You told me to do these things, to look for your friend, to look out for Anna and Jeb. To get you information. And your Circle is waiting. Just like you asked for. Just like you needed."

Kirk nodded slowly. "Yes. Just like I needed. And they came through for me?"

"Yes. They're waiting for my word. I came here to see if you still wanted to go through with it. You know you're throwin' away all the training you've gone through. You know they'll try to destroy you after this, no matter what the cost. You can never go back," Sylvie said seriously.

Kirk nodded. "I know. It—it doesn't matter." Kirk thought for a moment about his father, about how proud he was of Kirk's achievement, and felt a shiver of sadness run through them. "Not much, anyway," Kirk said.

"I always knew you were a traitor, a rat's ass fuckin' traitor'," Mr. Demon said inside his head. "If only I could I'd scream it out to every fuckin' wraith in hearin' distance. You slip up once, and I'll spill the whole can of beans, buddy-boy. I'll blow the whistle so loud they'll nail you seconds afterward. You better watch your step, you whining mama's boy. One slip, and you're mine."

Kirk's frown turned to a slow grin. "I must be doin' somethin' right, Miss Sylvie. Mr. Demon's got a firecracker up his butt."

Sylvie laughed. "It's not always reliable, doin' the exact opposite of what Mr. Demon wants. But it's a good indicator you're goin' in the right direction."

Kirk nodded. He flung open his grey cloak and took a step forward to wrap his arms around Sylvie and hug her.

She smiled. "I don't get too many of those. It's good to know you're still on the team, Kirk."

Kirk nodded. "Do you think we have a chance in hell?"

Sylvie shook her head. "Nah. But we do have a chance here. Now, here. Take this."

She gave Kirk what looked to be a little toy compass and a silver figure-eight pendant. They glowed from within, just a little.

"That compass will find Rick's soul. It's keyed to him," Sylvie said quietly. "Just give it a little juice if it starts to get dim."

Kirk nodded. "Lifeweb?" he asked quietly.

Sylvie shook her head. "A family secret, sort of. A different sort of magic."

Kirk nodded. "And the figure eight?"

Sylvie grinned. "That's not a figure eight. It's an infinity symbol. Don't give it to anyone but Rick: it won't work on anyone but him. Give it the juice, put it around Rick's neck, and get the heck out of there. Rick will be safe after that."

"What the hell? What will happen?" Kirk asked.

"He'll be taken out of there. Taken to where the Hierarchy can't get him," Sylvie said.

"Where will he go? Heaven?" Kirk whispered.

"Never you mind, Kirk Rourke. You just do what you're supposed to do," Sylvie said quietly.

Kirk nodded. His face changed as he remembered something. "Wait! Sylvie! I just remembered something. The Wolves: they're looking to get a big source of power. Some kind of massive energy source."

Sylvie nodded. "The ration of soulfire from Stygia. It's due on the next Midnight Express. It will be guarded, and—wait a second. They plan on attacking the express?"

Kirk nodded.

"They're crazier than I thought. Kirk, don't you get in the way of the Ferryman who runs that train. He will hurt you, and badly," Sylvie warned.

Kirk grinned. "You folks are really scared of those Ferrymen aren't you? They must be tough shit."

"Something like that," Sylvie agreed.

Kirk thought for a moment. "How am I going to get to Rick during all this?" he asked.

Sylvie smiled. "You know how to ride a train, don't ya?"

Kirk nodded. "What will happen if the Greymaster gets that power, Sylvie?"

Sylvie shrugged. "Who knows? I can't imagine he'll be any better a ruler than the Hierarchy."

"No, he won't. He's a bastard through and through. And his men are very highly trained. I think he'll rule the city like it was a military base," Kirk said quietly.

"You know I'm with you, Kirk. We all are," Sylvie said.

Kirk nodded slowly. "All the way?"

Sylvie smiled. "Yes. All the way."

Freda and Duke were encloaked with darkness, crouched at the outer edge of the Grey Wolves' security perimeter. Duke ticked off their current operation in his head: he had been in the 'Nam too, just like some of these guys. He knew what they were doing—looked like a standard convoy setup: a mortal moving truck and a pickup. Three skinpuppets (their aural glow black and grey with their possessors' own auras) hustled something covered in canvas into the waiting truck, and with a minimum of time wasted, they slammed the rear door down and moved out.

Duke turned and nodded to Jojo on the roof of a nearby building, who then vanished. He turned to Freda. "Let's catch the next train to Avondale, shall we?"

Freda nodded.

———

Jojo materialized next to Sylvie, smiling, his long fingers draped over her shoulder. She jumped. "Don't do that!" she said. "You scared me."

Jojo grinned behind his monkey mask. "They got movement. We ready to go. Hey, Kirk."

Kirk grinned. "Hey, Jojo. Thanks buddy. I—gotta go say good-bye."

Jojo nodded. "Give the little tot some of this—" he said, smiling, reaching out with his finger to give Kirk some Pathos.

Kirk nodded, accepting the energy. "Thanks."

Jojo nodded. "He's a good boy."

Kirk grinned and walked down the hall. He turned the corner and saw Cindi rocking the boy in her rocking chair, her arms shaking. He walked up to Cindi quietly.

Touching her, he gave her some of the energy he had for Jeb, and she immediately calmed down. He turned and touched Jeb, as well, crooning as he did so, and Jeb slowly began to wind down, like a steaming tea kettle being lifted off the stove, his cries less piercing, until finally the little boy grew quiet and snuggled close in between his mother's breasts.

"You be good, now, you hear? I'll be back," Kirk whispered. Jeb turned his head around to look at Kirk for a second and actually smiled at him.

Sylvie touched Kirk on the arm. "Come on, Kirk—it's getting close to time to move out. You'll be missed back at the warehouse."

Kirk pointed at Jeb, smiling. "Look! He smiled at me!"

Sylvie shook her head. "Kirk, you don't know nothin' about babies. He probably just got gas or somethin'. Come on," she said, pulling him into the hallway.

Kirk stopped at the door and waved good-bye to Jeb, who giggled at him. Grinning, feeling somehow recharged, he walked back down the hall to Jojo.

"See ya later, dude. Thanks for everything," Kirk said as he grasped the edges of his cloak and pulled it up around him. A cloud of black Tempest-energy whirled around him, and he was gone.

Kirk almost didn't make muster. He stood next to the Wolfguards as they waited for Greymaster to emerge from his quarters. Team Alpha had already left for the site. Team Beta was going through a final weapons check before moving out. Kirk felt the tug of the now-hidden mask as it was being moved. No wonder Greymaster wanted it in position before they moved out: it would distract the entire troop if it was constantly popping up in their thoughts. Kirk realized that sharing a common Fetter was a great strength and a great weakness at the same time.

Then the Greymaster emerged and all snapped to attention, even Beta Team, who were splayed out across the floor inspecting their weapons.

"As you were, men," Greymaster rumbled under his mirror mask. "Kirk. I looked for you earlier. Where were you?" Greymaster said quietly.

"I had to go get some juice, sir. Sorry for my absence," Kirk said quietly.

Kirk felt his father's eyes sweep across him even though he couldn't see them behind the mask. He felt the tingle of some Arcanos being used on him. "You didn't go runnin' to the Hierarchy, did ya, boy? Or back to that Sylvie bitch?" he asked quietly.

Kirk felt Mr. Demon well up inside of him and clenched his teeth as he forced the foul thing back down. "No, sir. Just around the corner."

Greymaster nodded. "Very well, then. You ready to kick some ass?" he asked quietly.

"Sir?" Kirk said softly.

"You heard me. You ready?" Greymaster demanded.

"Sir, yes, sir. I'm ready," Kirk said.

Greymaster nodded. Kirk wondered if his father had more in mind for him than just "command and control" like he had said earlier. "Very well, then, troops. Let's move out to the site. Let's go! Midnight approaches!"

The packs of Grey Wolves moved out, vanishing into the night as they did.

Kirk felt the compass and the eternity necklace in his pocket grow cold as they entered the Tempest, and realized that he felt ghost vibrations in his chest as he remembered what it was like, long ago, when his heart used to pound. He felt that way again, just like he used to feel before a big fight or before his main connection would happen. His heart beating quickly, adrenaline running through his veins—this was what it felt like. As he stepped out of the Tempest on the other side of the jump (one of the Wolfguards leading the way), he realized that some of the other wraiths there were also lit from within by the passion of the moment.

Kirk shook his head, looking at the railway with its third rail on the other side of the track and at the train station as normal, mortal trains arrived and departed on about a ten-minute cycle. Kirk was willing to bet that, somehow, tonight the mortal train wouldn't coincide with the Midnight Express.

"Kirk, I want to speak with you a moment," the Greymaster said, pulling Kirk off to one side. "You've got a special mission in this," he said quietly.

Kirk felt a cold chill go through him. "Sir. I'm ready, sir."

"Don't give me that drill instructor crap. I want you to listen to me. You're going to have to do something to impress the heck out of these guys, or they will never follow you," Greymaster said, quietly.

"Like what?" Kirk said.

"Like, you're going to have to save the day here. Now, listen to me, boy, and listen good. If you fuck this up, I'll have your ass in a sling so fast it'll make your head spin. I want you attach yourself to the Crystal Sphere that's going to be waiting on you on the other side of that train door and encloak it. Make it vanish, along with you. Then I want you to Flicker it one car down, either way. I don't care which. You decide. Pick a good car, though, boy. There's some foul cars on the express, places you don't want to go into at all. Then, just hold it until the backup gets there and off-loads the sphere. You might be attacked by some passengers, but I think you can handle that, can't you?"

"Sir. Yes, sir," Kirk said.

Greymaster nodded. "Tonight will be glorious, my son. We will rule this city, after this. And you will become recognized among my Wolves as the Firebird of prophecy: the bringer of the winds of change! Heh. I hate that prophecy crap. But it works—I've seen it too many times not to believe in it."

Kirk nodded. He watched as Team Beta boiled up out of the Tempest, then perched on the pylons which held up the south side of the station, across the way from the main platform.

Kirk looked at a bank clock just down the street: it read 11:48. He felt the rush of anticipation and, off in the distance, heard a lone whistle—a train call in the darkness.

6

GHOST TRAIN

Ghost Story:
The Midnight Express

When you've worked the railyards as long as I have, boy, you learn not to look down the track so many times. You deal with the train in front of you, not the one comin' down the track. Why's that, you ask? Well, because of the ghost trains that'll come down the track if you're lookin' for them. You don't believe me? They'll rush up out of the darkness on a full head of steam and nearly run you over. Used to be, when I was a boy, I'd see one pass by my window every night, just about midnight: the whole thing growlin', huffin', and puffin', rushin' by full of old cars that got themselves wrecked at some point. If you see one of those trains, boy, don't you dare look into the conductor's eyes: he's been known to scare a man completely to death before. Just you watch. Heh. Or don't watch . . .

The Midnight Express was on time, as always. It boiled up out of a Nihil and rushed onto the tracks near Avondale Station, heading for its first stop. The Grey Wolf agent on board was named Brenner, and she had asked to depart at the Avondale stop for "security reasons" when she boarded the train the night before. It had been a rough twenty-four hours for Brenner, who had to share the compartment with just about every freak of death she had ever seen. She was glad this was nearly over, even though she still had some work to do and the truly stressful part of this mission wasn't exactly over.

She had already managed to do what she had come to do: a small chip of the giant wolf mask, magically imbued by Dr. Teeth months before, had been placed under the sphere of soulfire in the Hierarchy freight car attached to the train. She had used her grey cloak to enhance her ability to Enshroud and move unseen through the Hierarchy's watchful security. She had even positioned herself so she would be able to run out and throw open one of the freight doors at the appropriate moment.

She felt the curious motion of the train change as they moved closer to the station. Any moment now, and all hell would break loose. Behind her wolf mask, she smiled. This was going to be *fun*.

"You sure you've got your orders straight, boy?" Greymaster said, looking down at Kirk.

"Yes, sir. I'm sure. You want me to nab the soulfire, cloak it, and move it to another car. I think I can do that. One problem, though. How do I find the soulfire in the train?" Kirk said, trying not to let his nervous voice or the demon inside him betray his true feelings.

"A fragment of the wolf mask should be in place near or on the thing. Just Argos in there to it. Even a green recruit like yourself should be able to do that."

Kirk nodded slowly.

Greymaster put a large hand on his shoulder. Kirk felt the man's terrible sword scrape against his side. "You ain't havin' second thoughts, are you, boy?"

Kirk shook his head. "I—I—just want to do good for you, sir." He realized it was only partially a lie. He actually did want to make his father proud of him, in some sick way. He couldn't forget the fact that here was the man who used to comfort him in dreams, who was always watching out for him, or so he thought. But then there was the Fetter, and what Anna had said about the Wolfman. What was that all about?

Greymaster grinned behind his mask. "Yeah, I know, boy. That's good. That's real good. When you're done here, I want to show you the good side of this life. You have to know that there are some sweet, really sweet, things you can do when you're a spook. Things you couldn't ever even think about when you were alive." He laughed. "You'll probably get a kick out of it."

Kirk looked up at his father, for a second wondering if the man's Shadow had taken control of him from the way his voice sounded. But there was no dark aura, no tangible sign that it held sway. Kirk had never seen the Greymaster's Shadow come out before and wondered morbidly what it looked like, what it did.

Kirk was amazed at all the thoughts running through his head as he waited for the train to arrive at the station. Time seemed to stand still. He was suddenly seized with a deep, gripping fear, a fear like he'd never felt before. As if cold hands were clutching around his heart. He had no idea where this feeling had come from (although some reasonable part of him had already begun to suspect Mr. Demon), but he suddenly realized that he would rather be anything else, do anything else than what he was doing. It was all he could do not to Flicker out of there and leave.

He wrapped his hand around the infinity pendant, holding on to it for strength. It gave him cold comfort, but somehow its certainty, and his promise to Rick, kept him in place.

Then he saw it: the train. Chugging down the line, a curl of black sulfur smoke boiling up out of its stack, the number thirteen illuminated by the glow of its single headlight. He thought he could even see the red glow of twin eyes in the engineer's compartment, the black robe of the Ferryman glowing from the fires that ran the engine.

Kirk felt the chill of his final decision wash over him. It was time to do what he was meant to do. It was as if the light of the train galvanized him into action.

"Prepare, boy. Don't fuck this one up," Greymaster said quietly, drawing his blade and vanishing from sight.

The train loomed closer.

"Train sighted. Get ready," Duke said.

Freda nodded, wordlessly arming herself. "I just hope the kid makes his move. Otherwise this is going to be a real short trip."

"Give the wolfies my love," Duke said, grinning.

Freda managed a wolfish smile from behind her mask. "Oh, I'm sure they'll be delighted to see me," Freda said. Jojo moved his hands over the mask she wore, crooning to it, feeling it changing. "What was that?" she asked.

"Just a little surprise for the wolfies, yes? Yes. Surprise!" Jojo cackled.

Freda shrugged her shoulders, but she knew better than to ask the trickster Jojo about his business. She posed like a striking cobra, waiting for the train to enter the station.

The light rain was still falling in the parking lot of the MARTA station when felony theft took place.

"Hey, man, what you doin' with my car, man?" Huey, a black man with an Atlanta Falcons T-shirt demanded.

"I'm takin' it, that's what," said the Grey Wolf possessing a hapless businessman who had obviously been working late and on his way home.

Huey grabbed the skinpuppet and slammed him up against his car. "Hey!" the skinpuppet yelled. A few MARTA police down the way moved closer to the scene, drawing their weapons.

"All right . . . break it up."

The skinpuppet turned toward the cops and began to mindlessly utter a stream of obscenities. Inwardly, his skinrider grinned: this should be enough of a diversion. He watched as a flood of mortals came walking across the bridge that spanned the main road and connected the parking lot to the station: the other team must've done their work clearing out the platform already. Clockwork. Everything was going as planned.

The train began to slow. Brenner stood silently next to the door of the train, watching carefully, her hand on the hidden souled revolver she carried with her always. She heard the Hierarchy guardians taking up position as the train came into the station: they had good training, she knew. She wondered if even a squad of Wolves could take them down. As she waited for the train to come to a stop, she wondered idly how they were going to move the soulfire off the train, but decided that was outside her ken. She was through here.

There was only one kink in the mission. A grey-hatted Hierarchy type had gotten on the train with her last night. She had watched him almost the entire time, but he had done nothing. She felt that he must be some kind of powerful wraith: his aura didn't show, and he was quietly ignored by all the wraiths on the train, even the crazier ones. He never moved from his place, seeming to sleep but not ever Slumbering. He read from a Relic book constantly: a book with no title on the cover.

Brenner had used every trick she knew to try and figure out who this guy was, but he was either too oblivious or too good at remaining incognito. This one loose strand worried her, but soon he passed into the realm of things she could do nothing about. She would remember to include him in her report to the Greymaster, however.

The train slowed and pulled into the station, perfectly aligning itself with the platform, which had suddenly emptied of skinlanders as waves of fear swept the frightened masses up the stairs and out of sight. The team of Grey Wolves was ready as Brenner leapt out and pulled open the freight car doors.

"Danger! Critical warning!" barked out one of the Hierarchy guards as the Wolves fired and advanced on the guards surrounding the tarp-covered sphere of soulfire.

———

"Go," Greymaster hissed, hitting Kirk on the back. Kirk nodded and surrendered to the power of his Argos, flickering across the Tempest in a matter of seconds and materializing in the freight car, which was filled with Grey Wolves and Hierarchy guards.

Throwing himself at the sphere, he threw his cloak around it. Only one Hierarchy guard, a green-coated soldier from World War I by his dress, turned and caught sight of Kirk as he embraced the sphere. The doughboy raised his rifle to fire—at nothing, as Kirk vanished into the Tempest.

Seconds passed.

"Disengage!" the Wolf leader yelled as the train began to move again. All of the Grey Wolves fighting in the train moved back, performing defensive maneuvers as they retreated.

Three Hierarchy guards jumped onto the platform, dark smoke surrounding them as their Shadows leapt into control. The Wolves kept fighting, knowing that these Centurions had been driven over the edge with rage and would not stop until they were discorporated.

Kirk materialized in a dark freight car. It smelled sickly-sweet here. The shadows moved independently of his motion. The only light was the burning green of the soulfire within the sphere, cloaked in a tarpaulin and his own grey cloak. He shook from the effort of moving the object. Suddenly, in the darkness, a Grey Wolf materialized as the train began to move. He froze, not knowing what exactly to do. Freda was supposed to be here, to make the connection, to take this thing off his hands. Where was she?

The Wolf shook its head. "You sure picked a spooky fuckin' car," came a familiar voice, but he couldn't quite place it. The Wolf walked toward Kirk, holding out his hands. "Great. You got it. Let me have it. Come on, boy, I don't have a lot of time."

Kirk shook his head slowly. "I . . . can't let you take it."

The Wolf pulled off its mask. "You don't recognize me?" Freda said, moving closer.

Kirk felt the tension leave him as he saw his friend. "You scared the shit out of me."

No room. There's no room here for you. . . . came a spectral voice from the shadows.

Kirk shuddered, as did Freda. "S-s-sorry. I had no idea. Just what is this place?"

Freda looked down, remasking herself. "Freight car from an Auschwitz train. Part of the Holocaust. Look, we can't do anything to change the Hell that these souls are going through. Just give me the sphere and let's go."

Water. Give us water. Please. Just a little water.

Kirk saw tendrils of shadow reaching out to caress the sphere, to seek a hole in the tarp and start draining the soulfire from it. Tearing the fragment of the wolf mask from it, he shakingly handed Freda the sphere. She nodded at him. "Get out of this car, Kirk. Go two cars up, that's the passenger compartment," she said, and vanished.

Kirk felt an icy chill grip him as he saw the sphere vanish with her. Now his Fate was sealed. He turned the mask fragment over and let it drop soundlessly to the shadowy floor.

Feed us. We're so hungry. Just a little food.

Kirk shuddered again as he vanished.

———

The train rumbled on, moving swiftly toward its destination with midnight. Kirk materialized in the passenger compartment. He sat down in an unoccupied seat next to someone who was sitting on the floor, clouded in his own Slumber. He held on to the compass and watched it, watched as the needle changed direction as they got closer to Rick.

He didn't look up as a figure dressed in grey sat down next to him and tried not to turn his masked head to see. He didn't want to know who it was; the fear in him still wanted to escape this place, and he was doing the best he could to stay calm.

"Hello, my boy," the grey-clad man said, easing back his flannel hat and pulling at his long white beard. Kirk involuntarily turned: the man's voice was familiar.

The voice, the face, the grey robes, the sickle symbol keeping his cloak pinned—these could only mean one thing: Hierarchy.

Kirk shook. "Are you Jebediah?" He whispered the name that had haunted him since he had fled the Citadel.

"Glad to see you know me, son," Jebediah said. It was definitely the soft, Southern voice that had asked about him in the Citadel, so long ago. The man wasn't wearing a mask now, and he smiled at Kirk. "I have come here to talk to you. It's important that you listen to what I have to say."

Kirk narrowed his eyes, not knowing what to think. "Look, uh, I'm just riding this train and I don't . . ." Kirk said.

"Don't lie to me, boy. I can smell a lie coming a mile away. That's my job. Now you just shut up and listen to me. I don't know how, just exactly, but you, my boy are a grand mistake. You shouldn't be here. The O'Rourke family Curse should have died with me," Jebediah said.

Kirk shook his head, confused. "What the hell are you talking about?"

"You heard me. You're an O'Rourke boy. Ain't ye?" Jebediah said quietly.

"Rourke, yeah. My dad said his dad dropped the O' part a long time ago," Kirk said.

"That's right—ashamed of his true heritage he was. Silly fool. Still, he had a right to be, perhaps, more so than his kin. His heritage was a curse as well as a blessing. The Curse that followed our line, grandfather to grandson, throughout history. I died so that there would be an end to it, killed by some of my Irish friends who did it in a ceremony from the ancient times. I swore not to carry on the Curse. And yet, somehow, my boy, somehow your father was affected. My grandson."

"My—my father?" Kirk said, shock running through him like a douse of cold water. The train shifted as it entered a tunnel, and the entire train shuddered as it ran through a moving MARTA train, insubstantial and unnoticed.

"You're my great-grandfather?" Kirk said quietly.

"Aye. You're quick enough when you want to be. Now, listen to me, for when the train arrives at the station I be no longer your kin and be then Hierarchy, and I must act as Hierarchy do. I know not where your father is: I've been unable to locate him, no matter how long and hard I search. But you must decide, as I did, to not further the Curse. I don't know how to end it, boy. I thought that everything I did would end it. It is a foul thing, and has cursed our family for many generations. But you must do all you can to forswear the Curse that makes us wraiths!" Jebediah said, his voice quaking with emotion.

Kirk looked hard at Jebediah from behind his mask. "And what am I supposed to do about that? Go to Oblivion?"

Jebediah shook his head. "I cannot advise you. I don't think that jumping into Oblivion will fix the Curse. I don't even know what originally caused it. But hush and listen again. You wear the mark of the Firebird. And yet the Firebird will bring you only great pain, great destruction. You must not use its power. It is the spirit of the curse, made manifest in you, the youngest male of the clan once known as Riorche."

Kirk squinted his eyes. "I don't understand what you mean. It's just a mask."

Jebediah shook his head as the train began to slow. "No, son. No it's not just a mask. It's also a sign, a sign that a prophecy is being fulfilled. You are the Firebird. You bring death, destruction, utter change. Behold the mark of the Firebird as it tormented me." Jebediah drew back the cuff of his jacket to show Kirk a bird-shaped scar raised as if it had been made by the touch of a white-hot brand on his wrist.

"See, there. And it will so claim you, if you do not put it aside," Jeremiah said.

Kirk felt the tug of his infinity pendant. He looked first at Jebediah, then at the slowing train platform outside his window, then back to Jebediah.

"Thank you, Great-grandfather, but I have to follow my Fate," Kirk said quietly.

Jebediah shook his head. "No, boy. You can change your Fate. Or, if you can't change yours, you can change your son's. Don't let the Firebird go free."

"How do you know about my boy?" Kirk said.

Jebediah smiled. "That's what Monitors are for, boy. To tell you things. I was the one who visited him. Tiny thing. Half-dead already. Do you really want Oblivion to claim that tiny soul?"

A flash of anger burned through Kirk. He stood as the train slowly came to a stop. For a moment Jebediah looked as though he would lunge for him, and Kirk remembered the man's promise about resuming his duty to the Hierarchy once the train stopped. Outside, on the platform, it was completely empty of people (cleared no doubt by the Hierarchy people upstairs), but filled with Centurions. Kirk wondered how he was going to escape this whole thing.

"Good-bye, Great-grandfather. Unfortunately, I can't stay and chat. I've got to start turning things around," Kirk said, adopting some of the man's Southern formality.

Jebediah just shook his head and hung it in shame. "Boy, you're not listening to me. If you would let me help you, come with me, I could—"

Kirk turned and, without looking back, leapt out of the train as it finally stopped, suddenly vanishing into the Tempest. This time, however, Harbinger Centurions were awaiting him in the Tempest. They swarmed around him, trying to grab his legs and arms, hoping against hope that he would have the desired soulfire that had gone missing. He held up his compass and fueled it with Pathos, following the bright shining light pointing to his destination. The light lanced through the darkness, burning arms and legs that got in the way. Suddenly he felt a connection at the other end, and he felt his entire body fold from the sudden acceleration toward his target.

Rick was hanging in darkness from his chains, completely unaware of his lot. Having materialized unexpectedly fast, Kirk had to take a moment to adjust to his surroundings. Clearing his head, Kirk touched the lock on the chains and tried to open them, shaping his fingers into picks like Dr. Teeth had taught him. He struggled with the padlock, feeling it start to click open. The chains fell to the ground with a clatter, the padlock went flying, and Rick collapsed to the cold cement floor. At the far end of the room a steel door opened, and a few Centurions came into the room as they prepared to move the shipment of new souls out to be placed on the Midnight Express: they hadn't noticed Kirk in the forest of chained souls.

"Clear this whole place out. We have to make up for the lost soulfire somehow. No holding back this time," came a Centurion's voice, and several wraiths began hefting the bodies in a fireman's brigade out the door and on down the line.

Kirk unmasked and peeled the thick Caul off of Rick's head, feeling his friend begin to stir. Rick shook his head once, then twice, then opened his eyes.

"Kirk?" he asked sleepily. "Kirk, is that you? Damn, man I had this shitty dream. You were dead, and I died in an explosion, and shit, it really sucked."

"Sorry to tell ya, dude, but you ain't dreamin'. This is reality," Kirk said quietly, holding up a length of chain. He hoped he wouldn't be heard, but the worker wraiths were making enough noise rattling chains and moving souls around that he didn't think there would be a problem.

"Oh, shit. I'm dead. Oh, well," Rick said. Kirk grinned. Rick had never been one to dwell on shit that happened. Rick looked up at Kirk. "What are you, some kind of soldier now?"

"Something like that. Look, Rick, I'm going to help you out. You're not like me. You don't have anything keeping you here. Look at you now: you're starting to get thin and see-through. That means Oblivion's pulling you down now that the chains aren't around you. What you need to do, Rick, is get the fuck out of here, someplace safe. I've got something for you, and I want you to take it and get the hell out of here. I got you into this mess, and—" Kirk said.

"I remember! You pulled the plug. Oh, damn! That was the worst, Kirk. I hated it. I hated you. Why didn't you let me live? I had a fuckin' chance," Rick said.

Kirk shook off his friend's vehemence. "Look, will you shut up and listen? I'm sorry you're dead. I can't help that now. All I can do is make sure you don't end up like these poor bastards. I can make sure you get out of here and get someplace where you'll be safe."

Someplace safe. That sounded so good to Kirk right now. His head was filled with images of his father, of his great-grandfather, of the battle. Of the Centurions and probably Grey Wolves who were now searching for him. All because he thought he was doing the right thing. He looked at the infinity pendant, and it glowed blue in the half-light of the room. The workers were almost done with the front half of the room, loading the souls onto dollies and pushing them off to the train. Kirk heard the train whistle blow once, like a warning. Kirk wondered for a second what the pendant would do if he willed it to function.

A voice boiled up from within him. "Try it."

Kirk felt his hand move to the pendant, alight with Pathos. Kirk watched helplessly as his hand closed around the pendant and it was set afire with blue flame. Suddenly it shot up into the air, held down only by the necklace it was on. It bobbed at the end of the necklace like a tiny steel balloon. Blue arcs traveled down it.

Kirk turned to Rick. "You have to take it. Pull your arms out of the Caul and take it. I can't . . ." Kirk tried to wrest control of his hand away from the beast inside him, to no avail.

Rick began to struggle. Now the light of the fire was illuminating half of the room, and workers began to point and call for the Centurions. Kirk wanted to curse, but even now, the Shadow within him had tightened its power and would not release its hold.

Rick broke his arm free from the slimy plasmic Caul and reached out for the necklace. He fell, face forward, onto the concrete, his fingers dancing within inches of the loop of blue-fire. Kirk growled wordlessly as he struggled to wrest self-control from the Shadow. He couldn't do anything to save his friend now: it was up to him.

"Fucking wonderful," Rick said, struggling, trying to break his other arm free and somehow right himself.

"Freeze!" called a Centurion from the door, and Kirk almost laughed. As if he was going anywhere.

Rick moved himself across the floor to Kirk and grabbed his leg. Pulling himself up with the one arm, he teetered in his ovoid Caul and turned around to grab at the necklace one final time before the Centurions could intervene.

Fingers danced through the darkness.

Blue fire illuminated Rick completely, burning through his entire Caul, as his fingers grabbed the necklace. For a second Rick rose into the air, burning off blue flame as he did. An infinity symbol burned itself into Rick's forehead, and even the Centurions in the room couldn't look directly at the fiery blue-white light. Looking down at Kirk, Rick smiled for the first time in a very long time. "I can see it now. It's all very simple," Rick said.

Kirk looked up at him. The blue-white light was like the summer sun melting an ice-encrusted lake; slowly he felt control returning to his limbs.

Rick looked down at Kirk. "Man, I never thought I'd say this, but hell. I forgive you. I forgive you . . . everything. If I had known—"

With that, the blue-white light surrounded Rick and he rose up through the roof, burning through the Shadowlands, rising up faster and faster. Even those who perched atop the Citadel reported later that the burning light didn't stop at the roof: it flew straight upward and into the black, stormy skies of the Shadowlands, until it couldn't be seen any longer.

Kirk backed up against the wall as he saw the Centurions advance on him, their hands on souled weapons that gleamed like stars in the shadowed storage room.

The blue-white flare of light that shot up from the Hierarchy was misinterpreted by many. The Grey Wolves thought it some sort of signal flare made of pure Pathos to warn patrols of the raid. Other wraiths thought it some sort of demon, or avenging angel rising up out of the Citadel, as if the Heretics had somehow managed to recruit one of the Unending to their service.

Far away, on the roof of the old Sears Building, Sylvie, Jojo, and Duke all knew what it meant: that Kirk had accomplished what he had set out to do. Sylvie smiled as she watched the light of Fate carry Rick away. She had no way of knowing where Rick was going, exactly. She just knew that it was someplace safe, which in the Shadowlands could be a kind of heaven.

Sylvie smiled. "Okay, let's go. Spread out and see if you can help Kirk," she said to the other two wraiths on the roof, and they vanished one after the other. Sylvie was proud to see that they had properly learned the Argos she'd taught them.

Sylvie was suddenly alone, but filled with warm energy as she realized that she had helped Kirk set Rick free. It was part of who she was: helping people was second nature to her. Even though it always gave her a large rush of passionate energy—triumph—she did not do it for the Pathos alone. She knew her place in the great Web, realized that what she did now affected all that she had done, all that she would ever do. She shuddered at the enormity of the pattern of all Fate-twines.

There was a coughing sound behind Sylvie as a figure flickered into view. The figure was wearing a black gown with a black veil. Turning around, Sylvie gasped as she recognized the symbol of the Lady of Fate on a ring on the woman's hand. "Greetings to thee, Lightbringer," the woman said quietly to Sylvie.

Sylvie curtseyed as best she could, shaking as she was. This woman was a Matron of Fate, a prophetess of great power. Her simple glimmerings were nothing next to the light that the older woman was able to see by.

"And also to you, ma'am. Did I . . . do something wrong?" Sylvie asked quietly, looking up, unconsciously using her little-girl eyes.

The Matron shook her head slowly. "No, my child. You did remarkably well. I am very pleased with you. Surely you can see your place in all of this?"

Sylvie shook her pigtails slowly. "No, ma'am. I've not got the sight to do that."

The Matron *tsked*. "We shall have to see to thine own education. Still, now I am come to bring a thing which has been left into my care up until now."

Sylvie watched as the Matron flung aside her cloak, revealing a tall scythe: the blade made of darksteel, the handle exquisitely carved with a battle-guard. This was no reaping tool, no farm instrument, but a weapon of battle.

"Beyond the darkness lies the fire. Beyond death lies the truth. Look ye to stop what must be stopped.

A circle has no beginning, but make this an ending, else the spiral will ever curve downward," the Matron whispered in her heavy Irish brogue.

The Matron gave the large scythe over to the keeping of the girl, who could barely keep it upright. "That is the weapon of the Firebird. I cannot shelter it any longer. It longs to be with its master. It will have its own way."

Sylvie nodded slowly. "What shall I do about the baby, Matron?"

She smiled. "Ah, yes, the child." Her face grew cold. "Kill it quickly, mercifully. Unless it has a proper home and family by the half-moon, it will die a terrible death." Only when she had pronounced sentence on the babe was she able to show her true feelings: a plasmic tear welled at the corner of her spectral eye. She dabbed at her eyes with a black handkerchief.

"What next, Matron?" Sylvie asked quietly.

"Ahhh, yes. Now, my dear bairn, you will know the true meaning of the word 'patience.' For you must wait. Wait, watch, and see. Keep your own counsel. The skein of Fate is so twisted now that none can properly unravel it. Where the Firebird is concerned, keep silent. Kirk must find his own way, now. There can be no turning back for him," the Matron said quietly, her voice chill.

"Yes, ma'am. I understand." Sylvie leaned forward to kiss the Matron's ring.

The Matron smiled at the young girl and placed her hand on the girl's head. "Now may the Laird bless ye and keep ye, and lead ye home should ye be lost," she said quietly.

Sylvie felt the blessing of Fate wash over her as the Matron did this, felt the woman's Pathos burn through her for a moment. Then all was well. She felt inordinately calm, even though a troop of Grey

Wolves could materialize all around her at any moment.

When Sylvie looked up, the Matron was gone, and only a cool wind carrying night smells reminded her where she was. Sylvie turned toward the east and waited. She felt the Fate-twines slowly turning, slowly unraveling, and knew that she must wait here for her destiny.

Kirk stood with his back against the wall, the Centurions advancing. He wished for a moment that he had been armed with one of the souled weapons, but had no such luck. He looked at his possible escapes: one door. The walls, floor, and ceiling were hard cement, painful to jump through.

One of the Centurions opened fire on Kirk, and Kirk saw time slow as the bullet raced toward him. Looking down, he saw the ammunition enter his plasm and penetrate it, burning a hole, moving through him. It seemed to be on fire. The bullet opened a conical exit wound behind him as he felt it leave his body. Another bullet ripped through his chest. Suddenly, the fiery pain from the first bullet hit him, followed quickly by the blazing inferno of torment the second wound caused.

Kirk bellowed out his pain, throwing back his head and nearly dislocating his jaws. He felt open, terribly vulnerable, totally out of control. His rage boiled out of the deepest parts of him, and somehow in all that pain he was able to reach up, out of himself, out to something far away.

Blazing light surrounded him. Fiery red-orange glow. Fire burned through the room, swathing him in licking flames, burning all around him. He raised his arms and saw them fan out into wings with fiery feathers. He turned to face the troops head-on, undaunted by their weapons. A puff of breath brought burning flames issuing forth from his mouth, melting souled guns and singeing wraiths with a consuming fire that only Oblivion could conjure.

Kirk lifted up one of the guards with his arm/wing and threw the hapless Centurion into, and through, a wall. The other two Centurions retreated, moving back as he walked toward the door. Somewhere in all the fiery destruction, he heard his Shadow laughing at him, but somehow it did not matter now. Kirk turned to view the entire room full of chained and bound wraiths. His vision blurred in rage: how could they do this to simple souls, souls who had died with visions of Heaven dancing in their heads? Why did they enchain all they touched?

With a gesture, Kirk felt fire pour forth from his claw/hand, watched as the flames engulfed the room, seeking after the chains themselves, moving like sinuous snakes of brilliant glowing orange, until they wrapped around the chains, setting the dead free.

Kirk heard his Shadow laugh with glee as, one by one, the will-less ghosts sank into the floor, falling into the Tempest. One by one they were lost to Oblivion, as the barrow-fires grew higher and surrounded the room. Kirk could barely think human thoughts: the fire in his brain was such that all he could feel was utter, overwhelming anger and rage.

Kirk took a step back and unfurled his great wings. They snapped smartly outward and he suddenly realized that he was flying, dizzily moving through yards and yards of cement, then pure rock as he rocketed upward.

"Now you're sure it will be safe?" Freda asked Meany, standing next to the Gypsy Wagon inside the World of Krafft.

Meany was juggling glowing skulls, end over end. "Sure. No problem. It'll be as safe as coffee. Safe as a dog's nose in a sledstorm. Safe as a pig in a blanket. Real safe."

Freda looked down, shaking her head. Why had Duke chosen this moron for guard duty? "Look, it's very, very incredibly important that you protect the sphere. If anyone's going to get any soulfire at all, we're going to need you to protect it."

Meany nodded. "Not to let anyone near the sphere unless he has a note from you."

Freda shook her head. "No, nobody's supposed to see the sphere. Nobody. Understand?"

Meany nodded. "Not to let anyone see the sphere except Nobody."

"No, no, not Nobody. Not anyone," Freda said.

"That's what I said. Not anyone except Nobody," Meany said, looking falsely puzzled. He enjoyed messing with Freda's head.

"Who is Nobody?" Freda asked, beginning to get exasperated.

"I don't know, I thought you were speaking hypothetically," Meany said quietly.

"I *was* speaking hypothetically! I said 'nobody.' As in not a single one." Freda could barely contain her annoyance.

"Right. But several can see it at once, right?" Meany asked.

"No! Nobody—oh, I mean . . . Well, dammit, you know what I mean," Freda said frustratedly.

Meany nodded. "Right. I know exactly what you mean. No problem, boss. You leave it to me, I'll take right care of it. Forget it even happened."

"Meany. You can damn well bet that I won't forget it. If you give this sphere away, I'm going to have to hurt you. Hurt you big."

Meany smiled. "You promise?" But he took the

sphere, and it vanished, and Freda got a sense that, just by looking into the clown's eyes, there would be no way in hell anyone would touch it. She worried a little that she'd have to beat the clown up to get it back, but that was something she'd deal with when she needed to.

It was dark within the truck as it trundled along the back streets of Atlanta, moving carefully so that no police car would accidentally stop it. So dark, in fact, that no one noticed the two figures materializing out of the shadows, grinning quietly behind their masks. One, hunched over, ran over to a steamer trunk and, just as quietly as he had arrived, motioned to the taller one to come and help him carry it. Only a sliver of light from the top of the truck shone down on the lion-head mask of the taller figure as he walked over to the steamer trunk and helped the smaller one heft it. It was very heavy and felt warm from the heat of the concentrated Oblivion that was contained within it. The taller one counted quietly in the darkness. "One . . . two . . . three . . ." and there was a brief flare of reddish light as the two vanished with the box.

Boiling up through the concrete and rock of Five Points Station came the Firebird. Passing by the living, who even in life felt a wave of heat from its fiery wings, it flew up into the dark sky of the Shadowlands, beating its wings and shouting aloud its birth cry.

There had been a night like this before, long ago, on August seventh, when the sky turned red in both the real world and in the Shadowlands—red from the burning flares of the guns besieging Atlanta.

Now the red tinge to the sky would be written off as a result of air and light pollution, nothing strange, but those who knew, those who were aware of more than just the everyday, would know that something was afoot in the lands of the dead.

Kirk exalted as the Firebird completely consumed him. He had never felt so full of power and energy, completely united as he was with the fiery being within him. He turned and flew—flew across the rooftops of the city toward a feeling, an instinct. Something that he needed, that he would need on his journey, was waiting for him.

The black-streaked fiery wings dipped on the downbeats, caressing the rooftops and searing through the night sky. No Legionnaire or Centurion gave chase, but as if in answer a great gonging sound echoed throughout the Necropolis, bringing with it a chill of fear. The gong was only sounded when something of great and terrible danger to wraiths everywhere was afoot. The Firebird had come: was the rest of the prophecy far behind?

Sylvie saw the gleam of the fire burning over the rooftops of the city. She held the basalt black scythe next to her side, barely able to handle its weight. She moved back, creating a space for the Firebird to land, for it was flying this way, its tail trailing a line of red light behind it. The Firebird backwashed with its immense wings as it neared the rooftop on which Sylvie was precariously perched and slowly, slowly descended with its claws to clutch at the rooftop. The fire immediately began to die down, a black streak at the center of the bird's body slowly taking on a man's shape and form.

Kirk stepped out of the burning flames, his face set and his eyes intent on Sylvie. His Firebird mask was gone, burned off his face by the power of the fire.

When Kirk spoke it was the Firebird, not Kirk's voice. "You hold the sacred weapon. Do you wish to give it up? To give it to me?" The Firebird's voice came hollowly out of Kirk's throat.

Kirk could feel the righteous rage, the thirst for pure destruction that welled up within him when the Firebird exerted itself. And he could also feel its strange humanity, as if the Firebird was some kind of conglomeration of a thousand different souls, all of them united in a single purpose.

Sylvie nodded. "I don't got the means to prevent you from taking this, Kirk. But I gotta tell you something. You're walkin' a dangerous path now. Your Fate is uncertain."

Kirk nodded. "That's as it should be. It's good to know that it's not tied up, not destined for a boring existence followed quickly by total nothingness."

"I warn you, Kirk. The path you choose will take you to the final death," Sylvie said quietly.

"Final death? You don't know how good that sounds right now. Did . . . did the others do as I asked?"

Sylvie nodded. "By now everything is as you asked. You must understand, Kirk, that we do not do this for the good of the Firebird. We do it because you are one of us."

"What is the Firebird? I—I don't understand," Kirk said quietly. "It's not Mr. Demon, is it?"

Sylvie shook her head quietly. "No, Kirk. No, it's something else. Something more powerful than the Shadow within you. It is your instrument of Fate, your higher self. Your Eidolon, made real in this world. That is why it burns so brightly. Still, it is a creature of destruction and fire, a creature that ultimately serves Oblivion."

Kirk nodded. "I—I—didn't ask for it to come. It just came to me—I was trapped. Completely. There was nothing I could do."

Sylvie smiled. "Kirk, one thing I've learned from Fate is that there are always choices. There are always pathways that are chosen and not chosen. People have tendencies that make them biased to a specific path, but they can decide to go against those tendencies. Only people who have stopped thinking, stopped making choices, are truly doomed," Sylvie said quietly, the wise words sounding very strange from her little-girl mouth.

Kirk felt the fiery being within him burning to be set free, and yet somehow he realized the truth of what Sylvie said. Looking out over the city, there was a hushed moment when all was at peace. He looked at the city he had grown up in, the city he had grown to both love and hate. He thought about his father, and his great-grandfather. For a bare moment, he thought about his little son and his sister. Turning back to Sylvie, he reached for the scythe she held. "I can't see another path. Not right now. I hope—I hope you can forgive me," Kirk said quietly.

"It's not my place to forgive you. I'm just here representing Fate. To tell you that there is a choice and not make you choose one way or another," Sylvie answered.

Kirk nodded absently, for the scythe was thrumming in his hands, almost moving and twisting like a living thing. He squinted at it. He looked up at Sylvie. "It wants something," he whispered.

Sylvie nodded. "Each weapon is a shard of the Firebird's egg, Kirk. Your father's weapon. Jebediah's blade. The scythe you hold. They long to be reunited. Each reunion will see the Firebird grow stronger."

"The Greymaster will be looking for me now," Kirk said.

Sylvie nodded. "You have sealed that part of your Fate. You must face him, Kirk. But you don't have to do it alone. You can summon your Circle and go to meet him with them."

Kirk shook his head. "Nah. This is my fight. I'll take care of it myself."

Sylvie tried to think of words she could say. It was hard for her: she saw the Fate-twines straightening down to two or three potential paths, but was forbidden to further help Kirk.

Kirk felt the fires within him start to burn again and he looked out across the city. Turning back to Sylvie, he tried to console her with a look, but she wouldn't return his gaze. As Kirk felt the fiery wings unfurl, he turned away from her and, with a single leap into the air, was gone, burning across the night sky.

Sylvie watched him go, holding on to her doll, suddenly feeling very small, very young, and alone.

It was dark inside the trailer. Mama Rourke was still out working. Anna was asleep in the back bedroom, clutching her purple dinosaur, the TV making snowy shadows on her face from the static. Kristy was asleep on the futon in the living room, still wearing the zebra-pattern teddy that she'd put on for her last client, who had been thankfully brief. She'd locked up her money in a strongbox and took a few pills to be able to get to sleep without the nightmares she was accustomed to having.

But there was one man who had the keys to the trailer who would not be denied. Not ever. J.T. loved to show Kristy how much he owned her, how much he could use and abuse her. Without a knock, J.T. slammed his key in the trailer door and opened it. A rush of cold night air came in, but that wasn't enough to wake up Kristy in her drugged sleep. He laughed to himself as he closed to door and slid the bolts closed. J.T. flicked on the TV in the living room, popped a porno video into the VCR, and rewound it. He went to the refrigerator and pulled out a cold beer, popping the top as he licked his lips, looking at Kristy's young/old body lying there, half-exposed under a blanket on the futon.

He sipped his beer for a moment, watching the video, fumbling for the belt on his trousers. He laid his dirty and stiff pants across one of the kitchen table chairs and kneeled down on the floor, moving one of his large and overly callused hands over Kristy's leg and up to her face, shaking her. "Hey, hey. Hey, baby. Wake up."

Kristy shuddered and awoke sleepily, looking up into J.T.'s eyes. She tried to smile at J.T.: he liked it that way, but she couldn't. She saw the light behind his eyes, the strange light that told her that he wasn't going to be easily gotten rid of tonight. "Hey, J.T.," she said, trying to sound friendly, but not being able to hide the irritation in her voice.

"Hey, baby, who loves ya?" J.T. said, smiling.

Kristy tried to shake herself awake. Her heart started to beat harder: whenever J.T. didn't ask her about her money right away, she got worried. That meant he was thinking about something else, and Kristy didn't want to think about what he was thinking about.

She started to sit up, and he pressed her back onto the futon. "Hey, where ya goin'?" J.T. said, grinning. "Don't you know I love ya?"

Kristy nodded, lying back, getting more and more afraid. Now he was getting pushy. J.T.'s breath smelled horrible. Looking past him, she saw nothing but the porn video he'd been watching. "Where's Mama?" she asked quietly.

J.T. smiled. "I don't know shuga. I guess she's out workin'. But I came to see my darlin' baby. Are you ready for your big daddy?"

J.T. wasn't able to see the red orange glow outside the window; the light was in the Shadowlands only. He wasn't able to see the black-robed figure carrying a huge battle-scythe walk into the trailer through the door. Kirk stood there quietly, the fiery light from his heart insulating him briefly from the evil words his demon would be saying about the scene that was going on on the futon.

Kirk felt the hate that he held for J.T. boil up out of the deepest parts of his soul. He wished that the scythe was real, that he could take J.T.'s head off with it. He saw the large, bulbous man's body roll on top of his sister, saw his fingers moving over her, ripping at her lingerie.

"Get the fuck off of her," Kirk said under his breath. J.T. stopped, froze. He looked around the room for a second. Somehow, Kirk was getting through to the real world. "That's right, you bastard. Get off of her, leave her the hell alone," Kirk said.

J.T. stood up slowly, looking around some more. He looked down at Kristy. "You just stay there, baby," he drawled, putting his pants on. She nodded, thankful beyond belief to get even this small amount of respite. She pulled the blankets up around her, looking at J.T. as he opened the trailer door and walked out.

Kirk looked at Kristy, hoping that he could get through to her, too. "You should leave this place, Kristy. You should get the hell out of here, go up to Aunt Sara's or somethin'. Go someplace else. Anywhere is better than this place," Kirk said quietly.

She shook her head like something had stung her, but didn't respond. She just pulled her legs up to her body, holding on to them, trying to control her shaking.

Kirk moved down the hallway, past Kristy's room, and phased through his old door. He looked down at his father's Marine sword on the floor, burning with his father's power. He lit up his hand with power and lowered it to the hilt of the blade, knowing that the energy would get his father's attention.

"I wouldn't waste your juice like that, son." A voice came from behind him. Kirk whirled just in time to block a heavy black machete that came down onto his scythe like a load of bricks. Kirk leapt up onto his bed, whirling the heavy scythe around to make a counterstrike.

"Good, good. Not good enough, however," Greymaster said, his ebony machete whirling in his palm like a sawblade and coming down on Kirk's arm. The heavy blade caught his arm and ripped into it, biting deep. Kirk yelped in pain. He jumped back, through the window, falling backward and landing in the gravel outside the trailer. The Greymaster flew through the window, diving after him like a predator-bird aiming at prey.

Seizing the handles on his scythe, Kirk pulled himself up quickly and felt the fire from within him burn up around his arms as he took a slice at his father, aiming the blade to reap his father's spectral head from his shoulders. The machete came up and blocked the strike, hooking in and pulling Kirk off balance, moving like a cobra to sneak past Kirk's guard and hit him once again, this time firmly in the chest.

Kirk felt the bite of the blade and wondered if this was darksteel. He worried that the Greymaster might be destroying him bit by bit as they fought. The unfamiliar scythe was more of a hindrance to him than a help, but he knew that this was a fight for his existence, plain and simple. Kirk realized that the eyes behind his father's mask were dark, full, with no pupils: completely controlled by his Shadow.

Kirk felt the scythe moving of its own accord, twisting and twirling in his hands as he defended himself against the terrible dark machete. His whole body shook as he took the force of a single blow on the basket-guard handle of the scythe, and he felt every muscle on his body strain as he lunged to slice at the Greymaster.

The edge of the blade ran along the Greymaster's outstretched arm and bit deep, but not deep enough. Kirk followed through, and the Greymaster saw a hole in his defense. A lunge by the captain was enough to drive the blade firmly into Kirk's Corpus, pinning him against a tree next to the trailer and holding him fast. With his mailed fist, his father bashed the scythe from Kirk's hands and it clattered to the ground, so much wood and metal now that it had left his hands. The Greymaster came down on the scythe with a single step and it shattered.

"So, my little Ferryman," James Rourke said under his breath, mocking his son. "I believe you have something of mine. And I intend to get it."

Kirk felt the fear within him, the fear of the man who was his father, and felt that fear freeze him like an icy vein running through his whole body. "I—I don't know. I can't tell you. It's gone," Kirk said.

"Gone. Far from it. Your Circle has it, don't they, boy?" James said, moving the edge of his blade to Kirk's throat.

"I don't know," Kirk said again. With a single thunderous slap, Kirk felt the man's mailed fist rake across his face. Although he couldn't feel the pain, the tremendous weight of the hand and the fact that the blade in him tore at his body even more was enough to make him whimper.

"I trusted you, Kirk. And you dicked me over. And I don't take kindly to being dicked over. Now, you are my son, and you appear to be some kind of

Firebird as well, but if you don't tell me where you put the soulfire, and help me get it, I'm going to destroy you and start working on your Circle."

Kirk looked at his father, looked at the man who held the face of his own personal demon, and shook his head once, slowly, but very definitely.

James Rourke laughed. He laughed wickedly, laughed with pleasure. He moved back from the tree, watching Kirk as he tried to squirm off the black machete's blade, to no avail. "You see, my boy, I know the Destroyer well. And I am sure that you know what his power's like. The Firebird's not just yours, you see. He's mine, too. See, that's what this pistol's all about."

James Rourke drew his Relic gun, the pistol that Kirk himself had recovered. "And that's why I'm going to blow you away with it. Sayonara, little boy. I guess the Firebird's going to have a new master now."

One bullet. Kirk shook with the impact. He felt the fire burn into him.

Two bullets. Waves of shock roared through him, a firestorm in his belly, in his shoulder.

Three bullets. Pain, white-hot heat. Burning death.

Four bullets. Now Kirk wanted to leave this world, leave everything. Oblivion beckoned to him like a chilling drink of pure poison, a tempting drink.

Five bullets. Chamber nearly empty. Kirk felt the Firebird leave him, felt the fiery heart that had been his flee. Instead, the bullets that were lodged in his body started burning anew, like tiny fires in his flesh.

Six bullets. Nothing. Darkness.

7

THROUGH THE TEMPEST

Jesus lover of my soul
Hide me, oh my Savior
Hide me till the storm of life is past
While the stormy waters roll
While the tempest still is high.
—Song from "sassafras, cypress & indigo,"
Ntozake Shange

Kirk fell. All that he was, all that he carried, fell from him. He lost all cohesion, falling through the ground, down into the Tempest. Instead of its traditional purple-blue tinge, the Tempest now held the color of Hell, the color of lambent flame. Bloodred and fiery blackened orange streaked out to surround him. A tunnel of fiery light engulfed him as he fell, and he heard laughing, singing, chanting all around him as he fell past the fires of Hell itself.

The feeling of falling was excruciating. It felt as though he would never touch bottom, that he would never be allowed the peace of unconsciousness or the finality of impact. Just falling, turning end over end, moving downward, feeling for the first time the true weight of Oblivion that tugged at his every pore, at every part of him. He could no longer feel the holes in his body, for he had none: he just felt the raw nakedness of his psyche exposed to the tender mercies of the sea of shadows.

The tunnel he was falling through seemed interminable. It was, however, no relief to Kirk when suddenly the falling slowed, and then slowly stopped, and he was instead standing in a dark hole, a dark cave somewhere in a world he had only had nightmares about.

Kirk sensed his Shadow around him everywhere, as if he had somehow fallen into the foul demon himself and was in the belly of that beast. Was this going to be his Fate for eternity?

He took a step forward, found black gravel and a path leading through scrub. Looking down at himself, he saw the blue uniform of a U.S. soldier from around the time of the Civil War: a Yankee. Kirk shook his head. He was sure that his hold on his own sanity was completely gone, that somehow the nothing had swallowed him up and that he would forever be in its terrible grasp.

Still, in Hell you do what you can to keep your mind occupied. He followed the path of gravel up a small hill and over the top, looking down into a valley and a scene that nearly turned his stomach.

Everywhere he looked he saw men dressed as he was, smiling and grinning and shooting guns into the air. He saw other men, and women, and children: they were dressed in buckskins and furs: Indians. U.S. soldiers rushed into the huts of the people living here and rushed them out, setting fire to the huts. A marshal stood up in his stirrups in the center of the clearing, reading aloud the dictates of his superiors, telling the assembled Indians that they were to depart the area for a specially prepared reservation out West.

Men, women, and children were forced from their homes as Kirk watched. Suddenly he looked up to see a tall man on a white horse carrying a service revolver. "Come on, boy, get on with them. You gotta get outta here, too. Let's move it! This ain't your land no more."

Kirk looked down at himself, saw the buckskins on his own body, the red war paint on his arms and hands, the feathers that were wound into his long black hair. He was now one of the Indians they were removing from this place.

One of the soldiers laughed as he taunted an older woman who was having trouble making it up the hill. "Come on, Granny! Come on! You gotta get movin', don't want to keep everyone else back. Come on, Granny! Let's move it! Hey, you—hey boy! Come on over here and get Granny to move her fat lazy ass," called the soldier, gesturing at Kirk.

Kirk moved over to help the woman up the hill. Her pitted face was ancient: she wore many necklaces and seemed important, dignity evident in her walk. She spoke a language Kirk had never heard before, and yet he understood her perfectly clearly.

"I am old, I have lived. You do not need to help me. I don't mind if they kill me. What will I do but live on? I know that I have won against them already. The bodies of the fallen will return. The fires of their hatred will always be returning to them."

Then there were gunshots; the soldier had grown impatient and no longer wished to wait for the old woman. She fell to the earth, a strange smile on her face, as fire rushed up out of her eyes and covered Kirk's senses, blacking him out for a moment.

———

Looking up, he saw a completely different scene. He saw the darkness of a night sky. A jungle was around him, thick with thousands of different kinds of plants and trees. The jungle itself seemed to breathe, and the breath that it was spitting out was thick and heavy and surrounded Kirk like a foul wet wool blanket, covered in the slime and sweat of a great festering beast. He moved through the jungle, clutching his M–16, trying to keep low, trying not to get shot at. Things were changing around him, and he knew that he had no control over his world, over his actions, that he could only move through this nightmare world and look for the way out.

His gun was cold in his hands and he knew that somewhere out there were quite a few men and boys who wanted him dead. They knew the jungle much better than he did, knew the darkness like an old friend, and were much better at crafting the indigenous weapons of war that the jungle offered.

All Kirk knew was that somewhere around here was a checkpoint and that he had to check in after his patrol. He had no idea how he knew this: the logic of the nightmare was clear to him, however.

He moved through the trees and into a clearing filled with GI's. A few of them saluted him. "Captain Rourke. Good to see you back," one of the men said. "Lose another patrol?" one of the men said from behind him.

Kirk turned around. "What did you say?"

No one was willing to own up to the comment. Kirk turned again, and out of the corner of his eye saw a man standing just out of sight: a man clad all in black.

Whispers came to him as he moved through the clearing, among the men, whispers of the thing in the trees, in the jungle. It was waiting for him.

"Everytime that old boy slept, his shadow would

come to pay court to me. Yeah, boy," came the whisper, in his father's voice.

"Captain!" the radioman called. "I got orders. Move up to new map coordinates and maintain position on that hill."

Great, came a thought unbidden to his mind. *More target practice. And we're the targets.*

"Let's move out!" Kirk called to his men as he strode into the trees. "I'll take the point."

They moved carefully over the intervening terrain, working together like the seasoned patrol they were. Kirk kept glancing to his left and to his right, expecting sniper fire at any moment.

As they were working their way up the hill, Kirk felt a twinge of uncertainty and saw the shadowy figure out of the corner of his eye again. Then, quietly, he looked up and saw a shorter brown man, maybe a boy, in his perch high above the jungle floor. He was clutching a sniper rifle and keeping quiet, taking aim at one of his wing men.

"HEY!" Kirk yelled, but it was too late. Gunshots erupted all around him. The man to the left of him fell with blood gushing from his eye. The man to the right of him took three shots at nothing before he, too, died. Gunfire ricocheted all around Kirk, but he was unharmed. More death, all around him: men falling like reaped wheat, and nothing, nothing at all that he could do about it.

Kirk looked at the gunman in the tree, unable to see his many brothers in the bushes, and screamed at him, felt the gunsight line up on his forehead, felt the bullet enter his head . . .

Looking up, he saw that he was young again. Sitting in his room, listening to his Metallica records, smoking some pot, talking to his girlfriends on the telephone. It was a typical Friday night for him: his mom out working at the factory, his sister Kristy asleep. This was before Anna, Kirk guessed, in a moment of clarity realizing that this was still a nightmare, still some terrible home movie that his demon had dreamed up.

Kirk kept listening to the record, and it kept skipping. Something about the skipping unnerved him, because it stirred up a very unpleasant memory, one that he had thankfully forgotten.

Something picked at the scab of that memory, threatening to reopen the old wound. Kirk felt cold fear wash through him as he shut off the record player and picked up his electric guitar, keeping the amp off so as not to wake Kristy. He played through some riffs, just fooling around, trying to calm himself. It was strangely pleasant to be back in his old body, back as he was before he died, before he had gotten into dealing, before . . . before tonight.

There was a sound in the front room, announcing his mother's arrival home. Kirk stubbed out his pot pipe and threw it into the cigar box he hid under his bed. He listened for her weary footsteps coming down the hall, but none came. Instead, he heard talking, laughing. *Oh, great,* Kirk thought, shaking his head. *She's gone and got another guy at some cheap bar someplace. Now I get to listen to the bedsprings creak all night.* But the thoughts were like the echoes of a far-off dream to him, because he was reliving it this time, just as it had happened many years ago.

Kirk heard the talking grow more intense. A chill of fear ran through him. He moved to the door, hearing the voices clearly for the first time.

"Come on, baby, you know you want it. How long has it been?"

"Not too long, but you just gotta give me a little time, I ain't no motor scooter you can just jump on. . . . "

"Come on baby, what do I got to do, send you an engraved invitation? I thought this is what you wanted, huh? Come on, baby, I'm real hot for you."

Then he heard his mother's voice muffled, as if someone's hand was clapped over her mouth. He stumbled down the hallway, looking at the shadows that danced from the light in the kitchen. He turned the corner into the living room and saw a man, some coworker of his mother's, tying her hands together with the scarf she always wore. The scarf that Kirk had given her for Christmas, last year. Her work uniform had been ripped open, her bra askew. She was struggling underneath him, fighting, kicking, but to no avail. Kirk could do nothing in his young body, nothing but scream at the man to stop. The words came from somewhere else, muffled to his ears.

The man turned to look at Kirk, and suddenly Kirk saw his father's face. His father who had been dead for several years. Somehow, he saw his father raping his mother. His mother, who would never speak of this night, who would carry the man's seed inside her and give birth to Anna nine months later.

Kirk screamed, and all was darkness.

This was a secret meeting, Kirk knew. No one from the tribe would've come to this meeting. It was forbidden to discuss what would be done here, but the elders had agreed that it must be done. The wise men and women had gathered around this fire and had described what must be done. The white men might carry the fire, they might carry the guns and the horses and all the power of their armies and their government, but they would not know the secret ways, the magic ways.

This was not a good path, and all those who were here knew it. They knew it was not proper medicine, that it was some foul, black sorcery that would doom them all. And yet, they knew that it was always best to curse quietly, to curse well, and to curse subtly.

The men had spent most of the day slaughtering trees around the campsite and cutting them into logs, just as the white men had taught them.

They took the logs and piled them high, piled them as high as they could reach. It was no longer necessary to worry about the fire burning out of control; this was not their land any longer, this was the war-ground. The wise ones moved among the warriors who had agreed to be here, to sacrifice themselves for the good of the people. They painted the Firebird on them, the symbol of their vengeance, the bringer of their curse.

Kirk stood and watched as they lit the pyre, as they danced around it, whirling and yelling out their anger, their hatred, their sadness. In their madness they leapt over the flames, finally catching afire and throwing themselves into the heart of the living flame, dying as they did. The air hung thick with sickly-sweet smoke as one by one they placed themselves on the bier of fiery death.

The Firebird grew up out of these flames, and Kirk watched as it reached toward the sky, toward the middle distance, and toward the earth. It was a creature of death, a creature of destruction, summoned to carry out a curse forever.

When the dance was over, all the wise men except one quietly departed. They knew that this curse would not drive the white men from the land. They knew that in many ways there wouldn't be any way they'd reclaim what they had lost, or if they ever did, it would not be worth anything to them: what good is a bunch of stone buildings and no living trees?

Still, Kirk needed to know something. He moved to the wise man, who bowed to him briefly and seemed to want to speak with him.

"Why are you letting me see this?" Kirk asked quietly. "Aren't I descended from those who drove you from your land?"

"Our enemy has become our ally. The circle has come around again. This is what happens with curses. They are hoops, circular. They keep coming around and around, until justice is served," the wise man answered.

"How can justice ever be served? This is futile," Kirk said.

The wise man looked at him sternly. "Justice is served when the right thing is done. Justice is served when one single man can change because of our curse. If one man walks a better road because we have cursed his kind and his city, then that is the object of the curse, and that is justice. But not one man has ever apologized for our destruction. Not one man has ever asked us for forgiveness and brought us gifts to appease us. Not one man has offered us restitution for the dead men, women, and children who have been lost to the Hungry Snake. So, the curse will continue, and our fire will spread again, to cleanse and start everything anew," the wise man said.

Kirk nodded as darkness overcame him again.

"Too easy. You've gotten off too easy. Now let's see a true test," a voice whispered behind him. Kirk turned, but no one was there.

It was still dark, then he was floating and in an old tenement somewhere in Atlanta. He saw Cindi sprawled out on the couch, her heroin works still on the coffee table in the living room where she had just used them. She was sleeping, while a caterwauling child screamed in the background. Kirk moved through the house to where little Jeb was screaming, and Kirk saw him not as a little boy but as the monster he had become: a thing with blackened skin, razor-sharp pointed teeth, a forked tongue. The boy was screaming, his diapers black with some combination of baby shit, blood, and some other goo. The howl was demanding, and Kirk didn't know what to do, how to quiet him. "Feed him," came a voice. Kirk shook his head, not seeing a bottle. "Feed him, Kirk."

Kirk shook his head again, then he realized the boy had quieted down when he brought his hand near. Kirk held up his hand and the boy watched his fingers move past, moving his head in time with his father's hand. The boy wanted something. Kirk moved his hand closer and the boy grabbed ahold with an unearthly strength. Kirk felt a pain like a beartrap closing on his hand as the boy bit down and began gulping the blood that poured from his fingers. Kirk watched as his own son drained the blood from his body, chewing on his finger bones and hand, biting them off and continuing to eat.

"Still want to let the brat live, Kirkie boy?" the demon said. "You could kill him, you know. Put him out of our misery."

"N-n-no! I won't!" Kirk said.

Demon whispered, "Now you can see why I didn't put an end to your skinny ass. Ain't fatherly love wonderful?"

Kirk jerked his hand back, and the boy started screaming again, straining against his baby bed to try and get at Kirk's fingers some more. A knife materialized in Kirk's hand. "Just do it, Kirk baby. Just do it. Do us both a favor."

The boy screamed and spat and hissed and tried desperately to climb out of the bed to get to Kirk. He shuddered as his own son licked up the blood that was spattered on his face and on the bed's rail.

"Ain't he a beaut, Kirkie boy? That's what he is

going to look like when we get through with him. Pretty boy. But you can put him down now if you want. Go ahead. Thrust the knife in," Demon said.

Kirk took the dagger and plunged it into the boy's heart, and a second later he was tiny, little Jeb, who could barely hold on to life. Kirk was suddenly standing in a hospital room with Cindi standing next to him in shock as he plunged the knife into his own son's chest. She screamed at him to stop, but it was too late: a little black blood was already flowing from the tiny corpse's lips. Kirk turned away, but the scene was still imprinted on his inner sight.

Then darkness, thankfully, took him.

"Is this all there is? Nothing but torture? Nothing but doom, death? Is this all there is for me?" Kirk asked quietly, in the middle of his own Hell.

He was sorry to see the darkness go: as frightening as it was, it was better than anything he had seen here yet. An altar and two fat black candles came into view. This place was once a beautiful cathedral, tall, perfect. And Kirk knew immediately where he was and what was going on. He saw the black streaks on the walls, smelled the vague scent of kerosene mixed with smoke mixed with holy incense.

He stood and watched the dark, smudged service, heard the burnt organ playing in a surreal mockery of its former glory. The Church had long ago abandoned the cathedral because it was just too expensive to pay property taxes on it, so it had gone unused for the longest time. The Dragons had made their home in it. They were a neo-Nazi group out of Forsyth County who had been making money by selling cheap drugs to the folks in Cabbagetown and Sweet Auburn. They hated Africans, Koreans, and everyone else, and Kirk hated them because they liked to bash motorcycles. He didn't like them getting close to what he considered his turf: the Five Points area and all around there. Yet they had moved in, with a lot of swagger and fuss, making their presence well-known and, some said, conducting strange religious services in the old cathedral.

Kirk saw himself pull up on his old motorcycle and saw his gang fan out around him, grinning as they each carried a can of gasoline or kerosene. The Dragons were off watching a movie at the I–80 Drive-In, so they had no idea that someone was about to put their favorite hangout to the torch.

Kirk watched as he ran up the steps, spreading kerosene as he went. He took a crowbar to the front doors and broke through them, moving into the vestibule and dousing the thick carpet liberally with the sickly-sweet smelling liquid.

He laughed with his buddies as he moved through the pews, turning them over, getting a thrill out of setting fire to the House of the Lord.

They grinned at each other as they moved on up to the front of the building, where they took a trash can (the altar having been removed long ago) and filled it with newspapers to make a new altar of flame.

Kirk watched as the two altar boys stood by silently, watching his younger self and his gang work over the cathedral. Kirk didn't have to strain to see out the front door as he and his gang ran outside. Mounted on his cycle, Kirk took a homemade Molotov cocktail and lit the rag on the end. "See ya, suckers!" the young Kirk yelled, and threw the bottle at the steps of the old cathedral. The fire caught quickly, and then raged up the steps and into the building. Kirk watched as the fire licked its way through the whole nave, burning up the walls.

Suddenly the fire was everywhere at once, and there was no place for Kirk to go. The fire burned him, just as it burned everything. He looked for the altar boys but could not find them anywhere: instead he saw a woman dressed in an ancient black gown, moving through the flames as if they weren't there. Kirk had never seen the woman before, but she seemed to give off an air of pure power and calm as she floated through the flames.

"This is what damned your soul to Hell, boy," the woman said quietly.

Kirk nodded slowly.

"Before this, you were able to be saved. But you burned a House of God to the ground, and for that you will suffer in the eternal lake of fire," the woman said to him.

Kirk could say nothing to his accuser, feeling the flames around him, but noting that her presence dimmed the fires just a little.

"So, that's why I'm here?" Kirk said quietly.

"No, this is just the waiting place. You wait for judgment, wait to be judged. Wait for the final days when God will return to claim thee," the woman said.

"Who are you?" Kirk asked.

"In life, I was Mary Riorche, your great-great-grandmother. I lived a simple life, a life of piety, and I was slain by the Curse that haunts our family," Mary replied.

"I keep hearing about curses here. The old wise man said that curses have a purpose. What's the purpose of the curse on our family?" Kirk asked.

"There is none that I can tell. Its purpose is lost to us. It is a sin that our family must carry forever, it seems. None can break the pattern. From grandfather to grandson, or now, in these times, from father to son. And ye, now dead, will be no father to that boy of yours. Ye surely must know that," Mary said warningly.

"How do you know so much about me?" Kirk asked. He felt a tremendous respect for her, despite what she said.

"I have been watching thee, Kirk Riorche. God has given me the knowledge of what ye are, of where ye are. He has shown me your path, and I watch ye. He protects me even now, even in this Hell of your demon's creation."

"You mean . . . you are not like the other things here?" Kirk asked.

"Nae. I am just as real—at the moment, more real—as you. I have come to see how you have fared in your Harrowing," Mary said.

"I don't know. I can't escape this place," Kirk said.

"That's because you've yet to find the thread that will lead you out. You must find the thread of Light to lead you out of darkness—you must reject the Shadow, deny him success. But, if you keep reveling in your darkness, you will never find that thread," Mary said as the fires burned up, making sparks, and burning his eyes as darkness fell on him.

Kirk was alone on a dark street. What could harm him here? He walked down the street, past shops that he did not recognize. The cars on the street were blurry, muddy, as if someone had put a filter on his vision. Each car that rolled by sounded like it was muffled, as if his ears were wrapped in cotton.

As he moved down the street he realized he was in a very bad part of town, one of the worst. Women hung out here, looking for tricks. This was where some of his dealers used to work the streets, usually getting busted, but always getting out in a few days or a week and getting back into pushing. He moved past them, one by one, remembering what Mary had said about turning away from his darkness. Still, he couldn't find any light here: there was no thread to pick up.

One of the girls called out to him. "Hey, hey, mister. Want a date? Want a cheap date?"

She came up to him, dressed in a black leather jacket with a skimpy camisole underneath, and a black leather skirt. Her face was smudged and badly done up. "Come on, mister, it's only twenty-five bucks. You got that, don't you?"

Kirk turned back toward her. It had been a long time since he'd been close to a woman, any woman, like this. She was pretty in her own tainted way. Despite her hardened exterior and tough-girl attitude, the way she smiled at him seemed strangely intimate and familiar. The way she clutched a silk rose in her hand was kind of innocent and sweet. Kirk couldn't help but wonder what she would be like, what it would be like to touch her.

Still, Mary's advice came back to him and he turned away. "Look, ahh, no offense, but, ahh, I'm sorry, I just . . . I just can't."

"Oh. Okay." Kirk looked at her again, in a different light this time. She looked much different: Kirk saw the lines under her eyes, the color of her eyes, the true color of her roots, the shape of her face.

Kirk felt a cold chill of ice run through him as he realized who he was looking at.

"Is . . . is your name Anna?" Kirk asked quietly.

She looked startled. "Yes . . . No. No, my name's Debbie."

"Which is it?" Kirk asked quietly.

"I'm not supposed to give my real name," she said. "Are you some sort of cop?"

"No. I'm just . . . I'm just a friend," Kirk said.

"Not any kind of friend I want to spend time with. Unless you've got twenty-five bucks," she said.

Kirk couldn't help but look in his "wallet"—he took out the leather billfold his nightmare had supplied him and ran his fingers through the cash there. There was three hundred dollars in the wallet. He reached in and pulled out all three hundred. Somewhere he could hear the demon laughing at him, encouraging him to buy her for the whole night, saying "Yeah, that's your little sister Anna-baby . . . ain't she sweet?" but Kirk wasn't listening.

"Look. This is all the money I have." Kirk said.

Anna looked at him. "I . . . I don't do strange stuff."

Kirk shook his head. "No. I am giving you this. Get off the street. Find someplace to go. I don't care where. Stop doing this. Your brother wouldn't want you to do this. Your mother wouldn't."

"My brother's dead. My mother is a whore, too," Anna said quietly.

"Well, you've got . . . you've got a little nephew. His name is Jeb. You need to go and live with him. Go and see Cindi."

Anna looked amazed. "How did you know? I used to go over and play with Jeb everyday—after I knew about him. Cindi didn't show him to Mom until he was three."

"Just do what I ask, okay? You need to go see Cindi. Give her the three hundred if you have to. Just get off the street. Okay?"

Anna nodded. Kirk waved at a taxi passing by and it pulled up to the curb. "Get in," Kirk said quietly.

"Why should I do what you say?" Anna asked.

"Because. Because, dammit, if you don't . . . I don't know what I'll do. You've got to, Anna. If not for yourself, for little Jeb. He needs his aunt," Kirk said.

She got into the cab. "You know, you remind me a lot of my brother, what I remember of him. You're all right. Here . . . take this to remember me by." She handed Kirk the silk rose, smiling at him as the taxi drove off.

Kirk looked down at the rose, felt the gentleness inherent in such a gift.

Suddenly the rose blossomed in an aura of silver light. The light grew and spilled over Kirk's hand, streaming down his body. Kirk could hear his demon screaming in the darkness as slowly, carefully, he rose up off the street, past the nameless buildings, rising up into the darkness of the night sky.

Suddenly, all was darkness, but this time there was peace.

8

THE RETURN OF
THE FIREBIRD

*Easy is the descent to the Lower World; but, to retrace
yours steps and to escape to the upper air—this is the
task, this the toil.*
— The Sibyl to Aeneas in *The Aeneid*

Kirk never thought he would be happy to see daylight
again. Even though it burned his ghostly eyes and
made him shiver with its intensity, he stood out in the
bright sunshine atop his school. He soaked up the
energy of the sun as he lay back on the roof, breathing
from the effort of raising himself up out of the darkness of the Tempest, of the Harrowing he'd just barely
survived. His body still bore the scars of his fight with
his father, but he was now in control. His scythe was
missing, but he was sane. He was soon able to crawl to
the shadows, where he felt a little more comfortable,
and waited as the sun slowly moved and ducked down
under the skyline. He had no idea how many days had
passed, if any, and had no idea where his friends
were, but at least he was there and in one piece.

Kirk felt a curious peace, something that he hadn't felt since his death. Something his Hell had given him was a kind of knowledge about himself, answers to many questions that he had asked of himself or of others.

He shuddered as he remembered the scenes that had played out in his own private Hell, but they had also given him valuable wisdom. Looking out into the fading sunlight, he realized that what he was experiencing wasn't something personal to him: the Curse of his family was circular, a cycle, from grandfather to grandson, from father to son. Kirk's father had given it to his son just as his grandfather had given it to his grandson. The way of Kirk's Shadow was powerful, as was the way of his higher self, but neither one was what Kirk wanted.

Kirk looked out over his city, the city where he was born, and realized that he stood between many great powers, all of them vying for his attention, all of them asking him to be a certain way, to do a certain thing. The Hierarchy wanted him to go to Oblivion. The Renegades wanted him to join them. The Heretics wanted him to do the right thing. And yet he knew that he could not please any of them and still be true to himself. He knew that nothing he did would satisfy any one group, and that he was tired of living for these massive powers. He would take the middle ground. He would follow his own Fate, make his own decisions. He also knew in his heart that there were a few things he must do, that had been prescribed for him to do, and if he ignored them he would suffer, as would the entire city.

For a moment he felt as though the entire Necropolis was his single vast Fetter, sick with the corruption and pain of a hundred years. He felt the weight of his duty on him, but also the light-headed feeling of being sure of his course now. Mary had shown him the way to pass through the fire of his higher passions. Anna, an Anna he hoped he would never know, had taught him how to turn away from the Shadow that threatened him. The only way he would succeed at all would be to follow his heart, to do what he felt was right, and nothing more.

As the last light fell behind the buildings, Kirk found himself wishing for his guitar, sighing as he remembered he'd left it back at the Wolves' warehouse. As the shadows grew long over the city, Kirk began jumping through the Tempest, moving from point to point, getting his bearings, and then making one last leap.

Kirk hadn't noticed the incredibly quiet, very patient Monitor who had been left behind several days before to watch the school building Fetter. The Monitor got down from his perch on a building across the street and made his way, through the Tempest, to the far-off Citadel.

The Grey Wolves' new hideout was in a now empty building which used to house a print shop. It was called the Ryco Building. It was particularly useful because it was right next to a train trestle (always a plus) and right down the way from the Jimmy Carter Library, so it was not exactly the kind of place you'd picture a bunch of Renegades setting up shop. No one had dared to go near the Greymaster since he learned about the disappearance of the soulfire. He was incensed; his Shadow seemed to be continually in control. There was talk among the Wolves, quiet talk but talk nonetheless, that the boss's Shadow had taken over completely, forever, and that they were now being led by a Doppelganger. But no one, not even Gunter, was willing to confront the old man to his mask. No one was willing to risk the wrath of that darksteel machete of his.

Word was that the Firebird had made off with the soulfire and that Greymaster had killed him before he had been able to obtain knowledge of where the stuff was being kept. The Grey Wolves were maintaining an extremely low profile in light of their recent failure. Even though the Hierarchy was freaking out (banging their silly gong and sending troops all over the place), there was not a single Wolf to be found in the whole city. That was because they were all hiding in the basement of the Ryco Building at Greymaster's command.

Meanwhile, squads of Hierarchy legionnaires fanned out through the Necropolis, bringing word to gather all the citizenry into the Citadel in preparation for a Maelstrom. The Anacreon of War had been in council for most of the night deciding what to do about the sighting of the Firebird, and they eventually agreed unanimously to sound full alert and open the doors of the Citadel to all Hierarchy wraiths in the city. This ruined social events that some of the more well-to-do wraiths were planning, but everyone had either heard of the Firebird prophecy, or had seen the outline of the fiery bird blazing across the sky an evening before.

The Heretics took to their secret catacombs, moving their people deeper underground and into the more powerful Haunts in preparation. The only exception to this were the Children of the Grand Dragon, who had been called up by the Greyboys to join together and meet in the basement of the Fox Theatre. They formed a rowdy Renegade faction that threatened to spill over into the living world with their shouts and demands for action.

Even the restless in the Oakland Cemetery were quieter than normal, seeming to prepare for a terrible battle that evening.

All was strangely quiet as Kirk materialized in the vast, empty warehouse where the Grey Wolves used to dwell. He stepped through the open bay doors and walked into the quiet concrete Haunt, feeling the comforting chill of the lessening of the Shroud here. He walked across the floor to the storage area and immediately wished for a light. Then he remembered his new-found powers and held up his hand. A blue-grey light burned from within his palm and illuminated the entire chamber. Looking over in the corner, he saw his ancient guitar still sitting there, untouched. He carefully examined it. He had learned enough from the Wolves to know that you never just gave anything to the enemy, and he figured the guitar was booby-trapped somehow.

But it wasn't, and he took the guitar up in his hands and felt the comforting weight as he slung it around his neck and plucked at the strings, tuning them briefly (and very roughly). He launched into a few practice riffs, moving his fingers up and down the frets, thrumming the strings without making a sound. He wished he had some soulfire for the guitar. It'd be nice to play it without having to feed it his own juice.

Kirk heard something go crunch out in the warehouse and stopped playing immediately. He ducked back against the wall and even went so far as to shape his left hand into a tight, sharp spike should anyone come through the door. The spike glowed for a moment from the small amount of juice he spent on it.

Step. Step step. Step. Footsteps coming his way.

He couldn't help but worry that the Wolves had somehow followed him back to the warehouse, had somehow known that he was here. He knew that, handspike or no, he wouldn't last long in a fight with a fully armed Wolf: the darksteel machete of his father's had left him with more lasting wounds than he wanted to admit to himself.

Kirk held his breath as he waited, and finally a figure stepped into the storage room. A green light bathed the room.

"Kirk?" came a small voice. It was Sylvie.

He released his breath and stepped out of hiding. "Sylvie!"

"Kirk! You're not gone!" Sylvie said. Her grin was very wide, her pigtails flying.

Kirk embraced his friend. "I made it through, Sylvie. And now I know what you were talking about. I had to go through Hell before I figured it out, but I did."

Sylvie smiled at him. "I'm glad, Kirk. I really am."

"How's Jeb?" Kirk asked quietly, not really wanting to hear bad news.

"He's— He's okay. There's some problems, but . . ." Sylvie said.

"What kind of problems?" Kirk asked worriedly.

"Kirk, they can't stay in the hospital forever. In fact, their Medicaid runs out in a day. Department of Family and Children Services is going to do an evaluation on Cindi tomorrow to see if she's fit to take Jeb home. He's stabilized, but he needs a lot of special attention. Frankly, Kirk, I don't think he has much chance if he doesn't get a nice place to live. I don't think Cindi can hack it."

Kirk shivered, remembering the hellish vision of his son. "I agree. We gotta do something, Sylv. And there's one person in the whole world that I'd trust to do anything like that. I am going to need your help to talk to her."

Sylvie smiled. "Oh, Kirk. You've—you've really changed. I don't know what happened to you, but you're very different. It's scary, in a way, but it's very good. I see the future getting brighter for you all the time!"

Kirk shook his head. "I ain't no different. I'm

just—I think I got my priorities straight, if you understand what I mean."

Sylvie smiled. "I think that's exactly what's going
on."

"Let's go, Sylv," Kirk said.

"Where to?" Sylvie asked.

"Would you believe the Probation Office?" Kirk
said, grinning.

Deep in the Citadel, an entire floor of the MARTA
station had been cordoned off during the day by
skinridden MARTA workers, and the area was being
used as a staging ground for the legionnaires who
were being assembled for the massive operation that
had been ordered by the Anacreon of War earlier in
the day.

Fearing a Renegade assault with the surety of the
coming Maelstrom (so reasoned the Hierarchy), the
Lord of War had decided to do a little preemptive
cleanup of the "known Renegade Haunts" in the
area of the Necropolis. All members of the Hierarchy
had been ordered to report for war duty at the
Citadel.

This included Jebediah, who reported wearing his
Mask of Honor and took the honorary title of
Centurion, in charge of a small group of Legionnaire
squads.

Sir Alisdair, a Knight of the Sickle, was clearly
upset that the Anacreon of War did not feel his
forces could handle the threat themselves and had
had to resort to calling up the levies. He charged
back and forth in the staging area, huffing while
seated on his horse and barking orders at the con-
scripts, most of whom were consigned to garrison
duty anyway. All except Magistrate Jebediah, of
course. His Mask of Honor was enough to gain him

an invitation to the knight's war camp, a pavilion that was set up to one side of the staging zone. It was here that Jebediah rested until his patrol was supposed to go out, and it was here that he noticed a very old and honorable Monitor named Gregor move into the tent and speak to Sir Alisdair in a whisper about a wraith rematerializing at the school where he had been positioned by one of Sir Alisdair's own patrols several days before.

Jebediah couldn't help but pick up on this: his own particular Fatalism was developed enough for him to pick out the "golden threads" of Fate that wound their way past him. He was discreet enough not to show Alisdair a flash of recognition when the information was imparted, but Jebediah knew that this could only mean that Kirk had been through a Harrowing and survived. He was half relieved and half annoyed: how simple this all would have been if he had been lost. And yet, the thread of Fate that Jebediah followed with his meager powers was definite, clear, and strong. Perhaps it was good that he did not lose to the Tempest.

Jebediah knew the first place he'd look when his patrol was set loose, however, for there was a last chance that the boy might be turned to some good purpose.*

It was getting close to midnight again: almost a full day since the Wolves' failure. Greymaster emerged from his brooding loft and begin to quietly growl orders—orders that were memorized and followed to the letter.

A pack of Wolves were set on the trail of Kirk's Circle, particularly the Gaunt called Sylvie. Another pack was set on the trail of Kirk himself, in case he had survived the severe damage that Greymaster had given him. A third pack was sent to all the corners of the city in order to discover what was up. Greymaster needed information if he was to turn this terrific defeat into a victory. He knew that the soulfire and the stolen explosives were still somewhere in the city. Kirk's Circle didn't strike Greymaster as intelligent enough to get rid of the stolen goods. Besides, the fact that they had stolen both of those items and none of the other weaponry meant a lot: obviously Kirk had been planning something very close to what the Greymaster had been thinking of himself—to use the soulfire to fuel a huge explosion.

Still, as reports began to filter back to the Greymaster, he realized that this was a particularly unique time in the city's history: two powerful groups of anti-Hierarchy wraiths were openly allying, and the entire Citadel was on alert. It was a perfect time to unleash all of his former plans. He'd just have to find another way to get them all to follow him.

The Greymaster's mind was cunning, sly, and incredibly sneaky. It took only a few moments to put the pieces together, and soon Greymaster was calling to Dr. Teeth, his Masquer, with very specific instructions.

Kirk almost smiled as he entered the old Floyd Veteran's Building, walking up the steps and riding the elevator with Sylvie to the fourth floor, to the Probation Office. Although he both loathed and despised the office and all that it had meant to him as a teenager, he felt like it was almost familiar, like an old wound: annoying, but familiar.

Still, there was one person in the corridors and labyrinths of the office complex inside the Probation wing that he did want to see. Her name was Jo, a fairly heavyset African-American woman who had made a career out of being a probation officer. She always made Kirk stop and say "African-American" everytime he said "black," just to annoy him. She had also insisted that Kirk call her "ma'am," the only woman who had successfully managed that in any kind of consistent fashion. For Kirk, she had been something of a rainbow at the end of a long period of utter hell in his life. Sure, she could throw him right back in jail, but it seemed like she actually gave a damn about him. She actually cared whether he made it or not, which was something his mom had never really voiced an opinion about. Jo had a sign in her office which was very appropriate for her. It read: "I'm 51% Sweetheart and 49% Bitch. Don't push it!" She was very good to Kirk until he showed signs of selling drugs again, at which point she would come down on him like a load of bricks and he'd stop again. For a while. He almost wished he'd listened to her in the first place: he might be alive today if he had.

Still, although he didn't know why he knew this, he had a strong feeling that Jo wouldn't refuse him help, even from beyond the grave.

Sylvie smiled at Jo when she entered the office, but Jo didn't show any signs of noticing her, so Kirk made his way into the office where she was filling out reports and forms on the various convicts under her loving care. The other really impressive thing about Jo was that she had never lost a probationer: she'd never lost track of any one of her charges. For some reason, she had this uncanny sense of when someone was even thinking about breaking their probation. And she'd get up in the middle of the night, in the middle of church, in the middle of a doctor's appointment, and demand to make a telephone call, whereupon she'd proceed to give the probationer a serious tongue-lashing and thoroughly spook them. She called it her "psychic beeper service," and it only took one use of the "psychic beeper" before Kirk believed completely in it. He tried to not even think hard about breaking probation, although he'd never actually tested to see if she'd call if he was just fooling around. Somehow, either her own brain or her "psychic beeper" knew when someone was about to skip out for real.

So, Kirk wasn't entirely surprised that she was able to pick up on his presence: after all, she'd watched him for nearly five years.

At first she only looked up and around the room, as if there was a fly buzzing around her beautiful Nubian features. But after a while, she was convinced that it was something different. Kirk didn't say anything to her directly, because he didn't want her to get scared like the volunteer in the hospital.

He waited until she settled down again and started doing paperwork, then he sat down in the chair across from her desk—the chair he'd always sat in and described (the boring version) of what he'd done the previous weekend.

"Kirk, I think she's some kind of natural medium," Sylvie whispered, and suddenly Jo looked up, looking around the room, still unsure of their presence.

Kirk nodded, grinning. "I think you're right," he whispered as softly as he could, and Jo stopped again.

Jo got up, looked around her office, and then wandered briskly out into the hallway to see if there was anyone there. When there wasn't, she shrugged her immense shoulders and stepped back toward her desk. Kirk had to have some fun with her.

"Psst," he said quietly.

She stopped, put her hands on her hips, and swiveled 360 degrees, looking in every nook and cranny for the source of the noise. At one point she looked right at Kirk, but kept on searching the room.

"Psst . . . Ms. Jo. Over here," he whispered again.

Jo got a huffy look on her face and put her hands on her hips. "All right. I don't know where you gots the microphone, but I ain't buyin' it no more. I want you to come out in the open where's I can see you, or just stop messin' with me. Is that you Clarice?" she called out to the open office.

Sylvie covered her mouth and tried not to laugh at the woman's expression. Sylvie couldn't remember the last time she'd had as much fun as this.

Kirk smiled. "No, Ms. Jo. It's me. You remember Kirk, don't you?"

Jo put her hands on her hips again and huffed. Then she closed the door to her office, walked over to her desk, and sat down behind it. She started going through her paperwork again, as if nothing had ever happened.

Kirk whispered again, "Jo?"

"That's Ms. Jo to you," she came back, clear and loud.

"Ms. Jo," Kirk whispered.

"That's me. What do you want Mr. Spook?" she whispered, so that no one in the hall would hear her talking to the air.

"It's me, Kirk. Kirk Rourke. You remember, don't you, Ms. Jo?"

"I—I think I do. Kirk Rourke. Oh, yeah! Narcotics. Possession with intent to distribute. First-time offender. I heard you were dead. Dealing drugs again. Heh. Serves you right," Jo said, looking at a book that she carried with her always.

"Not on your shift, though, Ms. Jo. I was straight and narrow then," Kirk said quietly.

"Bull pucky, Kirk. You were funnin' yourself, and funnin' Ms. Jo. You were just waitin' to go right back to dealin'. See you got messed up by a punk with an autofire gun. That's as it should be," Jo said, talking louder this time. She seemed to be handling the fact that she was talking to a dead person rather easily.

"So, do you always talk to your deceased probationers?" Kirk said, a little annoyed that she wasn't particularly frightened, but glad as well that she was able to speak to him.

"Kirk, honey, when you've been in the business as long as I have, you gotta learn to expect just about anything. I tell you what, this job ain't nothin' if not intrestin'. Not that I need a whole hell of a lot of intrestin'."

Kirk smiled at Jo. Sylvie waved him on, obviously excited that he had made contact with her.

Jo said, "So, what can I do ya for? You get in trouble with Hell and you ain't got a decent probation officer down there?"

Kirk smiled. "Nah, I ain't in Hell yet. Well, I visited, but it ain't my style, Ms. Jo. No, I got me a little black—"

"African-American," Jo interrupted.

"—African-American girl who's my guide and friend. Her name's Miss Sylvie. She's here, too."

"Oh, my. Well, I s'pose you don't take up much room, so I guess it's okay she don't have a chair," Jo said, throwing up her hands. "Okay, so I am going crazy. This is good, I've been waiting for an excuse for a vacation for a while."

"Wait, Ms. Jo—you can't go just yet. I need to talk to you about somethin' important," Kirk said hurriedly.

"Important, eh? Okay. If'n it's important enough to talk 'bout from beyond the grave, I guess that's what I'd call important. Here, let me put my phone on hold so I can talk to you without interference." Jo pushed a button on the phone, picked up the receiver, and put it back down again.

"So, how can I help you, Kirk?" Jo asked calmly.

"You can help my girlfriend. And my new baby son," he said.

Jo shook her head and looked up at the ceiling. "Oh, Lordy! A baby boy and yo ol' girlfriend. Oh, Lordy!" she said, shaking her head again. "Kirk, I just don't know. Didn't I tell you to keep that thing in your pants? Who was it? That Kirsten girl you was seein'?" Jo asked accusingly.

"No, ma'am. Her name is Cindi." Kirk felt about sixteen years old again, and suddenly felt ashamed that he was having to talk to Ms. Jo at all. Still, he needed her, and she hadn't said no yet.

"Cindi, eh? She an addict, too?" Jo asked.

"Yes, ma'am," Kirk said quietly.

"Figures. Figures. What's her last name?" Jo said, going over to her computer screen.

"Staples, ma'am," Kirk said.

Jo punched a few buttons, then waited for a moment. "Lordy, I don't know what You is doin' to me, but show me the right way ta go!" she whispered under her breath.

Sylvie smiled. "She's a good woman. She'll do what's right," she whispered.

"Shush ya whisperin'! I gots to think here!" Jo said, waving an arm behind her.

The screen paused, then filled with a lot of information. "Let's see here, Cindi Staples, pregnant eight months, convicted of driving under the influence of narcotics, in possession of a felony amount of crack cocaine. Oh, boy. First-time offender. I think that's Clarice's department. Looks like the judge hit her with one of those new child abuse statutes when you takes drugs while you're pregnant. Yeah, here it is, a court order that she undergo natural childbirth and not get any painkillers after the delivery. Ooh, boy! Talk about your cruel and unusual punishment! I've been a momma twice now, and you couldn't pay me not to get a shot of Demerol and a spinal block. I tell ya, that child's had it hard already. Well, what else do you want to know?" she asked.

"What's going to happen to her?" Kirk asked quietly.

"What's going to happen? Let's see. DFACS is scheduled to take possession of the child. Social worker's report shows she's not a fit mother. The little boy's got a fifty-fifty chance to live, by the DFACS report here. That poor boy. He didn't ask to be born a drug addict, now did he?"

"No ma'am. Ma'am, can you help me with him?" Kirk asked.

"What do you want me to do with him? He's a baby. I's done my baby time. I done raised two babies and I ain't about to start raisin' a third," Jo said, crossing her arms.

"But, Jo, you gotta know, the kid is gonna die unless he gets some serious lovin' care. And Cindi, well, she needs someone to look after her, too. Also, you 'member my little sister, Anna? She's in terrible trouble, too."

Jo crossed her arms. "What do I look like, Kirk? Super Woman? I don't think so! I see this kind of hard-luck case come across my desk every single day. Do you think that if I went out and got involved with every single one of them I'd have any time for myself or my plants or my boyfriends? I don't think so."

Kirk sighed. "How many dead people ask you for help?"

Jo thought about that. "Not many. Maybe you're the first."

Kirk spoke up. "Then, you've got to believe me. This is important to me. Very important. And . . . it's important to Atlanta, to everything. I'm sure of it."

Jo sighed. "How is a scrawny little kid and his scrawny druggie mom important to the city of Atlanta?"

"Trust me, Ms. Jo. Have I ever lied to you?" Kirk asked.

"Don't make me answer that question, Mr. Rourke. I'm sure that you would not appreciate the answer."

Kirk grinned and shook his head. He was losing; he felt there was nothing more he could do. He hated to see his little boy die, but he knew that there wasn't anyone else who would stick up for the little guy.

"Well, I want to thank you Ms. Jo," Kirk said, the sadness evident in his voice.

"Wait a minute now, hold on there, hold on just a second there, Mr. Rourke. Is that a tear I heard just now? Are you cryin' for this kid?" she asked.

Kirk nodded, but Sylvie motioned to him: clearly Jo couldn't see him, only hear him.

"Yes, Ms. Jo. I'm crying right now. I don't want to see the little guy go. I really . . . I really love him. I've never even touched him for real, and I still love him more than I can tell you. I just don't know what I'm gonna do when he's gone."

"You love this little crack baby?" Jo said quietly, shaking her head. There was a tear in the corner of her own eye.

Kirk sighed. "Yes, ma'am. I love him with all my heart."

Jo shook her head, looked up at the ceiling again. She started cursing under her breath, snapping off her computer monitor, getting her stuff together, filing her paperwork.

"Oh, great, Kirk, you've gone and made her mad," Sylvie said.

"No, Miss Sylvie, no, he ain't got me mad—well, not at him anyway. At myself. I just can't believe I heard what I just heard. Kirk Rourke, a hardened drug addict and pusher with a history of beating up gangsters, smokin' crack, and burnin' down churches, and he's standing here sayin' that he loves a little baby more than anything. Well, if that ain't why I'm a probation officer, I just don't know what is. I got to give that little boy a chance, and I got to give Kirk a chance to know what it means to be a real human being, even if he is dead already. So, dammit, you've convinced me. I guess I'm going to have to make the guest room into a nursery. And we'll look into this thing about Anna, too," Jo said, sliding on her immense black trenchcoat and grabbing her umbrella. "Now, how's about tellin' me where I have to go, and let's keep it quiet so that I don't get locked up myself for being crazy. Hear?"

"Yes ma'am. Thank you ma'am."

"Humph. You can thank me when you figure out how to change diapers from beyond the grave," Jo said, muttering under her breath as she walked down the hall.

Dr. Teeth had just barely been able to reassemble his laboratory when the Greymaster was suddenly standing outside his door, waiting for the good doctor's services. Dr. Teeth had erected the giant wolf mask in the back room and had set up his teaching skulls and his other equipment, and he walked among the instruments charging them with his Pathos, listening to the Greymaster's instructions as he went.

"I can tell you, sir, that your good son is indeed still in existence. I cannot seem to get a lock on his current location, but I do definitely feel that his life-thread has not been cut," Dr. Teeth said, grinning wickedly. "Furthermore, I have developed a few handy items in the interim which should be very useful in locating Kirk's Fetters from a distance. It was quite easy, actually, since we own one of his Fetters already. Frighteningly simple, actually. I have a few locators ready for your men," Dr. Teeth said. He was always careful to say "your men" or "the men," never "his men." Although the men feared him, he had no delusions of being able to rule this wild bunch of mercenaries.

"Excellent, Dr. Teeth! I have need of some of your Masquing skill, as well. I want you to make me a Firebird mask, just like the one Kirk wore."

"But of course, sir. That was my second priority," Dr. Teeth said, pulling off a black burlap cloth from a stand which held just such a mask, and bowing gracefully from the hip.

Greymaster smiled as he fitted the mask to his face. "Excellent."

Jebediah had accompanied Sir Alisdair's patrol. Their first stop was a little-known place of refuge for the Renegades that Alisdair had been watching for weeks, waiting for just such a moment. Jebediah shuddered at the absolute relish he heard in the voice of the knight as he listened outside the bar.

"Well, Miss Susie. They call you Proud Susie, is that not true?" You don't seem to be too proud now. I wonder why that is?" Sir Alisdair said, striding forward to fix the last chain in place. She was nearly clothed in chains, the foul black Stygian kind. The chains that would prevent her from leaving, prevent her from protecting herself with her Arcanos. The knight smiled behind his helm, enjoying her helplessness.

"You're supposed to be a loyal citizen of Stygia, a member of the Hierarchy. I'm afraid you'll have a hard time convincing the Magistrate of that—it's known you harbor Renegades, Heretics, and your Circle is famous for keeping souls out of the hands of the Hierarchy. You are a little conductor on the Railroad, are you not?"

"I don't know what the hell you're talking about. I can tell you this, mister. I run a clean joint. My wraiths are all citizens. I check their seals, I make 'em pay their tithes. What more can you ask of a citizen?"

"What more can I ask? Quite a bit more. How about, oh, loyalty to the Empire? Surely loyalty is within your capabilities. I realize that you're a lesser wraith, hardly more than a wastrel. Still, if one of the Renegades comes to your very door, I would think you'd report it to the nearest Warder. Why did you not do this?"

"I don't know what you're talking about."

"Fetch the wraith who was witness to this crime," the knight said to an underling.

Soon a hooded figure was brought before Susie. It was drooping and nearly transparent: they hadn't provided any juice in a while and the Corpus was in tatters.

Still, Susie knew the wraith before they even lifted the hood off. "Jessie." She cursed under her breath. Jessie, whose last Fetter was itself in danger of being destroyed. "Damn, Jessie. I would've helped you. You didn't have to go to them."

Jessie looked down at her feet. "I'm sorry, ma'am. I'm sorry, Miss Susie. . . . "

The knight nodded and a Centurion unlocked Jessie from her chains.

The knight spoke up, indicating his stool pigeon. "This loyal citizen says that she saw you harbor one of the outlaw Ferrymen here, just three days ago.

You also promised to help an Enfant, a new wraith who is an outlaw from the Empire already. The wraith called Kirk."

They had released Jessie, who stood, rubbing her wrists and her thick legs where the manacles had bitten into them. Susie looked as indignant as she could, chained as she was to the wall.

"I don't know what you're talking about. I'm not a mind reader, if that's what you mean. If a Ferryman comes into my place, how am I gonna know? It's not like I can do anything about it, anyway. Your Warders are never around when you need them," Susie spat out, and tugged against her chains. The immense amount of darksteel that was required to hold her great bulk against the wall jingled strongly as she moved.

The knight shook his head slowly. "Oh, my, Susie. You are quite the raconteur. I do so love your stories. Unfortunately, you must understand that I know your heart. Indeed, I know where your last Fetter is. If you don't help me located the outlaw called Kirk, I'll be sure that a certain stained-glass window is destroyed, and rather quickly. It would be a pity to see such a beautiful work of art destroyed. Such a pity."

"You bastard! I don't know anything about where he is. I—my tale-teller, Sylvie, has got him. I don't know where they are, or where they're living. I only see her once a month, anyway, on Story Night."

"And where, then, is the tale-teller to be found?" the knight's tone was polite and as comforting as a bed of shattered glass.

Susie looked to the knight, to the Centurion, and back to the knight. Her head lolled to one side where they'd slapped her: she could feel her body slowly starting to slip away, into the Tempest, losing cohesion. Still, she couldn't betray Sylvie to them. "I—I don't know—" she whispered.

A Centurion stepped forward. In his glowing glove was an ancient corn-husk doll: a living-world object that, to any humans standing in the pool hall at the time (not that there were any) would be seen floating across the bar top. "Sir, I make this to be one of the girl's Fetters. Shall I assign a Monitor to secure it so we can wait for her return?"

"No, that won't be necessary, Centurion. We'll find her using the doll, wherever she is." The knight smiled behind his helm. He drew his Stygian dagger, the darksteel blade seeming to suck in light from around it. He stepped closer to Susie. "Ah, my dear. It is, how shall we say? Unfortunate. Very unfortunate that you decided to lie to us. You see, if you had admitted to knowing where she was, I would've let you continue to exist a little while longer. Only now, well, I'm going to have to utilize my executive privilege. Do say hello to your Renegade friends once they join you in Oblivion, won't you?"

Susie screamed, as did many of the other wraiths in the bar.

The knight took the blade in his hands, kissed it once, and plunged it into Susie's belly. He watched as the darksteel sucked up Susie's life force, and then twisted the blade, drawing it up and across her neck. With no effort her head parted from the rest of her spectral body, and suddenly the chains fell limp as her form dissolved and flowed down through a crack in the floor. Susie had only screamed once, and after that had not uttered a single sound: she had just watched the carnage and wasn't even able to struggle when the blade finished her.

Behind his helm, the knight smiled again. He strode out of the bar and into the street, where his midnight black horse waited. "Do what you have to. Get me the girl called Sylvie," he commanded his Centurion. He turned to Jebediah, who was still waiting with his own honor guard. "Let us continue our patrol, my dear Magistrate. I'm sorry that you had to be near such an occurrence. I assure you it is not my normal way of dealing with the foul scum. This place is to be shut down!" he called out, and with that, his dark steed was off, riding through the storming swirls of the Tempest like a nightmare.

In the darkness, the Hierarchs left didn't notice a single thick-legged figure slipping away from them, vanishing into the shadows.

Proud Susie's bar was desolate as the Greymaster's squad moved through it. Jacko and Fritz were up front, on point, and Harlan, Dean, Kribbs and Rogers were backing them up in a V formation. Kribbs shook his head. "Fuckin' 'archs. Proud Susie din' never hurt no one," he cursed under his breath.

Harlan looked up at Fritz. "Any ideas, Fritzie?"

Fritz grinned and picked up a flinder of wood from the floor where the tables had been shattered. He shrugged, closing his eyes. Harlan saw juice burning within him and waited: he knew that reading Fate-twines wasn't something you rushed. He also knew that Greymaster would not be pleased if they found absolutely nothing from this raid—and, lately, his displeasure was starting to take a turn for the nasty. Harlan waited, shifting his eyes from the sentinels posted at either side of the doors and Fritz. When Fritz spoke again, it was in a voice different than his normal one: Harlan had been told it was the voice of Fate. It rang true.

"Hierarchy Centurions—and a knight of Stygia— were here. Here, Proud Susie was tortured. Here, Susie was lost to us, lost to Oblivion at the point of a darksteel blade. They are hounds, who hunt as barghests for another one—the son of the Firebird.

They hunt for a small black girl who carries the powers of dreams in her hand. They hope to find Firebird's son through her. They have her Fetter, a doll, with them. After that, the twines get too tangled to see." Fritz's Fate-voice tapered off, and he sagged a little as the power left him.

Harlan nodded. "That'd be Kirk and his friends. Great, they're looking for him, too. Let's secure the area and get back to base," he said, looking out the front window of the ruined pool hall and nodding to himself slowly. Kribbs looked up at Harlan.

"You think this will be enough for Greymaster to get the other Renegades together? To move on the Citadel? I'd like to see those fuckin' 'archs blown to Oblivion because of this," Kribbs said, looking Harlan in the eye.

"You forget, Kribbs. Susie was a black woman. Do you think the old boy Renegades, the Klansmen, are gonna give a damn about Susie?" Harlan laughed bitterly. "I loved this place, too. Hell, I did my first skin-ride right over in that corner. It was sweet. Still, Greymaster ain't going to order any attack until he's damn good and ready."

Kribbs shook his head. "I have this feelin' that ol' Greymaster and the 'archs have got an understandin'. It just seems to me that there's many times either side could'a attacked, and they just sit there waitin'."

Harlan shook his head slowly. "You don' know what you're talkin' about, Kribbs. Now, secure the area. This place could be valuable to us, and if the 'archs come back, I want to know about it. I'm going to call the report in."

Kribbs saluted smartly, almost facetiously. "Yes, *sir*, Lieutenant, sir!" he barked, growling under his breath, and stalked off to do his duty.

———

In a secret ceremonial chamber beneath the Fox Theatre, a large group of wraiths had gathered, bickering, yelling at one another, with no faction accepting a clear leader. For the Heretics here, the Sons of the Dragon who were at one time involved with the Ku Klux Klan; the Firebird, seen burning over the Citadel in downtown Atlanta, was the sign for which they had waited a long time. Greymaster's old Circle, called the Greyboys, had a loose affiliation with the Dragon-Sons because of their particular anti-Yankee, pro-White bent. The Dragon-Sons had a version of the Firebird prophecy that had the Firebird ruling them as the son of the Dragon himself, whatever that was. The Greyboys were loosely controlled (in the absence of the Greymaster, who all Greyboys still respected despite his departure from the group) by Aleck Heck, a Confederate lieutenant and hero of the Battle of Leggett's Hell (even though the Confederates lost that battle).

Aleck was up on the podium talking to the assembled. "I tell you my friends, it's August! And what does August mean to yew? I'll tell you what it means! The Naht of Fah! The Night of Fire!" Aleck yelled at the top of his wraithly lungs.

A chant went up, "Night of Fire," over and over again, until Aleck calmed them down.

"And that's tomorrow night! The sky will turn red as blood and already those Archy boys have predicted a Maelstrom. Got all their pantywaists in their big ol' Citadel, safe and sound. Now what about we go on over to the Capitol building during this supposed Tempest (sheyeah, right) and get ourselves some soulfire! Eh?"

The chant went back up, especially among the Greyboys who were fond of their rifles, "Soulfire! Soulfire!"

"I say that's what we do! And another thing—I—" Aleck started to speak, but his voice caught in his throat as he noticed the Greymaster at the far end of the room, flanked by three of his famous Wolfguards. Quiet fell on the room like a quilt across a bed on a winter night.

"What's this I hear about soulfire? You boys want soulfire, we got it. We're the folks," Greymaster said, continuing to walk down the aisle.

"That's na' what I heard," Aleck said, his voice going nasal.

Some of the Greyboys laughed, but most of them just looked uncomfortable.

"Oh, is that right? And what did you hear, Aleck Heck? That I had the soulfire but lost it from right in front of my nose? Heh. And you know me." Greymaster shook his head. "It's pathetic. Pitiful, really, how much you slobs will suck right up and spit back out."

"What are you tahkin' about, Greymaster?" came a voice out of the crowd, echoed by a few from all sides.

"What I'm sayin' is . . . well, you figure it out. Let's say you come into a great deal of soulfire. Are you gonna go yellin' and scah-reamin' about it to everyone? Why, no. You're gonna keep it real quiet. Why you might even tell a fib around so that not everybody an' his brother'll come lookin' for ya. Particularly those Hierarchy types!"

A roar went up among the crowd: they hated the Hierarchy almost as much as the Greymaster did.

"So! If'n you've heard tell that I lost all my soulfire, well you can just go right on spreadin' that rumor, and it'll be good for you an' me. But for now, I wanna show you just exactly what kind of juice I got to burn."

And with that, Greymaster changed. He grew. Not starting in any specific place, but growing to almost a head-and-a-half taller than Aleck Heck. His body was like a bodybuilder's: strong, tenacious, tough. He grinned widely. "Ain't never seen nothin' like that, have you? Well, it's a little trick I picked up from Dr. Teeth, and you better believe it feels good."

A general laugh went up through the crowd, with a few hoots and jeers. The Greyboys loved it: they had missed a strong leader like Greymaster and had started to hate Aleck's smart-ass ways.

"So, my friends, just what are y'all gonna do about this Hierarchy business? I tell you, it seems like you can't turn around without the Hierarchy pokin' their nose in your business. Everyone knows they're working with the Sweet Auburn folks to cut our power in half and keep us from ruling this fair city. What do you propose to do about that, Aleck Heck?" Greymaster said, using his huge form to good effect by bellowing louder than the smaller Aleck.

"He ain't nothin' but a whiner, Captain!" came a call from the crowd.

"Throw the bum out!" called an older wraith.

Greymaster took the podium next to Aleck and held up his hand so he could be heard. "I'm here to tell you that poor Aleck don't mean to be weak, but he just ain't got the force of prophecy on his side," Greymaster said, pulling back his hood and revealing his new black-and-silver Firebird mask. It was more of a helm, really, with the phoenix's wings erupting out of the sides and the long sinuous neck coiled around the top, red fangs gleaming, and the fiery tail tucked around his neck. It was beautiful work, and it had its intended effect.

All through the meeting hall, wraiths knelt on one knee in the traditional gesture of loyalty and fealty to one's lord. Even the normally rowdy, proud Dragon-Sons knelt on the floor, one by one.

Behind his mask, Greymaster felt the rush of power as he realized the combined strength that was gathered before him. Now, he thought happily, he had but to harness that strength and get it fighting as a single unit.

"Hurry up and wait! Hurry up and wait. I tell you, these county boys, that's all they want to do to you," Jo said under her breath, listening to the traffic that passed by the admissions station in the hospital.

Impatient, Jo got up and walked over to the nurse's station. "I don't suppose you've got that paperwork on Ms. Staple yet, have you?" Jo asked quietly, although the annoyance in her voice was clear.

"No ma'am. Not yet. Please just wait. Our DFACS person will be with you soon." Jo nodded and shrugged and went back over to her seat.

Sylvie and Kirk stood out of the way near her, so she could whisper to them from time to time. Kirk looked at Sylvie, who nodded. "Look, Ms. Jo, I gotta go do some things. Are you gonna be okay here with just Ms. Sylvie?"

Jo nodded to herself. "I believe we girls can get along just fine, by ourselves. Just you make sure you get back here soon. I ain't taken care of no baby by myself."

Kirk grinned and hugged Sylvie once before vanishing.

It was all quiet in Oakland Cemetery, which was a strange event by itself. Usually, each night, the ghostly drones, those ghosts without will or thought, would emerge from their crypts and march across the intervening spaces between their graves and attack each other, sometimes brutally. Alliances would form, falter, and fall, only to be reformed again another night. Only the Hebrew section was off-limits and peaceful: the rest of the cemetery was a battleground. Except for tonight. No horns were blown, no troops made movements from grave to grave. No brilliant colonel made a beginning cavalry charge with the dying of the day's sun. It was a kind of peace that was uneasy, a sickly quiet that forebode something much deeper.

Sir Alisdair, Knight of the Sickle, had been given the Horn of the Legions by the Anacreon of War. This treasured ebony horn was an artifact straight from the vaults of Stygia itself. The governor of the city wished to make it known to the Renegades of Atlanta that there was a reason why the Hierarchy ruled the lands of the dead, and that it was not just the soulfire that continually trickled from the city of the dead. It was the sheer force of numbers, organized troops, special reserves, and highly trained legions that worked together as closely and as perfectly as clockwork, with precision timing and accuracy.

His death-horse prancing at the gates to Oakland, the Death Knight blew the Horn of the Legions not just once, not twice, but three times, each note sounding louder, clearer, and stronger than the last. As the song of the horn reverberated across the marble tombstones and among the granite crypts, as if in answer there came a ghoulish humming, a howling, a kind of wordless song that built slowly, mounted from the lips of hundreds of restless dead. This was a moment of glory for them: once again they were being summoned up out of their homes and shelter and called into the service of their country. It mattered not that their country was of the dead, and that their service was a grisly, spectral one. They knew only the rush of the march, the call of the line, the tempo of the drumbeat. What they wanted was the thrill of the charge, the anguish of the skirmish, the triumph of victory. Somehow the horn reached out with its one-note song and convinced them all that the way to glory was to follow.

Jebediah almost felt moved to cross himself as he saw the legions of the restless dead move across the graveyard and, regardless of their former affiliations of Grey or Blue, black or white, watched the drones form up in perfect marching units. This was War's finest hour, and the Anacreon must have something invested in this, something beyond the mere pomp and ceremony of this large band of ghostly warriors.

Jebediah knew that the Necropolis would not know peace for many a day. A single ebony gem on his ring finger lit up, and he motioned to a Legionnaire to take his place as he went to attend to some business. Stepping into the shadows, Jebediah vanished.

The night air was uneasy and full of strangeness in Atlanta. Even in the living world there was a kind of crazy scent to the air. The gangs noticed it: the Red Dogs and the Black Falcons, the Hellbringers and the Kaz Society. The Triplezees and the Muck-lucks. The Fine Gentlemen and the Dragons: they all sensed it. Turf was turf, and the gangs of Atlanta had begun the evening by staking their new claims on new turf. Spray paint had put colors on walls, slogans on streets, marking new territory as the secret map of violence suddenly changed its boundaries. Quiet plans were made, whispered promises, silent curses, huddles, deadly plans. Cars were commandeered or stolen. A sporting goods store near Emory was broken into and emptied of its rifles and its baseball bats. Although the special gang task force unit had some hint of what was going down, they had heard rumors of a turf war for weeks, without any movement. How could this be the night?—a relatively cool, only slightly humid night in August. Hell, the moon wasn't even full. How were they gonna see to fight, even if they were only going to bash each other's heads in?

The watch commander ordered a couple of extra patrols, a few more beat cops posted in key areas. The Underground precinct remained open for an extra hour, but it looked like nothing was going to happen on this Friday night. Not at 9:00 P.M. Not at 10:00 P.M. Nothing. The streets were quiet; the little hooligans had obviously decided to watch the World Series instead of fuck around on the street.

Hooray for baseball.

Renegades are naturally superstitious: that's because, if they're gonna survive, they gotta be. There's always a reason behind the prophecies, the special rules of the Shadowlands. There's always some wisdom locked away. That's why the World of Krafft was full up on this Friday night, full up with wastrels, fence-sitters, a few Heretics, and some other freelance Renegades who weren't into the big rally going on downtown. The place was packed for two reasons. The first was that the Maelstrom gong had gone off the night before: the gong that the Hierarchy beat to signal the coming of a Maelstrom. Even though a Maelstrom had yet to show, most of the wastrel wraiths who had survived La Tempest Madrino, the Great Mother of Storms, were still alive because they had been near a particularly strong Haunt at the time, not because they were off lolly-gagging or skinriding. They recognized the imminent need for shelter at a time like this. All over the city, wastrels and those who had nowhere else to go were coming to the World, and Meany was cleaning up: he had hired two bruisers to help him with security and he was raking in the soulfire, Relics, and oboli. He had even made enough soulfire to start up the merry-go-round for a little bit, as long as wraiths were willing to chip in now and then to keep the thing going. The Hearse Riders were all here, a bunch of kids who loved the merry-go-round, who would play on it for hours if they could afford the juice. The other wastrels just liked the Haunt: a strange place, a quiet place, a safe place, and not one that was strategically important.

The other fairly terrifying superstitious omen that the wastrels of Meany's World kept repeating to one another as they filed up the huge, very long escalator was that the Scarletts had abandoned their post.

Down below, in CNN Center, there was a movie theater that showed *Gone With the Wind* on a continual basis, and the famous Three Scarletts of Atlanta (three lady ghosts who each believed they were Scarlett) never missed a show. That is, they never missed a show unless there was some bad business afoot.

Several Grey Wolves had arrived early in the evening and hung out around the World, apparently hoping to catch sight of someone from Kirk's Circle, but to no avail. They stayed as long as they could stand Meany's questions, annoying songs, and singing. He harassed them until they nearly broke out weapons on him, but no one broke out weapons on Meany, not on his turf. There were parts to that amusement park that he and he alone knew about, and you didn't want to cross him.

So, the Grey Wolves had left in the early evening.

Just as Meany had planned.

Freda and Duke had been hanging out in the Gypsy Wagon in the World for most of the day, playing card games of many differing types: Duke had been a soldier for most of his life and had learned that a good card game can help pass the time without making the senses dull. And you didn't feel too bad about leaving behind a pack of cards if you got jumped. Still, Duke was pretty darn proud of the deck of cards he had assembled: a complete poker deck. The only problem was that the backs were different because he had had a devil of a time finding a complete run. Even when he had tried to bring over a complete pack of cards by destroying one in the living world, he never quite got them all: some perversity of chance or ill luck always meant that an Ace, a Jack, or a Queen was left out.

Freda was beating Duke in a third round of draw poker when there was gentle knock on the door and Kirk stepped into the wagon. "Are we ready folks?" he asked, grinning.

Duke shook out his mane of hair and looked at Kirk. "Welly, wellly. Look at you. Been through hell and back. Well, my boy, I want you to know that we've gone through our own version of hell for you. Do you know what ol' Meany does to you when you're just hanging out with him? Geez, I never thought I'd see a whoopee cushion and a joy buzzer again."

Kirk grinned. "It's good to see you, too, Duke. Guys . . . Freda . . . Duke. Thank you. You've done an excellent job, and I owe you one."

"That's right, m'boy you certainly do, and you can start by lighting this here cigar!" Duke said, grinning, holding up a Stygian cigar and puffing on it as Kirk put a burning fingertip to the end.

Freda shook her head slowly. "I hope you know what you're doing, Kirk. I don't like the idea of the Hierarchy benefiting from what you plan to do."

Kirk nodded. He sat down next to Duke, across from Freda, and looked her in the eyes. "Freda, how did you die?" he asked quietly, never having had the time to ask her such a thing.

She shrugged. "It don't matter."

"Matters to me," Kirk said.

Freda gave Kirk a pained look, shot an angry look at Duke. "Why? It don't matter. It's over."

"It matters to me, Freda. I want to know," Kirk said.

"I was raped," Freda said. "The guy cut me up pretty bad."

Kirk nodded. "Yeah, somehow I got the sense that something like that happened to you. Well, did you take care of the bastard?"

Freda looked at Kirk, puzzled at first, then she grinned slowly and nodded. "Yeah. I took care of him. One night he decided to take a flying leap out a fourth-story window. Too bad he was better at falling than he was at flying."

Kirk grinned and nodded. "Got what he deserved. Well, you see, my dear Freda, this bastard—this Greymaster—he needs to get what's coming to him. He's got a lot to answer for."

Freda nodded. "You put it that way, and it makes sense."

Kirk nodded. "Makes sense to me, too. I used to be angry about it. Now I'm just decided. I'm going to take care of him like he took care of me. Like he took care of Mom. Like he took care of Kristy, my sister. I'm going to make sure that the buck stops with me. Stops now."

Duke looked at Kirk and nodded. "If you came in here screamin' for vengeance, I would'a told you to go screw yourself. But I know the kind of feeling you have. I've felt it before myself. It's like . . . Fate."

Kirk shook his head. "Nope. Not Fate. My choice. But I think that, for now at least, my choice's what Fate would have happen. I hope."

Freda put down her hand of cards. "Let's go, then."

Duke swore quietly under his breath. "And here I was about to win my first hand."

If it weren't for the sentries that Greymaster had posted up on the street, none of the Renegades would've known about the troops of Hierarchy soldiers moving through the city, "securing it" against "Renegade activity." The fact of the matter was there was barely a wraith at large in the city. The Maelstrom gong had seen to that. Greymaster had just finished revealing himself as the Firebird when a messenger stepped up out of the Tempest next to him on the podium. Whispering in his ear, in that closed-hand way that all Grey Wolves whisper so that not even other wraiths can hear, he told Greymaster about the legions of the dead marching down Peachtree. Smiling down at the gathered throng, impassioned by his words and the promise of free soulfire, and caught up in the power of the Night of Fire and the mythic Firebird, Greymaster was like an archer who, having notched and drawn a great and terrible arrow, had no other choice but to let it fly.

"My fellow grand and glorious Renegades! I have just been informed by my Harbinger that a force of Hierarchy dead has been sighted marching down Peachtree. The streets are quiet, the mortal world sleeps. Let us bring destruction to the enemy, and glory to ourselves! Remember Leggett's Hell! TAKE BACK ATLANTA!" Greymaster yelled, and with a single growling roar the Renegades assembled moved as one.

Kirk watched as Duke carefully assembled the blast pack full of plastique. It was a fairly simple fuse, yet it took all his demolitions skill to put it together. The entire steamer trunk was packed to the gills with the stuff. He took a Relic basketball that Meany had in the Gypsy Wagon and made an indentation deep in the middle of the claylike plastique in the trunk.

"That's where you're going to want to put the soulfire for the bomb. The detonator, here, has its own soulfire just in case." Duke held up the little plunger with the radio antenna attached. There was a half-moon of soulfire crystal attached to the side: it glowed like a deadly little night-light.

"Of course, unless the soulfire ball is in there, what you're going to get is a poof and not a bang. With the soulfire ball inside the trunk, what you're going to get is a huge *kaboom*. What I'd do is plunge the detonator and then Argos out of there as far as you possibly can. Then get to a shelter ASAP, because there's probably going to be a Maelstrom of some kind or another right after the bomb goes off. Understand?" Duke said, looking into Kirk's eyes. Kirk nodded.

"I'm going to have to face him back at the trailer— my old home. That's the only place where I know for sure he has a Fetter. I don't want you guys to be anywhere near that place, okay? I want you folks here, hiding out like the rest," Kirk said quietly but firmly.

His Circle-mates were never the expressive kind: they hardly knew what to say. Standing there, for a brief moment, Kirk thought Freda was going to hug him, but he thought wrong.

Kirk bent over the heavy steamer trunk, shouldered the backpack, and wordlessly stepped out of the back of the Gypsy Wagon.

As he walked quickly toward the shadows, ready to dive into them, he was brought up short by a figure standing amidst the detritus of the forgotten amusement park.

It was Jebediah, in his Confederate dress uniform, unmasked to face Kirk alone.

"I guess you're here to stop me," Kirk said slowly, his heart sinking.

Jebediah stroked his beard and took a step forward so that his face was out of the carnival light. "My dear boy, if I were younger, I would be taking you into the Citadel right now, taking you in and forcing you to swear allegiance to the Anacreon of War, to whom you so clearly belong. If I were just a little younger, I would've brought a squad of Centurions along with me, to clap you in chains, just for being a confirmed Renegade. But I've been living too long in this modern world, Kirk. I have seen too many things. I have had my fill of death, of killing. Did you know I've sentenced men to be sent to Oblivion? I've seen the way their eyes look as they contemplate that darkness. In my secret thoughts, my most private thoughts, I have thought that I must surely be destined for the hottest fires of Hell, should the Lord decide to make his judgment upon me. Still, looking back on my life, I have always been the one to try and do the thing which is right. Even in death, I have followed that particular dictum. And now I find myself without my favorite black-and-white rules, in a world full of only grey."

"So, you're not going to take me in?" Kirk asked hopefully.

"No, I'm not, my boy. I have come to realize, through either the curse or the blessing of knowing the secret will of Fate, that there are things which must be done, regardless of whether one man considers them good, or evil. These things are like natural storms: they come, they go, and they have a vital place. No, my son, my great-grandson whom I have never known, and now will never hope to know, I do not wish to apprehend you. What I wish to do is to ask you if you have thought about my words to you on the train. Have you marked well the Curse that follows our family?" the magistrate asked, emotion creaking his voice.

"Yes, Great-grandfather. I know what you're talking about. I think I know what this Curse is, and I mean to end it here, with me," Kirk said stridently.

"I am glad that you are thinking that way. And yet I hope that you are not struck with the same futile hubris that I was struck with . . . somehow, dear James, my dearest grandson, somehow he ended up cursed, as Restless as I am," Jebediah said.

Kirk nodded. "I believe I know why. I went down into the Hell of the Tempest, and I saw many things. One of those things was a scene of my father, moving through the jungle in Vietnam. There was a—a dark Spectre that haunted the woods all around him, that followed him and hounded him. That encouraged ambushes and skirmishes against him and the people that he led. As my own Shadow, the demon inside of me has my father's voice, could it be that this Spectre who haunted my father—would that be your Shadow, sir?" Kirk asked quietly.

"But—but I guard my Shadow well. Always. I have never let it loose without my knowledge. It is always bendable to my own will," Jebediah said, but as soon as he said that, his face changed, showing a look of sudden surprise.

"My Shadow . . . it laughs at me! As if there is some secret joke that only it can understand!" Jebediah said.

"We were told—in basic training—about how some people's Shadows can travel around by themselves sometimes, sometimes without you ever knowing. Perhaps this . . ." Kirk said.

"Impossible!" Jebediah interrupted. "That can't be. I . . . I would've known by now, surely. I would've been able to discern this terrible thing by now! After all the Pardoners I've visited!"

Kirk shook his head. "I have been in the worst of all Hells, Great-grandfather. I have seen the worst that the Shadow can be. And I know that he can do anything, or just about anything."

Jebediah just looked down, not meeting his great-grandson's gaze. Then he looked up and tipped his Confederate hat. "I do want you to take care of that little boy. I have been around to see him, and I find him to be a meager morsel at best."

Kirk nodded.

"And keep that father of yours away from him," Jebediah said, striking a terrific chill of fear in Kirk's heart.

The hospital was a madhouse. There were gang fights breaking out all over the city, and the ER was filled with gangsters, people with slices in their skin and bullets in their bones who would occasionally break out into little side fights while waiting to get sewn up from the first fight. Jo wasn't afraid of them, she just put on her probation officer's badge and look of frigid hell, but the people that she was trying to talk to, to get Cindi and Jeb out of the hospital, were too busy to see her. Her patience was near its end.

Sylvie's patience was also nearly gone. She strode across the room, carefully avoiding the gurneys moving back and forth through Admissions, and stepped into the restricted area where all the clerks were.

She stepped over to one of the clerks and, with a twinge of disgust (Sylvie never much liked to skin-ride), slowly sank into the large admissions receptionist. A moment later . . .

"Ms. Jo Evans?" the admissions receptionist said.

Jo smiled and sauntered over to the front desk. "About time."

The woman smiled. "What is it that we need, Jo?" she asked.

"What do you mean *we*? *I* need to get a girl named Cindi Staples and her rug-rat Jeb out of this hospital and take 'em home," Jo said.

The woman punched up a few keys on the computer keyboard and looked down at them.

"Oh, no, Jo. They're gone. They've been checked out already!" And for the first time Jo caught the hint of Sylvie's voice behind the receptionist's.

"Oh, really? Oh, my. Who got 'em?" Jo asked.

"Someone named J.T. Emerson. Address is 1316 Royal Pines Way. Royal Pines! That's where Kirk lived! Oh, no!" Sylvie said within the receptionist. Then the receptionist shivered as Sylvie stepped out of her.

Sylvie jumped up on the counter and slid across, jumping down to stand in front of Jo. "We gotta get out to Royal Pines. Now," Sylvie said.

The receptionist stared blankly at Jo for a second. "Did I call you up here for something?" she asked absently.

Jo smiled. "Oh, no, ma'am, I guess not. Thank you anyway."

Jo turned around and started whispering to Sylvie as she walked toward the elevators. "Okay, but this better not be any wild goose chase. I done enough chasin' wild gooses today."

Kirk wanted more than anything to Argos over to where Sylvie was picking up Cindi and Jeb and see how they were doing, but he knew that he had a job to do and that would just be putting it off. He turned to look at Jebediah in farewell.

Jebediah shook his head and offered his hand to Kirk, then pulled him into a rough embrace. "Kirk, my boy, I would wish you luck, but I have my limits. Just be sure that what you're doing is what you're supposed to do. I don't know how to tell it any plainer than that. Good night," Jebediah said, tipping his hat again, and slowly faded from view.

Kirk turned and closed his eyes, visualizing the trailer at Royal Pines, and stepped forward into a Nihil, the Tempest, and away.

The battle was raging in the streets. Renegade and Dragon-Son fighting together, side by side, against the more organized but less brutal Hierarchy forces. They climbed up and over cars, positioned themselves in the middle of the street and behind street sweepers, made flanking maneuvers through parking lots and down stairs and through parking garages. Several wraiths had sprouted wings and had begun fighting dogfight duels in the air, raking at each other with claws or slashing with swords and long spikes. Then the gunnery arrived on the scene and everyone took to trading pot-shots from behind heavy cover, choosing their ammo usage very carefully, utilizing stealth to its best advantage. Everyone was conscious of how much juice was burning up in the battle, and of causalities on both sides.

Curiously enough, the major players in the battle, the Greymaster and the knight, were both missing from the main fray, although none of the combatants had any time to wonder where they were.

Kirk had wanted to arrive before his father, had wanted to be there and set up his battlefield appropriately. But apparently someone—or rather something—had already been to Kirk's old home and left.

The trailer door stood hanging open. Inside was a shambles: the signs of a struggle and a hurried search were evident even from outside.

Kirk had been taught how to use his hands as entrenching tools, and the soft shadow-earth under the shadow-gravel wasn't hard to dig in. He dug down just enough with his shovel-hands to plant the steamer trunk after firmly attaching the soulfire sphere inside it and locking the trunk shut. He quickly covered up the hole and kicked gravel back over it.

It was at this point that Kirk heard a scream coming from another trailer—a scream that sounded curiously like his mother.

Kirk went around the back of the trailer and opened up his senses to the noises.

"Oh . . . oh, please stop. Please, we'll do anything."

"I've heard that before. I don't believe you. Besides, I like this. This is fun. I wonder how Anna will do."

"No! Not my baby! You promised!"

"I didn't promise anything. . . . "

Kirk clenched his fist. Somehow J.T., whose voice he now recognized, had dragged his mom into his trailer and was beating her.

Kirk snuck around the front of the trailer and phased through the door, stalking his way back through the tiny corridor to the rear bedroom, from which he had heard the noises.

He felt his demon clawing inside of him, laughing and jeering as he saw his mother chained to the wall with a crude set of hardware store chains and J.T. standing over her doing unspeakable things.

Kirk's anger flared. He watched his hands go from normal to flame-red and, in his outrage, slammed J.T. in the back.

He jumped, looking around. "What the fuck?" J.T. said.

He looked around, then he focused his eyes right on Kirk. What was he? Another natural medium? Or something different?

J.T. turned around and threw a heavy black wool blanket over his mother, then stalked past Kirk and went into another room. Kirk followed the man in: watching J.T. lie down on a foul-smelling bed (really more of a collection of rags), he nearly screamed as he saw a terrible black radiance surround J.T.

Suddenly, the Greymaster slid out of the fat bulbous body and, grinning, bowed slowly in front of Kirk, who was backing away from his father.

"Well, there you are, Kirkie boy. Nice to see you again. I wondered how long it would take before you showed up. We've been having a good ol' time. Unfortunately, everyone's all tied up right now. Why don't you look next door? I'm sure you're gonna see someone you know."

Kirk took the bait: he couldn't afford not to. He stepped through the wall of the trailer and gasped as he saw Cindi manacled to a heavy recliner and little Jebediah on his back in a large drawer.

"Gee, I guess you didn't realize that I had really good Monitors working for me, Kirkie boy. Yeah, boy, we were able to hunt down all your silly little Fetters. See here?" the Greymaster said, pointing to an ancient teddy bear sitting on the shelf.

Kirk whirled around to the Greymaster. "You bastard. I'm going to send you straight to Hell!" he yelled, growing claws from his fingers.

"Unh-uhn-unnh. Tsk, tsk. I wouldn't do that if I were you, Kirkie boy. See this grenade? It's real. One flick of my wrist and blammo—there goes your little boy, your widdle teddy bear, and your bitch. I'm sure you wouldn't like that."

Kirk looked down at a string tied to the firing pin of a grenade, and the other end to a steel ring that was within Greymaster's reach.

"Gee, I thought you'd be more amenable once you saw my little prize setup there. Come on outside, let's talk man to fuckup," Greymaster said, grinning, and stepped back down the hallway and out of the trailer.

Kirk phased through a window, burning some juice to recharge his body a little. He glared at Greymaster.

"What do you want from me?" Kirk said, fingering the trigger of his detonator, wishing he could blow the Greymaster to smithereens right then and there.

"What I want from you, Kirkie boy, is your pretty little light show. Your Firebird imitation. I want you to go help rally the troops downtown, so I can lead them in an attack on the Citadel," Greymaster said.

"You're fucked if you think I'm going to do that," Kirk answered.

"Oh, no, my boy . . ." Greymaster said, but paused as a passing car's lights pierced through him. "Oh, no, my boy, you're the one who's fucked. You see, if you lose all your Fetters, you're gone. Completely. I've got a team of skinpuppets set up at your widdle high school ready to blow it sky high as well. And I can break your bond with the Wolves at will. So all I gotta do is give the word and you're Fetterless."

Suddenly a floodlight came on and filled the yard of the trailer with blinding luminescence. A large woman wearing something which looked like a police uniform, and carrying a gun, moved across the front lawn and down toward Kirk's trailer.

"Oh, shit. You stay here, Kirkie boy. If you don't, it's kerblam on your Fetters. Got me?" Greymaster said as he passed through the wall of J.T.'s trailer, presumably to skinride the pimp again.

Kirk had a secret thrill when the woman returned, her face now glowing in the light. It was Jo! Jo was on the case. All he had to do now was get her attention.

"Hello there, officer," came J.T.'s drawl from the trailer. The Greymaster had his J.T. act down pat. "What's the problem?"

Jo turned and faced the huge man. "I've had reports of a break-in and some trouble in this neighborhood."

"Trouble? What kind of trouble?" J.T. asked.

Kirk made his way slowly over to Jo, then cursed under his breath as his foot knocked up against something hard and sharp on the ground.

Bending down, Kirk ran his hand along a shattered piece of wood and a smooth curve of metal. A slow smile crept across his face.

Jo stood with her hands on her hips, holding her gun down at the floor—but at the ready. "You're gonna tell me there ain't no trouble around here, when I can clearly see there is?"

"Shoot him, Jo!" came Kirk's cry, as J.T. moved faster than any man his size should have been able to move and made a grab for Jo's gun.

J.T. grabbed the pistol and trained it on Jo, who started to raise her arms.

Kirk took the smooth curve of steel and held it over his head. Bringing the steel down and releasing it, he threw the head of his old, broken scythe at J.T.

The scythe flew, end over end, and landed, point first, thrusting its way into J.T.'s forehead, which suddenly became Greymaster's forehead. J.T., devoid of his driving force, slumped quickly to the ground, and Jo was able to get the gun away from him. Greymaster screamed as the darksteel of the scythe blade sank into his Corpus, through his head, and screamed again as his motion caused it to move even deeper. Greymaster writhed on the ground, screaming in pain.

"Jo! Listen to me. You have to get Anna, and Cindi, and Jeb out of here now. Sylvie! Show Jo where my teddy bear Fetter is. I need her to take that, too."

Jo shook her head. "Teddy bear? Kirk, you too old to play with dolls."

Jo went into the trailer. She found Anna hiding in a kitchen cabinet, still shaking, and then Cindi and Jeb (luckily the keys to the shackles were hanging on a peg on the wall) and Anna's teddybear, as well.

Kirk watched with one eye on the Greymaster, who was starting to lose cohesion and trying to flow off of the burning darksteel, and with the other eye on Jo as she herded all her charges out to her Ford LTD.

Kirk could barely wait a second longer when he saw his father work his way free of the darksteel and reform quickly, sprouting several weapons from all over his body.

"Oh, so we're going to play smart-ass soldier now, are we? Well, let's do that. I'm going to kick your ass, just like I kicked it before," Greymaster said, advancing on Kirk.

Kirk smiled. "No, father you're not. Not this time."

Greymaster shook his head. "You just don't ever learn, do you boy?"

Kirk smiled as the Greymaster stood one step closer.

"No, Father. It's you who never learns. Surprise!" Kirk said as he thumbed the trigger on his detonator.

From far off to the west of the city there rose a giant ball of red-orange fire in the Shadowlands, a strange lighting effect that, just for a moment, entered the living world's view. Scientists would explain it as a strange effect of air pollution and city lights, but if any of them had been alive on August seventh during the Siege of Atlanta they would have recognized it instantly. The night the whole sky turned bloodred and the doom of Atlanta was foretold was one that the old-timers would remember forever.

Atop the boiling cloud of red-orange flame rode the Firebird, streaking across the sky like a rocket. Underneath its fiery contrail there seemed to be a welling up of flaming red clouds that suddenly began to boil up out of the ground.

A Maelstrom had begun.

Kirk watched as, far below, the great firestorm swept over Atlanta and burned across the city. Like a huge, rushing, virulent plague, the fire crept across the city, engulfing it completely. Kirk saw from within the veil of flames that surrounded him as the entire Underworld was doused with fires of purple, red, gold, and yellow.

It was a magnificent sight. Caught in the flood of fiery clouds, the huge Maelstrom cleansed all traces of the Dragon-sons, the Hierarchy troops, and the Greyboys from the streets of Atlanta.

Kirk watched as the great storm mounted, built to a crescendo, and slowly began to die down, banking its embers as, one by one, the buildings became visible again.

That night, all over Atlanta, fires broke out spontaneously.

But then again, Atlanta is always burning.

Afterword

Congratulations is due to Jeb M. Rourke, summa cum laude graduate of the Class of '16 from the University of Georgia. Mr. Rourke received his B.A. in Celtic Studies and Confederate History, and is pursuing a Masters in Emory's Theology department. We wish him all the luck in the world.

Excerpt from Jeb's summa cum laude speech at graduation:

And in conclusion, I would like to quote from one of my father's diaries. "At the heart of the Fire there is always Truth. Below the darkness, there is also Truth. But the truth we live is the truth we walk with day by day." I want everyone to know that I do not think I could've made it to the place I am today without the help of my father, who, even though he died before I was born, has always been a source of inspiration for me. Thank you very much.

FREE

CARD OFFER

To celebrate the UK launch of a hot new World of Darkness novel series, White Wolf Fiction and BOXTREE are making available, for a limited time only, one free trading card.

Send a **stamped self-addressed envelope** and **proof of purchase** (cash register receipt attached to this coupon) to BOXTREE Ltd, 2nd Floor Broadwall House, 21 Broadwall, London, SE1 9PL.

No photocopies will be accepted.

Offer valid in UK and Eire only. Please allow 8–10 weeks for delivery.

Name: _____

Address: _____

_____

Postcode: _____

Shop where book was purchased: _____

_____

BOXTREE

The World of Darkness™

One of the world's top five card game systems invented by White Wolf

Free card with each purchase

Dark fantasy novels – where man fights to control the beast within

Magic: The Gathering™

Series of four gaming fiction novels

Based on the highly popular trading card game

Special Offer – one free new card with purchase